D0851556

MARRYING MR. WRONG

ALSO BY MELISSA JAGEARS

UNEXPECTED BRIDES

Love by the Letter: A Novella

A Bride for Keeps

A Bride in Store

A Bride at Last

Blinded by Love: A Novella

TEAVILLE MORAL SOCIETY

Engaging the Competition: A Novella

A Heart Most Certain

A Love So True

Tied and True: A Novella

A Chance at Forever

FRONTIER VOWS

Romancing the Bride

Pretending to Wed

Depending on You: A Novella

Marrying Mr. Wrong

NON-FICTION

Strengthen Your Fiction by Understanding Weasel Words

FRONTIER
VOWS

MR. MARRYING WRONG

MELISSA JAGEARS

UTMOST
PUBLISHING
www.utmostpublishing.com

CHAPTER ONE

Wyoming Territory – Late Summer 1885

Oof.

A whirlwind of swishing skirts smacked into Timothy O'Conner.

His arms shot out to keep the woman from falling as the scent of lavender stole his breath. Glory be. His dreams had come true. Long, blond hair, creamy skin, eyes as blue as prairie flax—Gwendolyn McGill was in his arms.

Her hands anchored onto his shoulders, and she looked up at him as the whistle of the incoming train pierced the air. "I'm sorry. I wasn't watching where I was going."

His arms tightened around her, as if they'd decided to keep his dreams true just a bit longer—propriety be hanged. "Gwen."

She cocked her head.

How had he dared to breathe her name? No lowly ranch hand called the prettiest, wealthiest girl this side of the Mississippi by her first name, let alone a nickname. Especially since—as far as she was concerned—they hardly knew each other. But he knew plenty about her, more than he wanted to know sometimes.

She looked at him oddly. "Again, I'm sorry."

"No, it was my fault."

She attempted to pull away.

Why hadn't he let her go?

Thankfully he hadn't come into town smelling and looking like the ranch hand he was. And yet his clean, threadbare clothing seemed as if they'd contaminate whatever fancy fabric she was wearing. A deep blue cloth that set off her eyes, which were even more beautiful up close.

"You can let me go now. I'm all right."

"Are you?" He looked behind her, scanning the crowd scurrying about the station. "You were practically running, and you're not the type to run."

She pointed awkwardly toward the train. "I guess I was sort of running—that way."

"Oh? Well, trains don't leave that quickly. It takes time to disembark and—"

"I know how trains work." She let loose a chuckle which made his heart stop. That had been a real laugh. For the past several years, he hadn't heard anything but the fake laugh she used when flirting with men about town. The last time he'd heard her truly laugh had been the year he'd watched her mother chase after her by the creek behind their huge home. His parents had never played with him like that. He'd been content enough when they'd just—

"I'm on my way to meet Mr. Wright."

Timothy looked toward the locomotive, a sneer overpowering his lips.

He'd expected the young lawyer to return months ago and put a ring on Gwen's finger, relieving Tim of this ridiculous pining for a woman who'd never be his. But the longer Mr. Wright had stayed away, and the longer Gwen hadn't flirted with anyone since, the more his heart had been suspended in half agony, half hope.

Considering a new lawyer had set up in town last month, Mr. Wright couldn't be coming back for work. Which meant he had to be coming back for Gwen—the woman in Tim's arms.

Why was he still holding her? Tim let go and took a giant step back. How long had he kept her trapped against him? Seconds? Minutes? An eternity. "Sorry."

A worried wrinkle creased her flawless brow as she looked toward the passenger cars.

Had Mr. Wright seen them wrapped up together? With the smoke rolling across the platform, hopefully no one had. Tim smashed his hat down, shoving the bangs he always arranged to hide his blemished forehead nearly into his eyes.

"Well, excuse me, Mr. O'Conner, I must—"

"Are you sure?"

"About what?"

Oh, why had he not kept his mouth shut? It was disrespectful to question someone of her social status. And yet, when would he ever again be able to ask her what no one seemed to be asking? "About Mr. Wright."

"What do you mean?"

He didn't meet her gaze, too afraid to see the affection she held for the man they spoke of. Was there anything he could say that would make a difference? "I just don't think…" He huffed and glanced toward the train. "That he's right for you."

"Oh?" She straightened, tilting her chin.

Now he'd done it. Got her defensive. But what did she see in the man? Beyond the fact he was good-looking and wealthy.

Tim sighed. That was probably sufficient for most people. But he'd seen the two of them together enough last year to know Mr. Wright was not mesmerized by her. Nor did he seem to care why she pretended to have no interests other than whatever issued forth from his mouth.

Tim didn't quite know why she acted like that either, but he'd seen the depths that ran under Gwen's surface, once after her mother died, and once nearly two years ago—though Gwen hadn't known he'd seen her crying that last time, sitting on a rock by the creek, doubled over as if sadness had given her an ulcer.

Mr. Wright didn't strike him as the kind of person who would pray for her for weeks without any idea why she was crying. And if the gossip could be trusted, he'd not communicated with her the entire year he'd been gone. "He can't be the right man for you. Just like the six who came before him weren't."

She took a quick step backward. "Pardon?"

"The others who left you high and dry."

Her eyes clouded with hurt.

But it was true. There'd been Smith, Jefferson, Hendrix, Grayson, Thomas something or other, and Parks. Though Hendrix, the best of the bunch, had never strung her along, none had truly seemed interested in what made her who she was.

"Maybe so, but I don't know why…" Her face crumbled.

Had she no idea her phony flirtations attracted the wrong type of men? Maybe if he explained. Tim held up his hand and ticked off fingers. "Smith was too old for you. If you'd acted more mature, he might've been interested."

Her brows shot up and fire sparked within her eyes.

Goodness, she was gorgeous riled. But he couldn't stop now. "Hendrix couldn't take your clinginess or the fake way you presented yourself—you know that I know you don't naturally act like that."

Her eyes clouded a little, and she visibly swallowed. He'd wondered if she'd forgotten about that day, but apparently, she hadn't. They'd never talked about the time he was eight and had caught her hacking into a tree trunk with a broken blade in a mournful rage after her mother's death, when she'd hastily wiped away her tears after realizing he'd sneaked into her family's orchard to steal the rotting apples off the ground. She'd sent him home with a ham hock instead, then gotten into trouble over the missing meat. But she'd never told her father, knowing he'd have accused Tim of stealing.

His hand trembled at the memory, but he put up another finger. After that day, she'd gone on living a life he could never aspire to—though now, he wasn't sure it was any better than his. "You likely didn't have enough money to entice the nice-looking railroad boss. And the blond probably realized he couldn't afford the standard of living you'd require." Timothy glanced toward the train. "I'd not be surprised if Mr. Wright made seven."

"Thank you for that depressing prediction, Mr. O'Conner." She lifted her chin and glared at him, though he noted the moisture in her eyes. "I'm glad to know I've no qualities whatsoever to attract a man—"

"That's not what I meant." He reached for her, but Gwen's glare stopped him cold. He sighed and clasped the back of his neck instead. "You've got a lot of good qualities. You care about people. And you're stronger than I am." He knew what it was like to be judged by a father's failure. The talk. The wary glances. He had difficulty looking certain people in the eyes.

She'd found a way to hold her head high, despite her father being sent to prison.

The train doors thumped open, stealing her attention.

"Gwen!" A masculine shout turned Tim's head, and his heart sank. Time had run out.

She waved at the blastedly good-looking Mr. Wright before turning back to Tim. "I'm thankful for your concern, but I have to go now."

Before he could say more, she plastered on that beautiful, heart-numbingly fake smile and walked straight for Mr. Wright.

Why had he ever held onto hope?

It was such a worthless thing to possess.

Arm in arm with Eric Wright, Gwen willed her heart to settle. He'd been hard to convince to take a walk after he disembarked, but she'd practically begged, and he'd relented.

This was likely her only chance to prove to him she wasn't the empty-headed woman he'd left behind last year before her brother showed up and monopolized the conversation. And yet, the words she'd planned to say had all fled—the ones she could remember felt either trite or childish.

What if, no matter the words she chose, he didn't like the real her any better than he'd liked the flirty her—the girl she'd believed he'd fallen for until he'd left and never wrote back?

Thankfully Eric seemed content to take in the scenery as they drew closer to the creek that ran behind the church. The mountain ridges surrounding town were enveloped in a summer pollen haze and the clouds hung like fragile wisps high in the sky. The golden light infusing the air gave her hope that if she just got the words out, the interest he'd lost in regard to her would return, that she'd still have a chance at moving to Denver with him so she could start over.

Her past flirty ways had disguised the fact she wasn't a simpleton, aiding her in collecting enough information about her father's criminal activities to pass to the marshal, but her flighty façade had done *her* no good. After Father had been sent to prison and her brother had returned to clean up the mess, she'd not been able to instantly drop the act and had teased and flattered her brother's friend as she'd been accustomed to doing with the many men who'd come before him. But once she'd realized she liked Mr. Wright, she'd discovered herself imprisoned by her false front, ensnared by her own deceptions.

No one knew she wasn't really like that—except maybe Timothy O'Conner.

She shook her head. No, that day in the orchard had not been enough for Timothy to actually know her. And after that incident, they'd never socialized, despite attending school together.

And yet, Timothy had quite accurately described several of the men who'd left her without a second thought. But what of the good qualities he'd rattled off about her while his muddy hazel eyes had drilled into hers as if trying to convince her she was what he claimed? Well, she wanted to believe all those things about herself. But lately, the way the people in town treated her made her believe she was just fooling herself to think a man like Mr. Wright should've seen something worthy enough about her to have at least written once.

Up ahead, a cluster of birch trees shot up through a pink and green cloud of Woods' Rose behind the quaint little bench she'd commissioned in memory of her mother. With the trickling of the nearby creek and the backdrop of the purple-blue ridge bordering town, it would be an excellent place to declare herself.

She rubbed her hands against his sleeve to dry her sweaty palms. It was time to break this awkward silence with something. "Are your legs feeling better? It's been a long time since I've had to travel so far. How's Denver?"

Denver. She'd visited several times and considered it the perfect place to begin again. All the things she could learn to do there, the people she could meet, the ability to walk down the street and not be judged by her last name.

"I couldn't have picked a better town or job for myself." He led her toward the wooden bench nestled between the two flower beds.

Gwen sat and let out a shaky breath. "I'm glad you came back."

He raised a brow but sat beside her without asking the almost palpable 'why' that hung heavy in the summer heat.

"Of course, Bo has been looking forward to your visit since we got your telegram, too. For a while there, he'd begun to believe you were never going to speak to us again."

Eric shifted on the bench but took her hand and patted it—

like one might do to calm a doddering old woman. "Bo and I will always be friends."

She waited for him to mention her, but he seemed content to say no more.

The moths that everyone assumed occupied the space between her ears started to swirl behind her ribcage. "I hope we're still friends?"

He blinked hard but gave a short nod. "Of course."

"Then why didn't you write me?" She braced herself for his answer. If only he might say something that would prove he'd felt the same as she had before he left.

He looked toward the mountains. "I'm not much for writing."

Her heart lifted a little. Maybe she hadn't been the reason for his silence. "My brother isn't either. I got very few letters from him when he was at school."

Eric smiled slightly, but then looked back toward the mountains, a deep wrinkle creasing his brow.

A sudden urge to brush the lint off his shoulder and let her hand remain on his arm, give him a practiced smile, and tell him to stop being so very serious tugged at her. Though flirting might make things more comfortable right now, she would not allow herself to do so until he knew exactly what lay beneath her polished art of dalliance. "I'm sorry I didn't receive any letters from you when you were gone." She pulled in a deep breath and allowed the words to flow out, polished or not. "I know I might've acted in a way that may have made you believe my regard for you was shallow. I suppose it was in the beginning. But before you left, I'd begun to hope."

His whole face scrunched with apprehension.

The moths turned into big fat frogs that kicked their way down into her stomach. "I know I should've been more forthright about my feelings before you left, but I've…been forced to grow up since then." Maybe it'd be better if he believed she'd become a better woman this past year than try to explain why she'd continued to act like a cotton-head even after her father had been locked up. She'd chastised herself enough for her stupidity in continuing the ruse, for wasting the chance she'd had with him. "I know it's been a long time since we were together, but I'd begun to develop feelings for you."

"Feelings for me?" He shook his head. "You didn't seem to have feelings for me. Not real ones, anyway."

His tone indicated he doubted she could develop feelings for anyone. How could she prove he was mistaken before he walked away from her forever?

Before her mind was aware of her body's plan—her lips were upon his.

When he didn't react, she squelched the urge to pull back and run away. She pressed harder, curling a hand into his hair. The feelings he'd had for her would surely resurrect if—

And then his fingers slid down her jaw and his lips turned soft and all manners of heady sensations she'd never experienced made the whole world grow hazy. When he broke the kiss, she pressed a hand against her scuffed lips.

But the smile which had started to warm her face melted clean off.

His expression bore no resemblance to that of a man who'd had his hopes rekindled. He stood and stabbed a hand through his perfectly combed hair. "I can't do this."

"I'm sorry." Oh, what must he think of her? How had she thought kissing him would make him believe she'd changed one whit? "I know that came out of nowhere, but the feelings I had for you last year were real. I was hoping to marry you, and then when you didn't even write…"

He turned and paced a few steps then came back. But as soon as he opened his mouth, he turned and marched off again.

If only the ground could swallow her up. But instead, she pushed off the bench and went after him. "Eric. Could we not see how things might go—"

He shook his head and turned. "I can't right now."

9

"I understand. It's too soon after so much time away, and you only intended to be here a week." She put a hand on his arm though all she wanted to do was run away and curl up in humiliation, but that would get her nowhere. "But will you at least let me show you how much I've grown since you left—though a week surely isn't enough time to do so. What if I moved to Denver? I'm certain Bo would allow me if—"

"No." Eric put up a hand, rubbing his forehead as if he'd suddenly recalled something, and took a step back. "You can't."

She wrapped her arms around herself. How could he say no so adamantly after kissing her like that just minutes ago? But then, what did she really know of his feelings, his plans, his wants? He'd seemed to enjoy her flirting last year, but what if that's all he'd enjoyed?

His agitated movements were not those of a man who'd just been offered the chance to win back what he'd thought had been lost to him forever.

"I'm sorry. I'd thought…" She turned her head and blinked away the warmth rising behind her eyelids. Seemed she hadn't chastised herself enough over the way she'd handled things last year. Now she would lie awake for another handful of months, berating herself for this even bigger blunder. "Never mind. Pretend I didn't say anything."

"Gwen…"

His patronizing tone made her recoil. What had she been thinking to believe he'd ever felt something for her? He'd likely only put up with her flirting because she was his good friend's little sister. "You don't have to stay and assure me I'm a nice girl. That I'll find somebody someday somewhere or anything of the sort. You're free to go, Eric."

"I didn't mean to hurt you."

She glanced up and saw the confusion marring his face. He really hadn't thought about her at all if he could be so blind-sided by her hopes of renewing what she'd thought they'd once had. "It's all right. I want you to go." If he didn't leave soon, he might see her cry, and that would make it even harder for him to leave.

Thankfully he nodded, and without another word, turned back toward town.

She plopped down on the bench and winced at a pinch pulling at her scalp. She reached up and extracted a few loose hairpins, allowing the right side of her curls to cascade over her shoulder.

How was she going to spend seven days—let alone one— listening to Eric joke and laugh with her brother now? Or had she ruined Bo's visit, too? Staring at the plants in the flowerbeds she'd commissioned earlier this summer, she tried not to think about all the ways she'd messed things up and allowed the minutes to tick by until she could trust herself to breathe normally without releasing tears.

"Miss McGill?"

Gwen held in a groan. The town's biggest busybody would not make today any better. What was Mrs. Tate doing all the way out here anyway? As nonchalantly as possible, Gwen pushed her loose hair back behind her shoulder. Surely Mrs. Tate wouldn't be able to see how her lips still pulsed after her ill-fated kiss, though it was highly unlikely her eyes weren't blood-shot. Maybe she could blame that on hay fever if the woman noticed.

"Are you all right, Miss McGill?"

Keeping her face turned away, Gwen patted enthusiastically at the dirt at the base of a crooked flower. "Of course. Just out enjoying the sunshine."

The overweight woman stopped three feet away. "I don't believe you." She took a step and plucked a pin from the left side of Gwen's coiffure. "What happened?"

Failing to bluff well enough might entice Mrs. Tate to make up a story to spread about town. "I'm sorry, Mrs. Tate. I shouldn't have tried to deceive you. You're right. I'm having a terrible day and wished to be alone."

11

"Bet you've had plenty such days since your pa landed himself in jail. Don't understand why your brother didn't drag you away from here the moment he moved back. Is he not paying attention to you? He shouldn't sit around and let things get worse." The woman tsked and planted her hands on her meaty hips. "Nor should you. I saw what happened and you better do something about it before you land yourself in real trouble."

Why were people she barely knew telling her what to do today? First Timothy O'Conner, and now Mrs. Tate. But the woman was right, staying in Armelle was not best. Why did Bo seem unable to see that? "And pray, how should I do that?"

Mrs. Tate held out her hands to help Gwen up. "First, we get you cleaned up and looking like the lady you're supposed to be."

If Timothy could see something good in her, and Mrs. Tate was willing to help her when she was upset, maybe the towns-folk's opinion of her wasn't as bad as she'd thought.

CHAPTER TWO

Timothy O'Conner nodded a wordless thank you to Pastor Lawrence, who handed him a second crate to fill as they stood side by side in the church's narrow pantry.

After all the hours he'd put in at the Keys' ranch, all the money he'd given his mother, they still couldn't buy enough food. He'd hoped not to have to ask for food from the church again this month, but thankfully the pastor was the sort to help without judgment.

Though such judgment ought to fall on his father.

Ma should've known better than to put the cash Tim had given her under the mattress. Pa had discovered that spot once already, and when Pa needed money, he checked everywhere he'd ever found a coin twice over. He'd steal from the baby if he had to. Forget that Tim had worked long days in the hot sun with blistered hands for weeks on end. Wrangling cows. Fixing fences. Mucking stalls. None of it mattered—the last four weeks of his wages were long gone.

Tim sighed and placed a jar of what looked like green beans and peppers into his crate. Next payday, he'd take the afternoon off to ride into town and deposit the money straight into an account at the mercantile. Hopefully Mr. Owens would be

MELISSA JAGEARS

willing to make a separate account for his mother. Tim shook his head. Perhaps it'd be best to make an account in his own name and give his mother privileges. If Father found out Ma had a secret account, he'd demand to take it over, and Mr. Owens would likely relent.

Tim squatted to see what was on the shadowy bottom shelf. A whole untouched section of peaches. These hadn't been here weeks ago. Was the shopkeeper's daughter back? If these were her preserves…

He grimaced. It was an awful thing to be poor and starving, but Raven Owens's peaches could make a starving man willing to fast. Did ladies' finishing schools teach women how to can better? He picked one up and squinted at it. "Pastor Lawrence? Are these—?"

A door slam cut him off. Then female voices, one on top of the other, floated in.

"I better see what they need." Pastor Lawrence left Tim to his selections.

He put the peaches into his crate, then moved over. Jams and jellies were stacked two jars high, but the indecipherable print on the lids made him uncertain what lay within.

"What can I do for you ladies?" The pastor's voice boomed from somewhere in the sanctuary.

"Get prepared to have a wedding, Pastor Lawrence."

Was that Mrs. Tate? Weren't all her children married already?

"Pardon?"

"I said—"

"What?" Gwen's voice sounded incredulous. "Oh, Mrs. Tate. That won't help anything at all."

Tim froze.

"I'm afraid you're…" Gwen's words turned breathy. "That you've been mistaken—"

"Biddy and I both saw that young man of yours use you ill."

14

"Now, Mrs. Tate." Pastor Lawrence's voice cracked. "We don't—"

"Just look at her—evidence enough of what we saw. And doesn't the Bible say if single people can't control themselves, it's better to marry? And it ought to be done right away to avoid scandal."

Tim's eye twitched. If there was any scandal, Mrs. Tate and her friend were creating it. And yet, he'd told Gwen he'd had a bad feeling about Mr. Wright.

Seemed he'd been a fool to watch her walk off alone with him. But who she chose to spend her time with wasn't any of his business. And truly, he didn't know anything about Mr. Wright besides what his gut said—and what was the chance his gut would ever approve of a man who courted Gwen? He left the pantry to poke his head out of the pastor's office.

Gwen stood in the middle aisle of the sanctuary, wide-eyed, disheveled, tear-streaked.

One of his father's favorite curses bounced around inside his head.

"It was just a kiss, Mrs. Tate."

Tim's innards curdled. Knowing they'd kissed shouldn't have bothered him. The two had courted for months last year, but to know for certain that they'd...

He sighed. He had no right to feel one way or another about it. He'd allowed his feelings too free a rein earlier when he'd said things to her he never should have voiced.

Mrs. Tate pointed out the window in the direction of the creek. "What I saw was a clear indication these two need to be married quick, Pastor. My boy's gone after her beau. I told people she ought to have a chaperone. But does anyone listen to me? No."

Tim raised a brow. The problem with Armelle was people did listen to Mrs. Tate.

But would Pastor Lawrence? Would he go through with a forced wedding? The few times Tim had heard of such things, he'd figured they were nothing but exaggerations. But then, if they were real, they likely had someone as pushy as Mrs. Tate behind them.

The door opened as if on cue, and Mr. Wright stepped in, his face dark and pinched. Trailing in behind him was Mrs. Tate's forty-year-old son, Ivan, shotgun in hand.

Tim shook his head. Apparently, Mrs. Tate could act as entitled as his own father, believing things should happen just because they wished it so.

Though Gwen was indeed a mess. Had there been more to that kiss than she let on?

Tim pressed his lips together to keep from saying the word that had bounced around in his head earlier.

God, for Gwen's sake, don't let him turn out to be what my gut believes he is.

Eric gave Mrs. Tate a quick glare, then turned to the pastor, arms akimbo. "These women are crazy. And to send this man after me with a gun? Armelle really needs to hire itself another marshal to keep such insanity from ever occurring again."

Mrs. Tate waggled her finger in his face. "I know what I saw, and Biddy saw it, too. Besides, this isn't a marshal's business, it's a man of the cloth's. You must be made to do right by her in the sight of God."

Sidestepping her finger, Eric shook his head. "I don't know what you're talking about."

"I saw what happened on that bench. She might've been willing, but if you're not going to—"

"She wasn't on a bench."

Everyone turned to Biddy. Had she been there the whole time?

The much shorter friend of Mrs. Tate was holding up the spectacles which normally dangled across her ample bosom, inspecting Mr. Wright as if he were an insect in need of identification. "They were embracing in front of the station."

Tim froze. Biddy must've seen Gwen in his arms after they'd

bumped into each other. He had indeed held her too close for too long. If only she hadn't smelled like heaven.

Mrs. Tate harrumphed. "It wouldn't surprise me if these two weren't canoodling in all kinds of public spaces. With what I saw—"

"We didn't kiss in front of the station," Eric growled. He turned to the pastor and pointed at the women. "They're accusing us of things that didn't occur. There's no reason to listen to them any further. I'm sorry to have wasted your—"

"Just a moment, young man." The pastor held up his hand to cut Eric off. "Miss McGill, is what they've said true?"

Tim held his breath. Even if it was, he hoped she wouldn't admit it in front of these women.

"I…well, we were probably cozied up more than we ought to have been, but nothing to force us into marriage."

Tim grimaced. That'd be enough for Mrs. Tate to consider her guilty.

He stepped into the room. Maybe his presence might stop the crazy accusations.

Eric kept his fierce gaze on Mrs. Tate. "I will not let a bunch of feather-brained busybodies dictate—"

"That's him!" Biddy pointed toward Tim, squinting through her lenses again. "That's who I saw her cuddled up with, not this other one."

Eric turned in the direction Biddy indicated and he nearly recoiled.

Mrs. Tate shook her head. "Biddy, you're as blind as a bat. There's no mistaking these two men. Timothy's…well, he's an O'Conner, and Mr. Wright here turns all the young gals' heads."

Stiffening, Tim tried not to react to Mrs. Tate's thoughts of his lack of attractiveness. But then, what opinion had she ever kept to herself? Not that he could negate her opinion. He was an unsightly ragamuffin who couldn't even keep food on the table without the help of the church. Even so, his faulty looks and low social status were things Tim would rather not have pointed out in front of the girl he'd pined over for ages.

"But I did see her with that one. I just couldn't remember his name."

Mrs. Tate rolled her eyes at Biddy. "I'm sure she wasn't with Timothy. But perhaps she's been with more than one man today."

Gwen's face paled.

Tim stepped closer, holding up both his hands. "What you're suggesting about Miss McGill without a lick of proof is outside of enough."

Though he had five inches on the old woman, Mrs. Tate still somehow looked down her spare nose at him. "I know what I saw."

"That's debatable." Eric's voice rumbled low and menacing. He pointed an accusing finger at Biddy. "If this lady can't distinguish between me and him, nothing you two say is worthy of consideration. Besides, marrying under duress isn't legal. The law's not on your side. And I know the law. We're not getting married." Eric's words boomed off the rafters.

Tim raised his brows at such vehemence. If Eric wasn't intending to marry Gwen, what were his intentions?

Mrs. Tate's eyes nearly popped out of her head. "But you're willing to dally with her?"

The room went silent except for Eric's snarl. Gwen's knuckles whitened as she gripped the pew's back, but Eric's nose was too far up in the air to notice.

Pastor Lawrence gestured toward Ivan. "There's no need for firearms in the church. Put that away, and then we can talk about how our assumptions—"

"I'm not making assumptions." Mrs. Tate stamped her foot, as if that might make them believe her. "Mr. Wright—"

"But that's not who I saw." Biddy's voice joined into the fray. "It was the other one."

Mrs. Tate slashed her hand through the air. "That's not possible."

"Wild, baseless accusations don't hold up in court, ma'am." Did Eric not care a whit for how his words and actions affected Gwen?

Tim scoffed. "Neither does gossip, but it can sentence someone just the same."

Eric's glance snapped over to Tim.

Biddy pointed one hand at Gwen and fluttered the other at Tim. "Were you not with this man, Miss McGill?"

Gwen glanced at Eric, then Tim. "I mean, we were…he was—"

"I told you!" Biddy clapped, creating one harsh resound, like the slap of a gavel. "He's the one who ought to marry her."

"Timothy?" The pastor's tone was wary, yet also unbelieving.

"She was in my arms, yes, but—"

"See!" Biddy practically jiggled at being proven right.

"I caught her when she—"

"Then, young man." Mrs. Tate lumbered toward him, the disapproval Biddy lacked pouring from her narrowed eyes. "Are you going to step up and marry her?"

"Ma'am, I would if she asked me to." He shot a dark look at Eric. "But I'm afraid I have to agree with Mr. Wright. Your attempt to smear Miss McGill's character and force her hand is unchristian. I doubt this would be how you'd like to be treated if you were in this situation."

"Me? Smearing her character? Why everyone…"

The whole lot of them started defending themselves at once, making Tim growl under his breath at their inability to stay quiet long enough to listen to what anyone was saying.

Even if this mess got sorted out, Mrs. Tate had already caused irreversible damage by publicly airing her accusations. How would Gwen's reputation survive untarnished?

CHAPTER THREE

Timothy would marry her if she asked him to?

Gwen forced herself not to glare at Eric. Instead of telling Timothy there was absolutely no need, Eric was arguing with Mrs. Tate and her friend about law and duress.

Eric drew himself up to his full height, squaring off with a blustery Mrs. Tate. "All I'm doing by continuing to argue with you is lend credence to your ridiculous accusations. I'm done." He turned his back on them.

"Really, Gwen?" he whispered as he came by. "Me and him? I didn't think you could be that..." He shook his head, and before she could respond, turned for the foyer.

He couldn't believe she was...? Oh, no. "Eric. Wait."

But the foyer door slammed behind him, rattling upon its hinges.

"Now, Biddy." Mrs. Tate frowned at the smaller woman. "Why'd you drag Timothy into this? The girl's going to go back to chasing men now, thinking there will be no consequences."

Gwen pressed her hands against her swirling stomach. Because she hadn't wanted to lie in God's house, she'd admitted to what Biddy had seen, but for Eric to not even ask why she'd been in Timothy's arms? To simply believe the accusation of a woman who couldn't see past her own nose? How badly had she come across last year that he'd believe she went straight from one man to another so easily?

"Gwen."

Timothy's hand landed on her shoulder, but she shrugged it off. She had to catch up to Eric. After running down the aisle and into the foyer, she shoved through the front doors and into the harsh sunlight. Raising a hand to her eyes, she caught sight of Eric's taut shoulders as he marched toward the station.

"Eric!"

He didn't slow, though he must have heard her.

Though she'd been called onto the carpet for her lack of propriety already today, she picked up her skirts and ran. "Please, wait."

He glanced over his shoulder for only a fraction of a second.

Within moments, she caught up. "You said yourself those women are off their rockers. Why would you believe—?"

"Because you said it was true."

"You didn't ask me why—"

"You made me look terrible back there, Gwen."

She stumbled over something unseen. She had? "It's not my fault what those women said—not solely, anyway. You—"

He whirled on her in the middle of the road. "Don't accuse me of having any part in this."

"You think I did?"

"You were awful pushy about getting married earlier."

Pushy? "I *mentioned* my hopes of getting married, but surely you knew that's what I wanted last year, even if you doubted I truly loved you. But none of what happened back there was my idea."

He eyed her warily. "I knew you liked to play games, but I always figured you were rather innocent."

She stiffened. It would've never occurred to her to have contrived such a scheme. For him to even think she had...

"Hey there, Eric!" Her brother's call sounded behind them.

21

Eric turned away from her and crashed into Bo, giving him a hearty, chest-bumping embrace.

Gwen swallowed hard at how easily he'd turned his back on her but tried to pull herself back together.

"You just got in?"

"A few minutes ago."

"We've been eager for your return." The smile Bo sent her way died immediately. He stepped away from Eric and scanned her face. "What's wrong?"

She must not have pulled herself together well enough.

"Oh, nothing." Eric put his hands on his hips and chuffed. "Except for your town gossip deciding Gwen and I needed to get married immediately because of an innocent kiss. And then some bumpkin was pulled into it, accused of having designs on her as well. Ludicrous. I mean, if you'd seen the man, it's a wonder the pastor didn't laugh at the absurdity of it all."

"Who was it?" Bo's mouth curved into a heavy frown.

Eric shrugged. "I don't know. Doesn't matter though…"

Bo turned to her.

"Timothy O'Conner," she whispered, despite the fact Eric hadn't stopped talking.

"…They were making everything up. Your pastor needs to rein in his congregation. Slander and libel of that magnitude is no laughing matter."

Bo's expression indicated he'd stopped listening to Eric, as if Timothy's name had made him worried.

"He's right, Bo. They assumed things. Nothing happened." She glanced at Eric. How had he gone from accusing her of playing with both his and Timothy's hearts to assuring her brother nothing the women had said was true? "I was so intent on meeting up with Eric the moment he disembarked that I smacked into Mr. O'Conner. He caught me to keep me from falling."

Eric's eyes narrowed.

She couldn't have both him and those two gooses telling

people about town she was a two-timer. "That's all it was. I'm not interested in him."

His lip twitched. "But considering how he looked at you…"

She inhaled sharply. "He didn't look at me in any way that should worry you. We hardly know each other."

And yet, Timothy had looked at her with intense scrutiny.

Eric raised his hands and shook his head. "Fine. As I said, the whole thing's ridiculous anyway, nothing to worry about."

"I don't know about that." The storm in Bo's eyes hadn't lightened. "Mrs. Tate has more influence than she should."

Gwen's breath lodged in her chest. "But the town knows she's a judgmental gossip. Surely we ought to act as if there's nothing to what she says. Since everyone is desperate to work with you, any smear to my character should fade." Even if it took longer than it ought.

Bo's cheek only ticked.

Her heart fluttered. If her brother believed her reputation truly in danger, well then, maybe she'd finally be able to convince him there was no need to wait until her twenty-first birthday to give her access to the funds she needed to move away.

"Gwen, are you truly all right?" Bo's hand clasped her upper arm as if he were afraid she'd faint.

She glanced over at Eric. How could she say yes, when she was faced with enduring the next few days sitting in a parlor with a man who seemed to believe she was as wanton as Mrs. Tate did? Swallowing hard, she nodded. Maybe she could feign an illness, hide in her room, allow her brother some time with his friend before he realized exactly how much this town was about to turn against her.

"Good. Shall we?" Bo took her arm and informed Eric he'd send a servant for his bags as soon as they reached the house.

After years of practiced flirtations, she'd have thought it'd be much easier to put on a carefree mask, but thankfully her brother wasn't looking at her anymore. Bo questioned Eric about his trip, and he answered as if nothing life-altering had happened. As they talked, she concentrated on breathing, in and out, trying to believe this would all blow over as quickly as these two bounced between topics.

Eric pointed toward a man with dirty hair sitting on the boardwalk. "I thought you told me Armelle didn't have the riffraff problem Denver does."

"Most come up from Denver," Bo responded. "Your deputies send them packing, and they drift up here. Without an active marshal, they stay."

"I thought that one rancher was helping."

"Dent has few hours to spare, and the council hasn't been able to agree on who to hire." Bo's tone was less lighthearted than Eric's.

"Why don't you run for mayor and bypass that argumentative lot?"

Gwen pressed her lips together to keep from jumping in. Arguing politics in the mood she was in right now was likely not wise.

"I'm the one man who shouldn't run." Bo crossed his arms over his chest. "No one would vote in another McGill."

All right, so she couldn't stay silent. "I don't think that's true. Everyone's pleased with how you've handled the return of the land Father stole. And you have schooling and knowhow."

His jaw tightened. "Not interested."

"What will you do once you've cleaned up Father's mess, then? Become a man of leisure?"

"I don't think I'd mind leisure."

Her brother do nothing? She couldn't imagine that. But then, maybe he needed a break. He'd worked hard for over a year now and people were lining up to do business with him.

"With the real estate knowledge you've gained straightening out your father's affairs, I'd bet you have a good eye for what's fair." Eric strode down Main as if they were on a carefree stroll.

"I've got my eye on a piece of property on the outskirts of Denver. It's run down, mind you, but cheap."

"What do you intend to use it for?"

"After I hired a crew to renovate, I'd..."

And with that, they were talking as if she weren't there. That always happened when these two got together. Never before had she been so happy about it though. If she could just make it home, she'd excuse herself, hold her head a little too close to the lamp, and call up Mrs. Barton to take her temperature.

A few minutes later, Bo gestured for them to stop in front of the hotel and tugged on his tie. "Seeing as how Mrs. Tate believed you two looked a touch too cozy, perhaps it'd be best you stay in town."

"What?" Eric threw his hands up as if Bo were unreasonable. "We can't let a woman like that dictate our lives."

"I'll put you up."

Eric sneered for a second, but then shrugged. "Fine."

Wonderful. Perhaps she didn't have to fake the plague after all.

"But if you're that worried, perhaps I should cut my visit short."

"But how would leaving help?" She had to force herself not to clamp onto him. "Leaving immediately could lend weight to her accusations, make people think Bo believes her insinuations and asked you to leave."

"Gwen has a point." Bo's lips wriggled back and forth, as if trying to keep from saying more. "I don't think it wise for you to go home too soon."

Eric sighed. "I'd planned to stay the week, but perhaps we could leave early for Denver together. Why don't you come see the properties I'm considering?"

She tried to stare hard enough at Bo to get him to agree. Not only would that get them away from all the piercing eyes Mrs. Tate's rantings would likely send their way, but if they spent enough time in Denver, maybe he'd see how much better they'd fare far removed from the black cloud their father had enshrouded them in.

Her brother breathed deep and then looked toward the train. "Maybe."

Maybe? "Surely a visit—"

"We'll see." Bo cut her off, his gaze intense.

Why would he be against visiting? Even if he thought there was something untoward going on between her and Eric, they usually stayed with Mother's old friends, and Bo would be with them every minute. Though she now doubted Eric was the one for her, hopefully if she traveled down with the two of them, she could convince him she wasn't the kind of woman who set out to entrap men. She didn't need any rumors of her being a crazy person to contend with in Denver.

Bo took off his hat and swept his arm toward the hotel door. "Let's get you a room."

She stepped back. If her brother truly believed Eric had to stay at a hotel, going inside with them might bolster the busybodies' tongues. By now, Mrs. Tate had likely told plenty of people about her accusations. "I'll wait out here."

Could Mrs. Tate truly do more damage to her reputation than Gwen and her own father had?

CHAPTER FOUR

"Thank you." Tim grabbed the strange, long hinges from the blacksmith. What was his boss's wife inventing now? Tim shoved the odd contraptions onto the wagon bed then hoisted himself up. Whatever she was making, he had wood to pick up from the sawmill for her, too.

As soon as he finished pushing the animal feed sacks to the side, a wild movement out of the corner of his eye caught his attention.

Across the street, Bowen McGill was waving frantically.

Tim turned, but no one was behind him. Was Bo waving at him?

"Mr. O'Conner!"

Evidently, he was.

Tim brushed his hands against each other to knock off the feed dust and hopped to the ground. Why would Bo want him? A week had passed since the crazy day Biddy Lockheed had accused him of being inappropriate with Gwen. He'd figured Bo had been as incredulous as Mr. Wright about Gwen wasting a second on him and had forgotten all about it.

Unfortunately, Tim hadn't forgotten. The feel of her seemed embedded in his skin.

Would Bo ask what happened? His part at the depot had been innocent enough, but try as he might, he'd not been able to stop wondering about Gwen's disheveled state after her walk with Mr. Wright. Tim had determined to give her the benefit of the doubt, but what if there'd been truth to Mrs. Tate's accusations? He ran a hand through his long hair. He knew better than most that one could not make sound judgments based off looks.

Bo locked eyes on him and nodded, as if telling Tim to wait.

He took a moment to swipe at his sleeves, though doing so would not improve their appearance. They were stained and patched in so many places that a little dirt probably improved them. Next to Bo, he'd look bedraggled. The man wore an immaculate suit, a starched white shirt, and a silk tie the color of a green apple.

Tim dragged off his hat as the spit-polished man approached. They'd not been friends in school. Town kids like the McGills didn't play with country kids like him.

Bo stopped in front of him.

"What can I do for you, sir?"

Bo raised an eyebrow slightly.

Surely he was used to being called 'sir' by people his own age, likely even those older than him, considering his status.

Bo scrunched his mouth as he scanned Tim's threadbare shirt before taking a quick breath. "I wanted to ask you about something that was said the other day, when Mrs. Tate dragged you and Mr. Wright to the church."

Tim stiffened. "There was no truth in what those women said about your sister. They—"

"I know that, but I heard you'd offered to marry her?"

His heart froze, and his fingers turned to lead. "Um, I— Mrs. Tate and Mrs. Lockheed were trying to force them into a wedding. I'm not sure I thought through any of what I said. Just wanted to keep your sister from getting hurt any more than she already was."

"Hurt?" Bo cocked his head.

"She seemed quite upset that Mr. Wright wasn't keen on walking her down the aisle." *Unfortunately. What did she see in the guy anyway?*

Bo looked away and gave a slight shrug. "All right then."

Did Bo have no intuition when it came to the men his sister chased? Did he think letting her continue to gallivant around with such men with no oversight would end well?

"I guess there's no—"

"Aren't you tired of watching her go after men who don't want her? I know it's none of my business, but surely you haven't wanted her to end up with any of them."

"What?" Bo startled. He scanned Tim from head to toe.

Right, he wasn't qualified to have an opinion on the lofty set. Why hadn't he kept his mouth shut? He held up both hands. "I understand Mr. Wright's your friend, and I don't mean to judge, it's just…curiosity. I don't understand why she keeps setting her cap on men who'll only break her heart."

Bo stared at him for a second, but then looked toward the McGill mansion while running his thumb along his jaw. "I'd figured she was always too enamored to notice."

Tim shifted on his feet. "Do you truly believe Mr. Wright's good for her?"

Bo shrugged. "He's smart, a friend of the family, has enough money to keep her as she wishes—suitable. Before this, I… Well, I'm not her father. I can't tell her what to do."

"I wasn't suggesting you tell her what to do, but she needs someone who…" He waved his hands around, searching for a word. "…can advise her. Someone to tell her she doesn't have to settle."

"Settle?" His brows winged up on that word.

That probably did sound crazy since Eric Wright was the handsomest, wealthiest bachelor to ever set foot in Armelle— other than Bo. "I'm sorry. I should've kept my mouth shut." He put his hat back on. "I'm afraid I need to get going. Don't want the boss wondering what took me so long."

Bo opened his mouth, but then shut it quickly and gave him a curt nod. "All right, then. Good day."

Tim tipped his hat. "And to you as well."

After Bo moved out of earshot, Tim blew out a breath. What had gotten into him this week—saying what he thought to people who didn't care a lick what went on in his head? At least he'd reined in his tongue enough to keep Bo from guessing his true feelings.

After getting the boards from the sawmill, Tim drove to the mercantile. Before he returned to the ranch, he needed to see about putting money on credit for his mother. His boss had given him a bonus yesterday, likely because he'd seen the new holes in his pants, though Ma had sewn them up well enough to be serviceable.

He ought to at least check if they had ready-made trousers skinny enough to fit. He pushed open the door.

"Hello there!"

He nearly jumped out of his skin at the boisterous greeting.

Raven Owens smiled at him from less than two feet away. Did she think him deaf? Of course, she'd never been known for subtlety. He willed his heart to settle. "Miss Owens, I'd wondered if you were back."

That jar of peaches he'd taken home had been awful. Ma hadn't even tried to force his siblings to finish their "treat" once she'd taken a bite.

Raven smiled wider, her blond hair lighter and curlier than he remembered. "Yes, last month. Where have *you* been?"

"Working." He tried to hide his smirk. Her brashness was often amusing. "I'm a hand at the Keys' now."

She slapped him hard on the shoulder. "Good for you. Got money in your pocket, then? What d'you come in for?"

He quickly scanned her. Seemed she still didn't care if her clothes were fashionable. Today, she sported a bright orange dress with brown trim. The skirt was slimmer than what most women wore, likely good for work—and though practicality had its merits—he didn't want her advice on clothing. "I just came in to look."

She shoved her hands into what must have been deep pockets since half her arms disappeared. "Let me know if I can help with anything."

"Sure."

Once she'd crawled back into the display window, he headed toward the clothing but stopped short in front of the full-length mirror and frowned. His limp, dark hair and mottled face were what annoyed him most about his reflection, but they weren't the only things that made him less than appealing. What business did he have looking down on Raven's fashion choices? He definitely needed more than pants. Did anyone else in town wear clothing so threadbare it'd surprise no one if the fabric just gave up and fell off?

What would he accomplish by spiffing himself up, anyhow? No matter what he did, he'd never attract a woman like Gwen, nor gain the traits Bo had rattled off about Mr. Wright. Bo had mentioned nothing glowing about his friend's personality, goals, or character, just his connections and possessions, as if those mattered.

Tim turned away from the mirror and stomped over to the pants. What he needed to do was find a woman who didn't care about looks and money. He glanced toward Raven, who was on her hands and knees behind the display window, sneezing as she wrestled boxes around. He shook his head. If he could look past her hideous orange and brown dress, he'd likely note she was a lovely woman in her own right, but he was stuck on someone else.

Why couldn't Gwen just get married already and crush the irrational part of him that refused to kick her out of his heart? Until the ridiculous hope he harbored was dashed to bits, he had no business thinking about marriage. No woman deserved to be courted by a man yearning for another. Hopefully, someday soon, God would send along a woman who'd capture his attention so thoroughly, he'd suddenly realize Gwen was nothing but a distant memory.

With a sigh, he picked up a pair of pants. He had better things to do than ruminate over a woman. Ma had always said so whenever she caught him daydreaming about Gwen instead of attending to his chores. And Ma was the reason he knew marrying "up" didn't equate to happiness. She'd ended up sinking even lower in the ditch she'd tried to crawl out of when she'd caught Alan O'Conner's eye.

Tim took another look at Raven and then at his frayed cuffs. Maybe instead of keeping a lookout for someone to take Gwen's place in his heart, he ought to work on himself. Once Gwen married, he'd need to be ready to turn his mind toward someone who'd be happy to have him. Though he'd never believed clothes made a man, he didn't want a woman to be embarrassed to stand beside him, either.

Considering Mrs. Tate had basically called him ugly the other day, he had plenty of work to do.

CHAPTER FIVE

Thunk...whump.

Gwen steadied her hand, took a deep breath, and let another knife fly.

Thup.

The blade stuck deep into the wood. She'd never be as skilled as her uncle at throwing—or even her mother for that matter—but the thrill of sticking one was no less satisfying than the first time she'd done so. Unfortunately, the summer she'd begged her mother to teach her how to throw was the last one they would ever share together.

After walking across her room, she wrenched the three knives out of the block that leaned against the back of her closet then returned to her desk to take out her sharpening stone. After a few minutes of rhythmic, furious honing, Gwen stopped to look at her mother's portrait. If only she were here.

Caressing the worn handle of her mother's favorite knife, Gwen inspected the chipped point. She ought to retire this blade to save it from further damage. She tucked it away in her jewelry box, hardly able to see through the moisture glazing her eyes. Would Mama be happy to know she'd not given up knife throwing despite Father banning all tomboyish activity as inappropriate and dangerous?

She shook her head. Father had never forbidden Bo from throwing knives. And mud pies weren't dangerous at all—or at least they shouldn't have been.

Gwen lowered her head into her hands and closed her eyes, pushing against the invasive memories, to no avail. She'd known Father would disapprove of her playing outside after the rain with her mother, but she'd begged Mama to go barefoot in the mud with her anyway. Of course, how could a nine-year-old know that stomping through puddles would change their lives forever?

The day after Mama had died from pneumonia, Father had outlawed all socially unacceptable activities, but now that he was no longer here, why hide her knife throwing? Bo likely wouldn't care, and Father wouldn't be back for years. He was no longer around to treat her as if his lonely life were all her fault—though she wasn't sure she disagreed.

The years that had followed Mama's death had been so cold. Her mother's warm embrace no longer available to snuggle into, her father's love for her gone.

Yesterday, Eric had said goodbye with just as little warmth, like she was nothing to him.

Gwen thunked down the last knife. Blowing out a breath, she pushed away from her desk. She ought to talk to Bo. He'd not acted as if it was odd Eric had traveled all the way from Colorado to do nothing but chat with him, that his friend hadn't seemed bothered that she'd stayed in her room and read each time he came over.

So why had Bo not accepted Eric's invitation for them to visit him in Denver?

She put on her slippers, then started the long walk across the house and down to the first floor. Once she reached the open door to his office, instead of knocking, she leaned against the jamb, waiting for him to look up from his writing. Stacks of contracts, deeds, and folders lay scattered across his desk, the wastebasket full of crumpled paper. Though nearly a year had passed since their father had been escorted to prison, Bo still worked hard to compensate the county folk who'd fallen victim to Father's scheming.

And what had she done to help Bo? Nothing. Maybe she shouldn't be so miffed that Eric wasn't eager to marry her. All she had offered him was a pretty face and a bank account— both things men were supposed to want, but seemingly didn't… or at least not from her.

She sighed heavily. No reason to burden her brother with another request for him to fulfill. She pushed off the doorjamb.

"Gwen? Did you need something?"

She gave him a little wave. "Don't mind me. You have plenty to do without me pestering you."

He closed the ledger in front of him and beckoned her forward. "None of this is more important than you."

Her heart hitched. Now she felt terrible for interrupting his business with her petty worries. But she had to talk to someone before she broke all her knives.

She moved to the chair in front of his desk. "I'm confused is all. Did I imagine Eric liked me last year, or did I actually do something unforgivable between now and then?"

"I don't think you did anything unforgivable, nor do I think you imagined things last fall, but time tends to change things." Considering Bo wouldn't look her in the eye, he was keeping something to himself.

"So you don't think I'm no longer worth pursuing?" What if he said 'yes'? She didn't want to go back to pretending to be something she wasn't. She slumped in her chair. What did it matter? Who in this town would have her now?

Bo sighed and looked her straight in the eye. "That's not it. But I'm afraid there're other women involved now."

"Other women?" Her stomach dropped. Eric had never mentioned other women—of course, why would he?

"He kept talking about two ladies he knows back in Denver. One, a hotel staffer who refuses to give him the time of day—"

"I suppose she's beautiful?" Gwen rubbed a hand along her goose-prickly arm.

Bo scrunched a shoulder. "His expression suggested as much."

"And the other?" She clamped onto her sleeve.

"One of his partner's daughters. She's set to inherit quite a sum. Eric joked about matching me up with her—though she apparently looks like a turtle."

"A turtle?" She frowned. "That's not very nice."

"Not everyone is blessed with your fine features."

"But if he joked about setting you up with her—"

"I think he was worried if he admitted considering the match for himself, I'd try to talk him out of choosing a woman strictly for money. After mentioning the lady's inheritance, he made a comment about yours, as if probing to confirm how much you have. Since he hasn't been forthcoming about his intentions, especially after the episode with Mrs. Tate, I kept my mouth shut."

But Eric's job should have provided him with plenty of money. "Is he in debt?"

Bo shook his head. "He's interested in real estate. Asked me to invest, but I don't think it's wise when the properties are too far away for me to look at."

"So, if I have neither his heart nor enough money, he didn't come up to visit me at all." What a fool she'd been.

"I think he did, but when things went awry… Well, suffice it to say, I think you're only an option now."

She looked away, afraid to let Bo see how much those words had smarted. "It's nice that *somebody* has options."

"You have them."

She scrunched her face. "Not if I don't move. Though I love you very much, I want to get married one day, and there are no *options* here."

"What about Timothy O'Conner?"

Surely he hadn't believed Biddy's accusations this whole time. "There's nothing going on between me and Timothy."

Bo remained quiet, staring at her as if she'd confess there was truth behind Biddy's overactive imagination.

"I know I got myself into a predicament this past week, but that's because I'm still *here*. I know…" She swallowed hard before admitting to what she'd yet to voice aloud. "I know how I've acted in the past has not worked out in my best interest. And that means the only reason why someone around here would be interested in me is my money—"

"Gwen, you're exaggerating—"

She held up a hand. She'd tried to argue this before, but maybe it'd work this time. "If I move to Denver, there'll be *options*, as you say. I can start over there, no mucked-up reputation to contend with. Surely Mr. and Mrs. Ledbetter would take me in for an extended visit."

"I still don't like the idea."

His frown made her frown. She didn't want to leave him alone since she was all the family he had left—at least out west. But one day he'd marry—his reputation was stellar. He could have first pick of any young lady who crossed into Wyoming territory. "There's no future for me in Armelle other than running your household—and that will end when you bring home a wife. Mrs. Barton is just as capable of running things as I am until that time."

"But what about Timothy?"

Had she not explained well enough there was nothing to Biddy's accusations? "What does he have to do with anything?"

"Why not give him a chance?" Bo twirled a pen between his fingers. "If he can't win you over, then I'll consider helping you move to Denver."

Had she heard him right? Bo wanted her to entertain marrying a ranch hand, who likely owned no more than two shirts and quite possibly lived in a hovel? "You mean you want me to allow him to court me?"

"Yes, that's what I mean. Give him three months."

"Three months?" Her mouth went dry. Surely she'd missed a piece of this conversation. Why would Bo…? Her heart kicked up. "He hasn't asked to court me, has he?"

"No, and I doubt he ever would."

Her heart settled back into place. But if Timothy hadn't asked, why would Bo consider such a match? "You know he's poor, right? He's not from our circle, our class, our—"

"It's not the Middle Ages, Gwen." Bo leaned back in his chair and crossed his arms. "You can marry outside of class."

She leaned back as well and rolled her eyes. "Sure. And the next time a duke comes through Armelle on his tour through America, I'll ask him to court me, too."

Bo's expression didn't change.

Maybe she just didn't understand men—not Eric, not her brother, and definitely not Timothy. "I'm sure he's nice, but anyone and everyone could see it wouldn't work." She sighed. "I'd only end up breaking his heart—if he even wanted to court me." Which he wouldn't since he had literally counted on his fingers why no man would. "And I can just imagine the amount of wild conjecture that would occur about town. You do remember what Biddy Lockheed basically accused us of, right?"

Bo cleared his throat. "How could you be certain it'd end in heartbreak? Why not consider him?"

She'd thought her brother more empathetic. "I'd not consider him because the only reason I'd do so was in hopes of getting you to agree to let me go to Denver. And that's not giving Timothy a chance—that's using him. Surely you can see that's wrong."

"I think he deserves a chance to prove himself worthy of you."

Had they become chums recently and she'd not noticed? "You think Timothy would actually be good for me?"

Bo's jaw tightened as he gave her a curt nod.

"But how? No one in town would put us together—besides Biddy. Why, we'd only be setting him up for ridicule if he actually agreed to court me."

"I can't force you to do anything, of course. But if you don't give him a chance, I'll not help you move."

She screwed her face up at him. "How is that not blackmail?"

Bo shrugged. "I'm not refusing to care for you or even walk you down the aisle with Eric at the end of it, if it came to that. But I want you to be happy—truly happy. I know you'll not play with Timothy's feelings just to get to Denver if you decide you can't give him a chance. You're not uncaring."

"I'm glad you think I have at least one good quality."

"You have plenty of good qualities." He lifted an eyebrow and shook his head. "Why you insist on hiding them behind fluttering eyelashes, I'll never know. Do you see me going after women who act like you do?"

She looked away from his intense stare. She'd thought he'd been too busy to notice the ladies making eyes at him. Was that something he purposely ignored?

Could she actually give Timothy a chance? No, this was ridiculous. "If I did as you requested, and he won me over, can you tell me you'd be happy with me marrying someone who has so little?"

"You'll have money when you turn twenty-one—as you know since you keep asking for it early. But if you don't withdraw any, the interest alone is enough to keep you clothed and fed."

"How do we know he'll not squander what I have? It's not as if his family is known for handling money well." From what little she knew, they had no money to handle at all. "Have you not heard the rumors about his father?"

"I've had dealings with the elder Mr. O'Conner, which have given me pause, but I've interacted with Timothy enough to believe he's made of different stuff." Bo sent her a fierce look. "If *we* can be different than our father, surely he can, too—and he certainly gives off such an impression."

She squirmed and looked away. Bo was right, but Timothy didn't make her heart flutter, and he had nothing she'd been taught to look for in a man. Though Father hadn't made every decision with her best interest in mind, he'd advised her toward a certain type of man for good reasons—for without money, a woman's life was pure drudgery—especially out west.

Bo sat forward in his seat. "The few times I've spoken to him, he came across as too cautious to spend a windfall wildly, especially since I've heard he gives all his money to his mother."

So perhaps he could afford another shirt. "But you can't tell me you have no worries at all about Timothy's prospects."

Reaching for her hand, Bo waited until she reluctantly gave it to him. "I want more for you than simply to be secure. I want you to have a taste of a man who thinks about *you* rather than what's best for him. Someone who doesn't consider you an option among many."

She frowned into the silence. Perhaps Timothy could offer that to someone, but he acted more put out with her than interested. "Is there no other man in town who you think could treat me so?"

He cocked an eyebrow. "Are there any men left you haven't flirted with?"

She bit her lip to keep from telling him she'd never thrown herself at drifters and old men. "I'm not guaranteeing anything if I consider this, correct?"

"If you don't tell him you're guaranteeing anything, then of course you're not." Bo steepled his hands. "Part of courting is taking the time to discern whether a man has the ability to do as he promises, whether he'll turn out better than his parents, whether he can make you happy. Don't assume he's a bad match —find out. That's all I'm asking."

If she discovered Timothy was what Bo thought he was,

could she live so humbly? If she never married, she'd likely have to do so anyway. "I'll have to think about it."

"Which only assures me I was right—you'd only do this for the right reasons."

She'd wanted someone to have more faith in her, but maybe she wasn't ready to live up to it. She pushed herself out of her chair. "I need to wash up for dinner."

"Of course."

After she gained her room, she grabbed her knives. Could she really open her heart to Timothy just to fulfill her brother's whim? She turned toward the mirror, trying to imagine Timothy beside her.

She couldn't—they just didn't go together. And how shallow did that make her? What did she know of him besides what he looked like and where he came from? But a marriage without attraction…

Well, would that be worse than a marriage entered into for investment purposes?

She threw a knife and almost missed the board. Did doing as her brother requested mean she had to believe a happy ending was possible? If she spent time with Timothy, would she see whatever it was Bo saw?

Spending time with someone didn't sound as serious as courting.

After throwing for a few minutes, she readied herself for dinner. She'd tell Bo she was willing to try. She'd not flirt. She'd not encourage. But she could take the time to get to know Timothy.

However, the moment he began to believe she felt something for him that she never could, she'd step away—three months or no. Surely all Bo needed to see was that she'd tried. And when he realized he was wrong, he'd help her move to Denver. Because that was what needed to happen if she had any chance at having a family to tend instead of making gouges in her closet wall for the rest of her life.

CHAPTER SIX

Closing the outhouse door behind him, Tim frowned at the torn-up catalog in his hand. He'd started tearing off the top page when he'd gotten distracted by the advertisements, guaranteeing this cream or that lotion could cure his every affliction. He'd spent so much time poring over the manufacturers' claims, he'd been afraid someone might bang on the door and ask if he'd fallen in.

But what if these products worked? Of course, he hadn't the money to buy them all to figure out which ones did. He dropped the catalog to his side. No reason to spend a dime on any of this when Ma could use every cent he made.

To the right, a light in the cabin behind the boss's house flickered dimly against the morning light. Mrs. Key must be tinkering—which was good. He hadn't seen the boss's wife out in her cabin for a while now.

If anyone would know which of these things might work just by looking at the ingredients, it'd be Corinne. He took a step toward the cabin but stopped. Would she think him vain?

Was he vain?

Fiddling with his suspender, he pulled at the tight fabric. The Keys had given him these and a new pair of boots last

Christmas. Though their gift was likely nothing more than a simple act of kindness, perhaps they wished he looked more presentable. He had purchased a new set of work clothes a few days ago. But his acne and oily hair? He'd battled those for years. Once he got Gwen out of his heart, he didn't want to spend forever fixing himself up so he could ask a gal to court. If he was going to do anything about his skin though, he ought to start now.

Hoping the men had all finished using the outhouse and wouldn't miss the catalog for a while, he walked over and knocked on the cabin door. After hearing a muffled reply, he pushed his way in.

At the table in the center of the room, Corinne held her pen above a well-worn notebook, her brows skewed up in question.

He cleared his throat but couldn't dislodge the lump. He waved the catalog in front of him before he could talk himself out of asking. "I happened to be reading this and…" He forced out a fake chuckle. "I thought some of the claims ridiculous. Figured you might enjoy a laugh, considering you know what chemicals do and all. Though maybe I'm wrong and these things could work."

Corinne's brow remained creased, not looking at all amused. Did she have a headache?

He should've paid more attention. "I'm sorry. I shouldn't have interrupted."

She shook her head, the usual glint in her eyes beginning to return. "What were you looking at?"

"Oh, just these bottles which apparently contain the fountain of youth." He took a step back. "But as I said, didn't mean to be a bother. I—"

"Get yourself back in here, Timothy." She waved him closer. "Let me see."

He handed over the catalog.

She glanced down the columns, likely surmising in an instant what he'd been wondering. After placing the catalog on

43

the table, she trailed a finger down the right side of the page. "These all have acids in them for eating away at whatever causes blemishes. This one has witch hazel which would be for soothing inflamed skin. It has—"

"Oh, I wasn't in need of a science lesson. Never was too good at the subject."

"No?" She looked up at him, her eyes flashing with mischief. "Well, you couldn't have asked me about these at a better time. There's a concoction I'd like to try on someone." She turned back to her notebook and flipped through her pages. "But pointing out people's flaws and asking for permission to try to fix them wins me no friends. Especially since I couldn't promise I'd succeed, but now that you're here…"

He should've known she'd turn him into an experiment. But what if something in her notebook would work?

"Mind if I run a few tests?"

"Will whatever you make show up in a catalog one day?"

She smiled. "Maybe."

He glanced at the jars lined up on the back shelves, full of different colored liquids. "What are you going to try on me? I don't want to smell like a girl."

"I haven't mixed up anything yet."

So then, she'd not really had something to try out, but had wanted to keep from sounding like she was taking pity on him. "Then I'm sure you have more important ideas to get to first."

"They're all important." She tapped her notebook. "I don't make prototypes of my ideas unless I'm ready to work with them. Last year, I bought some of those fountains of youth, as you call them. I'll have you use them first and see how they work. If they fail, we can see if my concoctions do better. And if they do, I'll know they're worth sharing with Uncle. He's constantly asking me to invent things he can market to women." She huffed. "As if cost-saving farm equipment wouldn't appeal to women."

"I don't know. Does the stuff you want me to try look like

this?" He pointed to a bottle decorated with an image of a lady with bouncy ringlets and long eyelashes. "If I use that in the bunkhouse, Rascal and Sal will laugh me out of it."

"Why keep from doing what you want to do because of what others might think? I'd not be out here if I did so."

It'd be a sorry day if she quit tinkering to appease someone's silly idea of what women should and shouldn't do. The stepladder she'd invented was the one he fought the other ranch hands for nearly every day. "I suppose I could help you out." And if her experiment helped him attract a good woman in a year or two, so much the better.

Of course, his face was probably the least of his problems. Aside from poverty and his problematic father, every female in the county knew he'd been rounded up with the rustlers last year. He'd been forced to sell his horse to cover the fine he'd received for keeping what he knew of his friends' criminal activity to himself. His eyes still grew misty on occasion over the loss of Blue. She'd been the only valuable thing he'd owned that his father had never had the guts to take away from him to pay down debt.

Corinne mumbled to herself as she started pulling out drawers, but then suddenly, she seemed ready to topple over.

Her color didn't look right. He moved closer. "Are you unwell?"

She waved him away. "I'm good." She covered her mouth for a second, and then her face pinked up again. She took a deep breath and handed him back the catalog. "What I want to give you must be in the house."

"You don't have to leave work for my sake. I can—"

"You ought to know by now I won't allow you to back out of volunteering so easily." She gave him a wan smile before pulling him toward the doorway.

He shook his head but didn't dig in his heels. "Have I ever told you I'm happy you're the boss lady and not the woman Mr.

Key's cousin hauled up here last year when he tried to take over the ranch? Did he ever end up marrying her?"

Their visit last summer had worried everyone on the ranch. That woman would've sent him packing the moment she'd gained control. She definitely wouldn't have tried to help him.

"A couple months ago."

"That's a shame."

Corinne hiccupped a laugh as she marched him across the lawn. "Sour cherries come in pairs, you know."

"I suppose even scoundrels have their soulmates."

"Rubbish."

That made him stop. "You don't believe in soulmates? But you and Mr. Key—well, your situation couldn't have been better orchestrated by the Almighty than if prophecies had been written about it."

She grinned, though it seemed it took some effort to do so. "I won't deny God had a hand in us getting together, but do I think Nolan was created for me? No. Humans make too many mistakes for God to bother with that."

"What do you mean?"

"You know I'd planned to marry someone else, right? And I would have, if given the chance. So if God had made Nolan for me—poor Nolan. Yet in order to save the ranch, he would've married somebody else since I wasn't around. And that woman wouldn't have been his soul mate, right? And then her soul mate would be at a loss, and so on. I don't believe God would be so cruel as to let one person's lapse of judgment keep countless others from finding happiness."

"Sounds reasonable." Corinne always made good arguments, and this one set his heart at ease. This ridiculous feeling that Gwen was the only one for him would pass with time.

Climbing up the back stairs, Corinne reached for him. "Come on, no feet dragging."

She pulled him into the kitchen, where Nolan was sipping coffee at the table. He raised his brows at the two of them.

At least Corinne had dropped his hand before his boss started glaring.

"The stuff I want you to try is upstairs." She swished away on mission.

After she disappeared, Tim searched for somewhere to stand out of the way. He would've sat, but his boss was still eyeing him. He cleared his throat. "It seems once your wife has a project in mind, she's going to make it happen, whether you like it or not."

Nolan set down his mug. "You're the project this time?"

He shrugged.

Nolan went back to reading his newspaper, but not before Tim caught a glimpse of a smirk.

The stairway echoed with Corinne's returning footsteps. "Here." She crossed the room, carrying a jar—an enormous translucent pink one with flowers printed on the label. "Directions are on the back. Follow them exactly."

Tim strangled the container in his fist. How on earth could he use this in the bunkhouse without being laughed clear out of Wyoming? But if this concoction helped him hold his head up higher, look people square in the eye easier, he'd figure out a way to use it without anyone noticing. "Thank you."

Turning, he fled out the back door, shoving the bottle deep down into his pocket. Passing by the necessary, he stopped to throw the catalog back inside. Maybe he should have simply used those worthless pages as God intended.

CHAPTER SEVEN

"Feel free to talk to my men, but I…" Corinne took her hand off Gwen's arm, pressing it against her chest as they stood in the Keys' entryway. Then she moved to the front door hurriedly and held it open. "I can't help right now. I'm sorry, I…"

"Mrs. Key, if my request is an imposition, I don't want to be a bother."

"It's no bother. I'll help another time. Maybe tomorrow?" With that, Corinne pushed the door open wider. "But you can ask my men what you'd like today."

Stepping back out onto the Key's front porch, Gwen watched the slightly older woman scurry away, her skirts swishing across the wooden floor as the door shut between them.

Ten minutes ago, Corinne had seemed willing to show her around once Gwen had told her Bo had mentioned a rancher might ask her to court one day and he'd wondered if she could handle such a life, being as spoiled as she was—the ruse Gwen had concocted so following Timothy around wouldn't appear too strange—but then Corinne had pushed her out the door.

Gwen tried not to let it bother her. The former town laundress had always seemed nice, and she'd said she would show her around. Maybe this was simply a bad time of day—Corinne *had* acted distracted since the moment she'd answered the door.

Gwen turned and breathed in the pine and sage-tinged air that came down from the mountains, which didn't seem so far away out here as they did in town. She'd wanted to speak to Timothy at some point, but she hadn't expected to pester him on her first day. But since Corinne had given her permission, she might as well get to fulfilling her brother's request. Now where would the ranch hands be?

Descending the porch steps, she couldn't help but hop off the last one. Her tomboyish getup would've annoyed her father, but a split skirt was so freeing. It'd been too long since she'd worn one. Maybe she should sneak off to the tree line and climb one for old time's sake.

The sudden memory of her mother rescuing her from the top branches of a giant oak made Gwen's eyes smart. This was no time for crying or tree climbing. She banished the mental image and scanned the yard.

Near the paddock, she caught sight of Timothy on a horse circling an older gentleman holding the animal's tether.

She smiled at the high fence surrounding the men. Perhaps climbing wasn't completely out of the question today. She crossed the yard, scaled the fence, then perched herself upon the top slat. Kicking one leg, she let out a heart-happy sigh.

The older man in the corral encouraged the horse to go faster. On their next go around, Timothy glanced in her direction, but turned his attention right back to the horse, as if he'd seen nothing unusual.

Of course, with her hair in a braid and one of her brother's hats on her head, he'd likely assumed she was Celia. If any young lady spent more time outside with the animals than inside a house, it was the Hendrix girl. She'd been in town last week, and Gwen had figured patterning herself after Celia might help her get close to Timothy without him suspecting her true intentions. She'd headed straight to the seamstress and told her to fashion a similar outfit: a split skirt, vest, and sleeves with no poof, but with fabric more suitable to her coloring.

Her braid was light blond though, not auburn like Celia's, so Timothy should've noticed upon first glance—but he was a man, after all.

After he took another turn about the corral, paying her no mind, she observed him more closely. What about him made her brother think she ought to consider marrying a lowly cowpuncher?

"Whoa, there." Timothy pulled the reins gently, yet firmly. When the horse shied, he kept his seat easily and started the roan around again. Riding a horse, Timothy did appear more confident than she'd ever seen him in town or in the years they'd been together in school.

After three more circuits, he dismounted and handed the older man the reins. He gave the horse's neck a gentle pat before the animal was led out of the corral.

Turning, Timothy started toward her, casual and self-assured, until halfway over when he missed a step. He recovered, but quit walking, standing heel high in a muddy hole.

He pushed his hat brim up and scratched his head for a second before smashing his hat back down again. "Good morning, Miss McGill. If you're looking for Mrs. Key, she's in the house."

"I've seen her, but I wanted to talk to you."

He didn't move.

"I've thought about what you said to me when we ran into each other at the station—about why I run after men who don't want me. So I've decided I need to work on myself, learn a few things about what it is to work."

He didn't even twitch, just kept standing in that puddle.

"I am a Wyoming girl after all, so if a rancher ever took a shine to me, I'd probably have just as bad a luck keeping his attention as the city men who've courted me before. But I know nothing about how ranches work. And since you're worried about the caliber of men I'm pursuing, I figured you could help me learn the skills a quality rancher would want me to have."

His jaw worked as if he were rolling tobacco around in his mouth, though she was fairly certain he didn't chew.

What if he wasn't willing to help? How else could she spend time with him without flirting—which seemed to be something he despised.

Timothy cleared his throat. "If a man doesn't want you as you are, why bother?"

Exactly…and yet, she sighed.

Did Timothy not know what it was like to be lonely? Her brother seemed to think she might end up a spinster the way she was going—and Timothy seemed to agree.

She turned her face to the ridge, hoping Timothy wouldn't see how near she was to tearing up.

Though Timothy and her brother might be right about her chance of ending up alone, she was too young to resign herself to such a fate. And though she didn't believe Timothy was her man, she'd always longed to learn new things—especially things one couldn't do stuck in a parlor. "The big ranchers around here wouldn't be interested in me—given what my father did—but a small rancher with potential might overlook my connections. However, such a man would need a skilled wife, such as Mrs. Key or Mrs. Hendrix, until he could hire on. Considering the Hendrixes' baby is six months old, I didn't want to pester them, so I came here."

"You'd…" He tipped his head down, causing his hat's shadow to obscure his eyes. "You'd be willing to marry a man who had nothing?"

"Nothing but a ranch." She couldn't very well live in a bunkhouse.

"You truly want to learn what a rancher's wife does?"

"That's why I'm here." This had been too easy. He would show her around, she'd learn a few things, he'd see she wasn't made for this life, and Bo would send her to Denver. Once out of Armelle, hopefully she'd discover what she was meant to do, who she was meant to be with.

"Come with me, then." Timothy turned on his heel and marched through the gate.

She hopped off the fence and scowled at his retreating back. Though a rancher likely didn't escort his wife around on his arm, he surely wouldn't leave her in the dust, either.

Timothy stomped across the yard and up the back steps of the house. "Mrs. Key!"

She scurried to catch up. "Oh, I already obtained her permission to wander about the ranch and learn what I can."

After knocking on the door, he turned toward her. "Wandering around won't help you know what a rancher's wife does, you learn that from a woman."

Corinne opened the door, wringing a limp dish towel in her hand. She appeared even paler than earlier. "What do you need?"

"Miss McGill here wants to learn how to be a rancher's wife. I believe you'd be better at teaching her than me." He let go of the door and tipped his hat toward Gwen. "I trust she'll do well by you, good day."

He brushed past her and strode out of earshot within seconds.

Why, she could kick the man, dumping her so unceremoniously on a woman who looked positively ill. She turned to Corinne. "Are you all right?"

But the older woman didn't answer—just rushed back into the house.

"Mrs. Key?" Gwen followed her in but stopped short the moment she heard Corinne getting sick. Gwen cringed and sucked in air. Without her father around to frown at her tomboy ways, she'd been excited to come out here and get her hands dirty again—but this sort of "dirty" hadn't been what she'd envisioned. But then, a rancher's wife would surely have to deal with worse—sick employees, animals dying, blood, manure.

With a swallow, she started into the house. "Mrs. Key?"

Bending over the sink, Corinne leaned heavily against the counter.

Gwen scanned the room. What did Mrs. Barton do for her and Bo when they were sick? After grabbing a towel, Gwen picked up the tea kettle. It swished. Pouring water into the cloth, she offered the damp fabric to Corinne. "Would you—"

Hunching over, the woman retched violently into the sink, and it was all Gwen could do not to run out the back door and follow in kind. Instead, she dropped the towel onto the counter, pulled back Corinne's loose hair, and tried not to breathe through her nose. "I'm so sorry, Mrs. Key. If I'd known you weren't feeling well…"

"No." Corinne took the cloth and wiped it across her face. "I'm sorry."

A rush of staccato thumps sounded behind them.

"Corinne, honey?" Nolan stumbled down the stairs, barely put together in slacks, undershirt, and no shoes, one of his feet a strange brown color.

She'd never seen Mr. Key's fake limb before. For some reason, she'd thought it would resemble a pirate's peg leg like those in storybook illustrations. Evidently, Nolan's fake leg had a foot.

He limped toward his wife as if he'd not noticed the stranger standing in his kitchen. "I heard you getting sick, but I was in the middle of strapping myself in."

"It's all right." Corinne waved him off, but she'd relaxed once he'd touched her.

Nolan peered over his wife's bent head toward Gwen. "She's not been feeling well. Maybe you could visit another day."

She forced herself not to mention his wife likely wouldn't want a visit tomorrow, either. She knew enough to guess this sickness might not go away soon, possibly not for nine months, but who was she to bring that up?

Corinne took in a deep gulp of air, pushed the hair back

from her face, and tried to smile. "I don't know when I'll be able to help you with any sort of instruction. I can't keep up with the house as it is, let alone do anything outside." She turned to her husband. "I'm sorry to keep you from your work."

"Nonsense." He pressed a kiss atop her head.

Gwen stepped back from the tender scene. Though she'd set out to learn things about the barn and animals in an attempt to spend time with Timothy, how could she claim she intended to learn what a ranch wife did yet run away from one who needed assistance because it didn't get her what she wanted?

Besides, Bo had not ordered her to keep a log of how many hours she spoke to Timothy. Whether it was one or fifty, it likely wouldn't affect the foreseeable outcome anyway.

"Let me help you, Mrs. Key. Tell me what you need done, and I'll try to do it."

CHAPTER EIGHT

Bursting out of the cellar, Tim sucked in a deep draught of air. Dirt, lichens, mud, and grass. So much better than whatever intoxicating fragrance Gwen was wearing.

Every day this week, she'd dragged him into doing something one person was plenty capable of doing, but after just one look from those blue eyes, he'd been helpless to say no. And somehow, she'd found him again despite his disappearing early this morning to the east paddock. He'd thought he'd be safe, but she'd snookered him into coming back to the house.

The cellar door wouldn't open, she'd said. Mrs. Key wasn't feeling well enough to help.

He'd been too slow in coming up with an excuse to stay in the field, so he'd walked back with her, flipped the latch, pushed open the door. What she'd found hard about that, he'd never know.

But then she'd snatched his sleeve and asked him to help her find the butter pickles. He'd tried to tell her he didn't know what was in the cellar, but he'd caved to her pitiful 'please'—and then they were together. In the near dark. With her smelling like that.

As they scooted canning jars around, she'd peppered him

with ridiculous questions. What color he liked, if he could live without sugar, if he preferred the smell of rain or sunshine.

As if one could smell sunshine. Not that the answers he'd given her had likely made much sense—well, maybe about as much sense as her questions—because she kept bumping into him. Each time he'd pick up a jar, she seemed to think he needed help figuring out what was in his hands, as if he didn't know what pickles looked like.

He inhaled deeply once again. Yep. Sun smelled like nothing. Silly woman. Next, she'd ask him what he thought purple tasted like.

He needed to escape.

Near the barn, he caught the movement of a black shadow. The Keys' dog turned the corner. Was he limping?

Checking on Mickey would be as good an excuse as any for getting as far away as possible before Gwen called him back down to ask if he preferred fresh or aged cheese.

Mickey disappeared into the barn. Even better. Tim strode across the yard, hoping to slip inside the weathered structure before Gwen noticed where he went.

It was hard enough having her out here insisting on "ranching lessons," hoping *he* would help her become desirable enough to catch the eye of the next man she set her cap on. But why was she now treating him as if he were acceptable company? He might work on a ranch, but that didn't make him fit to socialize with the ranch bosses. And even if he could, he'd never want to drink coffee with Gwen's husband, that's for sure.

Tim stepped into the barn but didn't see the dog. He usually curled up in the sunlight that shot through the gaps around the loft doors. "Mickey?"

A rustling came from the first stall. Ambling over, Tim frowned upon seeing Mickey licking his front paw. "What's the problem, boy?"

He stooped and inspected Mickey's foot. A thorn of some kind had broken off in the pad between his claws, a thistle by the looks of the bits and pieces stuck to his fur. "That's no good." He scratched the dog's head. "Wait here."

Once he entered the tack room, he frowned. Someone had cleaned and organized it. He crossed to the drawer where he'd last seen the tweezers. Not there. Corinne wouldn't have rearranged their stuff. She nearly went into fits of apoplexy when people touched things in her shop, let alone moved something.

Gwen had struck again. Sighing, he opened the next drawer and rummaged around. Why had she taken the saw blades off the wall and put them in here? Someone was going to get their fingers sliced.

Shaking his head, he began pulling things out and onto the counter. Gwen really had no clue about anything involving work. And no matter how diligent he was in avoiding her, she seemed intent on finding him, begging him to show her how to do something, expecting him to magically change her into something desirable.

He closed his eyes and swallowed hard. Why did she insist on him helping to make her more desirable than she already was? It wasn't as if it were working.

"Timothy?"

He let his head fall back and shoulders droop. If only his boss would send him off somewhere for a week or two.

"Are you in there?"

Maybe she'd go away if he stayed silent. Was it horrible to pretend he hadn't heard her so she wouldn't walk up next to him, smelling like a flower garden, looking to him as if he held the key to her future—a future he tried hard not to think about?

Ignoring her might not be nice, but sometimes, a man's sanity had to be protected at all costs. After a couple minutes' silence, he quietly slid out the next drawer. The tweezers. Finally.

"Timothy?"

He froze. Her tone indicated she knew he was in the barn and was miffed he'd not answered.

Seemed hiding was no longer an option. "I'm in the tack room." After shutting the drawer, he returned to the barn's main room. "Dog's got a thorn in his paw. Give me a minute and I'll help you with whatever you need this time." He winced a little at the impatience in his voice. But maybe she'd notice and find someone else to assist her.

She stepped into a ray of soft sunlight, which created a muted halo atop her head. "Do you need help?"

"No, thank you." With that, he turned his back on her to keep himself from staring at her golden beauty and headed for the first stall.

Kneeling, he patted the dog's head. "All right, fella, let's get this taken care of."

"Are you certain I can't help?" She walked up behind him and leaned to look over his shoulder, her warm breath tickling his ear.

The hairs on the back of his neck bristled at her sudden nearness.

What he needed was for her to go away—far away. "I'm sure Mrs. Key has a salve you could put on him once I take out the thorn. Why don't you go get that?"

"I wouldn't know what salve to get, and Corinne's napping at the moment."

Corinne was napping in the middle of the day? When had she ever done that? Though he and the other hands had bristled for days after the boss's new bride had decided to help around the ranch, she'd proven herself beyond helpful within weeks. Worked harder than they did sometimes. Gwen, on the other hand…

"Tell me what container it's in, and I'll see if I can find it."

"Do you know which cupboard Mrs. Key keeps the medicines in?"

"Of course, I've been in that cupboard a lot this week."

Who'd needed medicine? His stomach sank. Could Mrs. Key's out-of-character napping have something to do with it? "Why?"

"Well..." Gwen's hand fluttered to her chest and she turned to stare off at nothing. "Mrs. Key's been trying out different herbal combinations."

His skin flushed cold. Had Corinne told Gwen about her attempts to clear up his skin? If only the ground would swallow him up this very minute.

"She's not felt well lately."

So Corinne was experimenting on herself, too? His chest loosened a little.

Wait, was that why she was always shoving Gwen out of the house? Come to think of it, Nolan had taken over cooking again. When was the last time he'd seen Corinne working in her little cabin? His boss would be devastated if anything happened to his wife. "Is she all right? Has Doc Ellis seen her?"

"She's seen him." Gwen bit her lip but said no more.

His heart knocked hard against his chest. "Is it that bad?"

A funny little grin wriggled onto Gwen's lips for a fleeting second. "Yes and no."

"How can an illness be both?"

"Well, she'll recover at some point."

"Are they sure?"

Gwen's eyes sparkled and her lips wriggled again.

How could Corinne's illness be a laughing matter?

Oh, wait.

If he hadn't had tweezers in his hand, he'd have smacked himself in the forehead. He had enough younger siblings to have pieced that together himself. His mother never bothered to inform them when she was in the family way until she started showing, but it never failed that months before, Ma would start sleeping half the day away. "I see."

But why hadn't the Keys told the men?

Perhaps Nolan was worried. Women often died in childbirth, and this would be Corinne's first. "Tell them I'm praying for her."

Gwen's face lost its mirth and turned all soft.

He pivoted back to the dog. Dang, Gwen was pretty when she liked something she heard.

"Since I'd rather not disturb Corinne if I can help it, what does the salve look like?"

"I don't know, but you could find iodine, surely. It might not be what Mrs. Key would put on it, but it'll suffice."

"Do you need it right away or could you teach me to do what you're doing?"

Had she been so pampered she'd never pulled her own splinters? Or maybe she'd never even had one. "There's not much to it, though if the thorn's deep, it might bleed. If so, you just put pressure on it."

"For how long?"

"Surely you've bled before. Rich people do bleed, don't they?"

She rolled her eyes at him—likely the most improper thing he'd ever seen her do, other than that time she'd come into the church, hair all disheveled, cheeks rosier than he'd ever…

He strangled the tweezers. He would not allow himself to think of what she and Eric had likely done that day.

"Yes, we bleed. I just thought maybe it was different for an animal."

"Basically the same thing."

"Then could I?" She held out her hand.

Gwen was probably hoping for a win at something, considering she seemed incapable of most of the chores she'd been given. Rascal, the Keys' oldest ranch hand, had spent hours cleaning up after her this past week. He would surely grumble all night after learning how she'd "straightened" the tack room.

Tim handed over the tweezers, caving to that look in her eye —the one desperate to please.

"What do I do?"

So she had truly never used tweezers? He let out a slow stream of air. "Hold his foot, pinch the thorn, pull."

"All right." She kneeled beside the dog and took his paw. However, she was too mindful of the dog's desire to keep control of his paw to make him stay still. "Come on, doggie, you'll feel better if you let me—"

"He shouldn't *let* you do anything. Force him to do what you know needs to be done."

If Gwen's glare could burn a hole through him, it would have, but within moments, she'd returned her attention to the dog. "All right, pup. I won't ask you this time."

And though this time she anchored his paw between her knees, Mickey whimpered and she turned soft. The tweezers only glanced across the thorn before he pulled away.

"As much pain as you might cause him, it'll be worse if you leave the thorn in."

She handed him the tweezers. "You do it."

Oh, for Pete's sake. He reached for the instrument but stalled. Her eyes were the deepest of blues—which he'd known —but they also looked so sad and defeated.

Though she'd attempted to dirty her hands more than he'd ever thought she would, a bit of pity welled up for her. Just like Mickey, she had a thorn keeping her from living the life she wished. But getting her to be anything like Mrs. Key would be far harder than a simple pluck of the tweezers.

Gwen was on a fool's errand. While he could admire her desire to learn, it'd be best she found a city man who'd let her pour tea, paint, or whatever else rich women did. But with her this close, and the sun playing in her hair, making the shadows of her long lashes splay across her flawless cheeks…

He snatched the tweezers from her hand and gathered up the dog.

How had he ever let himself yearn for the fairy-tale princess he knew he'd never end up with? And since she couldn't even open a sticky door, collect eggs in less than a quarter hour, or care for an animal's basic needs—what kind of fantasy had he got himself wrapped up in?

One that kept him from looking for the right woman. He needed to pine for more than a pretty face and a stubborn streak to help him weather the hardships of life.

After pulling the splinter, he handed her the tweezers. "Put those back in the tack room for me, would ya?"

"You don't want me to get the iodine?"

"No, I'll do it." He stood and patted his leg. "Come, Mickey."

Before she could ask him to help her with anything else, he hustled out of the barn.

Stepping into the fresh air, he strode toward the house, the dog at his side. "Boy, I hope you've learned from that thistle. No matter how lovely something is, how pretty it smells, if it won't improve your life, you shouldn't cuddle up to it."

A lesson he and Mickey both needed to get through their thick skulls. The sooner, the better.

CHAPTER NINE

"I'll go gather the eggs," Corinne said with a heaviness in her voice.

"Are you sure?" Gwen frowned at the last of the breakfast dishes she'd had to redo since they'd come out greasy. "Didn't you say you were tired?"

"I'll take a nap afterward." She gave her a wan smile before heading outside.

Gwen swallowed hard. She'd dropped three eggs yesterday —likely why Corinne was bothering to get them herself.

But how did anyone manage to get away with all the eggs intact with that hellion of a rooster around?

Of course, when she'd backed out of the coop kicking at the malicious animal, hollering like a banshee, she'd smacked into Timothy.

He'd just shaken his head at her and walked away.

How he and Corinne weren't scared of those giant talons stabbing them from behind, she didn't know, but running from an overgrown handful of feathers had only given Timothy one more reason to look down on her.

"Good morning, Mrs. Key."

Thinking of Timothy seemed to have conjured him up. His

booted footsteps thumped across the porch. "I've heard you're dealing with a sour stomach. I'm glad to see you out." His voice drifted in through the open windows. "Are you feeling better?"

"A little. But I'm afraid I haven't seen the last of it."

"The men and I wanted you to know if dinner needs to be blander for you, we don't mind."

"That's sweet of you."

"Is there anything specific we can pray about?"

Gwen wrung the dish rag and slapped it onto the hook. Though Timothy had no designs on Corinne, he was certainly invested in making her happy—more so than Eric or any other man who'd courted her had ever done.

"I'm fine," Corinne said, even though anyone looking at her would know she wasn't.

"Glad to hear it. Now tell me, where are those rocks you intended to stack around the flowerbeds?"

"Oh, don't worry about that. I'll get to it."

"Don't make me waste time looking for them." His voice held more teasing than Gwen had ever heard from him. "You don't want me stacking the wrong ones, do you?"

Why was he being so much more genial to Corinne than her? All week, she'd tried to come up with ways to talk to him, but he'd acted ready to leave their conversations as soon as they began.

Corinne chuckled. "You're incorrigible."

"Ma just calls me ornery."

"I can see why. But if you must, they're the flat reddish ones by the well house. There should be enough for both iris beds."

"Thank you. I'll have that done today."

The sounds of their footsteps, Corinne's light and sluggish, Timothy's determined and loud, hit the stairs and then muffled once they stepped onto grass.

Gwen could understand why Corinne had a soft spot for Timothy. He was proving to be a man many ladies would want —skilled, conscientious, showing genuine concern for a woman.

Whereas she was proving herself to be the worst potential mate for a rancher, or even a lowly ranch hand.

Instead of drying the dish in her hand, Gwen set it down and braced herself against the sink. Though she'd never thought herself prideful, his determination to pay her no mind was unsettling. Yet why should she expect him to fawn over her? Because she was pretty and wealthy?

Glancing out the window as the curtain fluttered in the summer breeze, she caught a glimpse of Corinne disappearing into the coop. Though reasonably attractive, the older woman didn't care for fashion, had work-worn hands, and had been a struggling laundress until last year.

Gwen frowned. The masculine admiration she'd received over the years couldn't compare to how the Keys' ranch hands treated Corinne. Their regard for her was deep and real.

Gwen sighed and tied back the loose curtains. *She* was nothing but window dressing. Her beauty was an unearned gift from God, and yet she expected to be fawned over like a queen for it? She let out a derisive chuckle. How had she ever thought hardworking men like Timothy would jump at a chance to wed her? Even if he were attracted by her bank account, he was smart enough to know that once spent, all he'd have left was her. And he seemed to have no interest in someone so useless.

She put away the last dish and hung her apron. Maybe she'd go stare down the rooster until her fear of him eased and she could gather eggs without running. Though succeeding at what any six-year-old farm girl could do would likely impress no man.

Throwing the door wide open, she headed toward the coop. Would Corinne have the energy to teach her how to butcher a rooster? Surely no one would mind if the scrappy bird ended up in a pot.

A feminine whoop sounded from the paddock.

Celia Hendrix was reining a horse to run a tight circle, a rope twirling above her. She threw the rope and snagged a calf.

Timothy was inside the fence, hollering something that

Gwen couldn't make out. But the look on his face as he spoke to Celia while she untied the animal was one he'd yet to give her—a look of camaraderie, as if viewing an equal, even though she was two years younger than him.

Would learning how to rope earn his respect? Surely, the ability to accurately throw knives had to be similar. Gwen watched as Celia jumped back into her saddle and rode off again.

Her next toss was a miss.

"Aim right at the back of the neck, keep your fingers pointed where you're throwing," Timothy called after her.

"I know, I know." Celia reeled in her rope and took another turn around the corral.

Turning to watch Celia trot past, Timothy caught a glimpse of Gwen. He sighed and moseyed over.

Was she that much of an inconvenience?

"Do you need something, Miss McGill?"

She pointed toward Celia. "I want to learn to do that."

His brow creased and he glanced back over his shoulder. "To do what?"

"What Celia's doing."

His face scrunched as if he couldn't comprehend words. "You mean rope?"

She nodded, but he shook his head.

"Ranchers don't expect their wives to know how to rope."

Probably not, but after this week, another failure wouldn't matter much. "I'd like to try anyway."

The creases in his forehead deepened. "But ladies don't rope."

Celia's loud whoop interrupted them. She'd pulled down the calf again.

Gwen pointed at Celia, who'd jumped down to untie the wriggling animal. "She does."

"Well." Timothy took off his hat and ran a hand through his too long hair. "Celia ain't exactly a lady."

Why must he insist on talking her out of everything? If she climbed into the corral and grabbed a rope, would he give up trying to dissuade her?

Gwen stepped onto the bottom fence rung and frowned. Too bad her split skirt had been wet this morning, but it was now or never. Hitching her skirts, she flipped over one leg, then the other. She cleared the top, but the moment her foot hit the ground, her hem snagged and her ankle twisted.

Tim's hands clasped her upper arms, and she puffed an errant strand of hair from her face as she steadied herself. Then he took a step away—a giant step. Just like he had the last time he'd caught her. Having to be rescued so often was becoming annoying. It wasn't as if she were clumsy.

"Are you all right?"

Though her ankle smarted, she wouldn't let on. "I'm fine. So, can you teach me how to rope?"

His expression was blank.

"Please, Timothy."

His chest puffed out like he would capitulate, but then he about-faced and held up a hand. "Celia!"

Gwen screwed up her lips. He was going to push her off on someone else again.

Celia trotted over on her pretty white horse, glancing between the two of them.

Timothy gestured toward Gwen. "Miss McGill wants to learn to rope. Could you show her—"

"Can't." One of Celia's auburn braids slipped over her shoulder as she scanned the horizon. "I shoulda left already. Since Jacob's obsessed with the new polo ponies and Ma with the baby, I have to make sure Spencer's keeping up with the animals, and he usually isn't." She shifted and tipped her dirt-encrusted hat at Gwen. "Sorry, but I've been in enough trouble this week."

With that, she trotted past, leaned over to open the gate, and let herself out.

Gwen shot a smile up at Timothy. He'd have to help her now.

But instead of the scowl she'd expected, his gaze roamed her face. He almost seemed...captivated. Maybe he didn't find her repulsive after all.

She let her smile inch up.

He looked at her mouth for a second, but then turned and walked off. "I don't have all day. I've got rocks to stack."

Well, clearly she had no ability to discern what was going on in his mind. Why did he dislike her so much?

He snatched a rope off a post and pulled it loosely through his hands. "First thing you need to learn is how to make a coil. Hold the tail here, reach down about an arm's length, and fold it over somewhat, turning it like this so it'll lay nice."

She ought to ask him to do that again, but she didn't want to stop him since he'd never before given in so easily to one of her requests.

"Once you got the rope coiled nice and smooth, hold the knot out here and build your loop like so."

Goodness, he did that fast.

"Pull down, make a shank the length of your arm, and hold here. You'll align your finger with the knot as you circle it over-head." He stepped away and started spinning the rope. "As you swing, keep your finger coming back to the target, which is the back of the neck. Twist your wrist to keep a nice open rope, then when the loop tip lines up with your target, throw." He let go and caught a fence post.

Though it appeared easy, she wasn't about to get her hopes up that it was.

After he unhooked his inanimate quarry, he held out the rope. "Here."

"You mean, you think I should try already? I didn't catch half of what you said."

"You know as much as any boy who picks up a rope." He

pointed at a sun-bleached skull mounted on a sawhorse. "Try for that when you're ready."

How to keep her shaky hands from betraying she suddenly wasn't so keen on him teaching her after all? She would fail, over and over again. Which was the last thing she needed to do in front of him.

After giving her a few pointers on coiling her rope and how to swing it, he stepped back, arms crossed.

What had he said about the actual throwing part? She stared at the skull, trying hard to recall how Celia had done it.

After a few turns of the rope nearly over her head, the rope landed with an awkward thud several feet short of the sawhorse.

"Your form's fine. Keep trying. Remember, the target is the back of the neck." He turned and headed off.

He was leaving her? "Wait! How will I learn this by myself?"

"I figured it out by trial and error. You can, too."

"How long did it take?"

"Weeks." He stopped and lifted an eyebrow as if he knew she'd give up. "You sure you want to bother?"

Squaring her shoulders, she answered by turning her back on him and pulling in her rope for a second attempt.

Her next throw landed even farther away from the skull. Keeping herself from checking if Timothy was still watching, she dragged the rope back for another attempt.

Weeks? Surely those "weeks" were pockets of time he'd found between school or chores, so likely just a handful of hours.

She had nothing better to do while staying outside while Corinne napped. If she worked until lunchtime, maybe she could learn something useful enough to impress somebody.

As the sun inched higher, she attempted to calculate how holding her arm in one position or another landed her rope, how different tosses changed the shape of her loop, how much force she had to exert to get close to her target.

Hours later, parched and sore, Gwen threw with even more

determination, though she needed to wait between throws because her shoulder was screaming. When she raised her arm again, her muscles seized. Was it possible to throw with her other hand?

As soon as she switched, Timothy called out from behind her. "Nolan's made lunch, told me to come get you."

She huffed, glaring at the skull in front of them.

He stopped beside the fence. "You haven't been roping since I left, have you?"

"Of course I have." She gritted her teeth, hoping to keep the pain out of her voice. "I'm putting in my weeks' worth of time."

"If you haven't worked those muscles before, you're going to be really sore in the morning. Maybe you ought to take a break."

Too late for that. Not only did her arms and upper back hurt, but her ankle still throbbed. She switched the rope back to her right hand. "I don't want a break until I've earned one." With that, she threw again, snagging a horn.

"Well I'll be, you did it!"

She stomped across the yard to unhook the skull. "I only got one horn."

He held out both hands as if imparting a blessing upon her. "Miss McGill, that's more than any of us would've expected of you. You should be pleased with yourself."

"Watch again, then." She stopped back to the spot she'd been standing for the last half hour and threw.

Missed.

"See? You praised me too early. I've yet to get consistent."

"You're being too hard on yourself. No cowpuncher ropes their quarry one hundred percent of the time."

"They're roping live, moving cows. Not a dead one on a stick."

He gave her a wry grin. "True, but you've done well for a

morning's worth of work. With more practice, you'd surely become…"

"Useful?" she supplied.

Shaking his head, he rubbed at his chest as if he were experiencing heartburn. "Not sure how useful it'd be. As I said, ladies aren't expected to do this."

"But Celia does."

"Well, that's Celia, and that type of woman…well, she's not your type."

She tried not to let it hurt that he clearly liked Celia's type better. "But she's the kind a rancher would want."

"Don't know about that. Ranchers don't marry because they need another hand. They hire those."

"So then, you've never thought of marrying Celia?"

Crimson crept up his neck as he glanced in the direction she'd gone.

"So you have. Which means—"

"It only means most men—at one time or another—think of all the available women as potential brides, especially when you live out in the middle of nowhere with few options."

Options? She sneered at the word choice. "So you've thought of me too, then?"

Shaking his head, he bent down to pick something up off the ground, his hat obscuring his face. "You're not an option for any of us, Miss McGill."

Was there really so much wrong with her? Of course, she'd not have considered a ranch hand for a potential match either, but to not even be thought about in passing?

Straightening, Timothy crossed the paddock, grabbed the spare lariat, and swung it over his head, throwing and snagging the skull with ease. "Next time, keep your finger pointed at the target."

She gritted her teeth to keep from grumbling. He'd already told her to do that.

Without stopping to retrieve his rope, he headed back toward the house.

She sighed as she watched him walk away. Bo had been dead wrong about her having a chance at winning Timothy over. With every passing day, he seemed more and more annoyed with her, even if he'd caved and given her a compliment today.

Though maybe Bo hadn't really sent her out here to find a husband, but rather be served humble pie. To learn that some men—especially this one whom she'd once thought beneath her consideration—felt exactly the same way about her.

CHAPTER TEN

The pine laden breeze blew across Tim's damp shirt and ruffled his horse's mane, bringing a small amount of relief from the heat. The sun beat down hard against the vast swells and dips of summer grasses interrupted by occasional buttes, canyons, random rocks, and the sporadic lines of willows and swamp oaks guarding precious bodies of water.

Out here, there was space—and more space. Even the mountains, though they blocked the western horizon, disappeared miles beyond what the eye could see.

And out here, there was no chance of stumbling upon a blue-eyed blonde with a face like that long-lashed doll his sister always admired high up on the mercantile shelves. If it hadn't been for Gwen, he and his sister would've thought the amount of ruffles, ringlets, feathers, and lace sported by that porcelain figurine fantastical. Though over the past few weeks Gwen had left her finery behind for more practical clothing, ringlets and long lashes seemed to suck him in as much as they did his little sister.

If only Corinne wasn't in the family way and hadn't decided to keep Gwen around for help. Not that she seemed to be much help, but womenfolk apparently enjoyed having company while in misery.

This morning, he'd told Corinne he'd pray for her, but he already did. He prayed she got well quickly and could send Gwen back home. Her presence only perpetuated *his* misery— dangling something in front of him he couldn't win, like one of those rigged carnival games.

Earlier today, the look on Gwen's face when she'd nearly begged for him to declare her useful had caused a hard pit to form in his chest. He might not know everything about her, but one thing was obvious—she tried hard to mold herself into whatever the man she was after wanted her to be. This time, it was an unknown rancher she hoped to impress one day, but still, a man who didn't know *her*. She was so busy being what she thought men desired, did *she* even know who she was?

He shook his head and took in another deep whiff of clean pine air. He was out here to escape Gwen. Thinking about her defeated the purpose.

Kicking his heels into the side of his mount, he started down an incline into the rocky ravine he'd decided to search for the Keys' missing cow and calf. Three days had passed since anyone had seen the pair.

"Halloo!" A faint call echoed against the nearby rocks.

Not yet below the lip of the crevasse, Tim turned his head and glimpsed a distant figure. He directed his horse to back up then squinted at a man's silhouette.

Rascal?

What was he doing out this far?

Hopefully the Keys weren't angry about his lengthy disappearance and hadn't sent their oldest cowhand to fetch him. He'd expected to be chastised for leaving without telling anyone where he'd gone, but he'd figured with the additional work he'd done on Corinne's flowerbeds, no one would care if he'd needed to put some space between himself and a pretty, little cocklebur.

Because that look Gwen had given him earlier...? He'd almost mistaken it as desire.

He'd clearly not been away long enough to stop thinking about her. Hopefully Rascal wouldn't drag him back to the ranch.

Tim lifted his hat and waved. "Over here!"

Rascal changed direction slightly.

Upon first coming to work for the Keys, Tim had been leery of Rascal since he'd have blended in well with Father's crowd, rough around the edges and cynical. The sixty-year-old had worked with Nolan's family since he was a boy, but over the past year, Tim had slowly grown to trust Nolan's oldest ranch hand himself—for he knew all too well how people could pull the wool over everyone's eyes—even the very people they hurt.

"You're certainly out here a fair piece." Rascal reined in his mount beside Tim's and scanned their barren surroundings.

"Been searching for the cow and calf Sal noticed missing days ago."

"You should've told someone. We were worried about you." Rascal's statement didn't sound full of censure, but it was there.

"Sorry 'bout that, but I'd had a memory of seeing some heavily flattened grass out here on my last ride, so I decided to check. Figured it was deer at the time."

He'd not tell Rascal that memory hadn't resurfaced until an hour after he'd wandered about aimlessly trying to figure out an excuse for his absence.

The way Rascal eyed him indicated he wasn't buying the story. "You ought to come back to the ranch. Miss McGill's been working hard at roping. Seems to prefer your teaching over mine."

Tim fought to keep from rolling his eyes. She didn't care who taught her, as long as she was making strides toward attracting the man she hoped to snag. "Couldn't help her anymore today. Had to check on—"

"That's a fib if I ever heard one."

Maybe looking for two missing animals wasn't dire, but it was certainly more useful than teaching Gwen how to rope. "I gave her pointers before I left."

"Are you out here hiding from the girl?"

Tim stiffened. "I've more important things to be attending than teaching her how to rope. Besides, it's ridiculous. She'd be better off attempting to learn what womenfolk do inside the house, don't you think?"

"Don't dismiss her just because she didn't grow up scrapping for everything like Mrs. Key. Ain't Miss McGill's fault she's been blessed to have people wait on her hand and foot. Her aim ain't half bad, you know."

He just shrugged. He'd lose this argument if he kept it going —especially if Rascal already suspected he was running from her.

Rascal plucked a long grass stem, plugged it into his mouth, and scanned Timothy from his hat to his worn boots. "You aren't thinking she's got her eyes set on you, are ya?"

Tim pulled his horse's reins to the right, putting more space between him and the old man. "Of course not. Everyone knows she'd not stoop to marry me." He pointed to the ravine, eager to direct Rascal's thoughts elsewhere. "You see that bent grass under the oaks down there?"

Before Rascal could answer, Tim kicked his mount to start back down the incline. He called over his shoulder, "I'm going to look for signs of that cow and calf." His horse's hoof slipped, sending a trickle of rocks ahead of them. "No need to come with me though. I'll check and be right back up."

Rascal's shoulders drooped, but he folded his hands over his pommel to wait.

Tim encouraged his horse to continue down the steep descent. "It'll be much less scary going back up, Midnight, I promise."

Once he made it to the trees, Tim slid off his saddle and ducked under the heavy boughs of a mature swamp oak.

The only animal tracks and scat around were that of deer, coon, and jackrabbits. He was remounting his horse when a glint caught his eye from the undergrowth.

After stomping the weeds down, he leaned over and plucked a metal object from the dirt. After he'd rubbed it clean, an intricate, but tarnished tip off a bolo tie lay in the palm of his hand. Not the simple metalwork one might find on a tie available in a typical mercantile.

He returned to his horse and rode back up to Rascal. "Have you ever seen someone wearing something this fancy?" He tossed him the metal tip.

The old man frowned at the long hollow piece that ended in a small dangling medallion with a star engraved onto it. "No. But maybe it belonged to Mr. Key's cousin. He snuck around a lot last year with all his attempting at sabotaging the ranch."

"He was too dandy to be this far out, don't you think? Can you imagine him picking his way in and out of that ravine? Plus, I don't recall him ever wearing a bolo tie."

Rascal handed the tarnished silver back to him. "It belonged to somebody more dandified than us, that's for certain. That cost a pretty penny."

Tim swiped the surface with his calloused thumb. "Could've been out here for years. I'll give it to Nolan anyway. Maybe he'll recognize it." Tim pocketed the piece and noted Rascal was waiting for him to ride alongside him. "Tell the Keys I plan to scout a few more hours. Probably won't make it back in time for dinner."

Or rather, he planned not to be. That way Gwen would definitely be gone when he returned. His heart had endured enough for one day.

"That's not the only reason you're out here." Rascal's bushy eyebrows arched high, as if such a statement would get him to confess.

Maybe he would somewhat. "Sometimes there's nothing better than a ride to clear your mind."

Rascal's brows didn't descend. But then, the older man shrugged. "No one'll blame you for calling off your search if you decide to eat dinner hot."

"Might do that, but don't wait for me."

Nodding, they parted, and Tim headed north to the next stand of trees.

Though Gwen had left before dinner every day so far, he'd heard the Keys invite her several times to stay and eat with them. With his luck, the day he'd allowed himself to imagine for just a fraction of a second what it'd be like to lean down and kiss her, would be the day she'd decide to stay for dinner.

And right now, knowing she'd never be able to see past his appearance and lowly connections, he wasn't keen on sitting beside her in the one place he'd finally begun to feel comfortable and accepted, just as he was.

CHAPTER ELEVEN

Taking aim, Gwen peered down the rifle's sight, let out her breath, and shot.

With the sun hanging low, she had to squint to see how she'd fared. Another hit, much closer than the last. Her groupings were getting tighter. Shooting was far easier than the roping she'd tried last week. Enough like knife throwing, she'd advanced quickly.

After glancing toward the cabin to confirm Corinne didn't need her for anything, Gwen reloaded.

She'd stayed to eat dinner today and had enjoyed the banter between the Keys and their men. The setting was so informal and simple, a rough-hewn table set right inside the kitchen. They'd chatted and teased as if they were family. Oddly, Timothy had been missing. Though maybe not so odd, since he'd been absent a lot lately. Half the time she couldn't find him.

After dinner, Corinne had felt better than usual and had been intent on working. She'd disappeared into her cabin and waved off Gwen's help, telling her to continue practicing if she wanted.

Corinne had agreed with Timothy's assertion last week that

a rancher's wife didn't need to learn to rope. She'd yet to have a reason to use a lariat but did often wish she shot better. Pests in the coop, coyotes preying on animals, bad men lurking when good men were away—all reasons a woman on a ranch ought to be confident with a gun.

So Corinne had been nice enough to teach her what she knew earlier this morning and had given her plenty of bullets to practice with. When Rascal had come over to investigate the constant gunfire, Gwen had forced pointers out of him, too.

She frowned up at the sky, which was filling with cloudy brushstrokes of darkening pastels. She'd hoped for instruction from Timothy, or rather, she'd hoped he'd come over and grunt with approval like the foreman had.

Glancing at the nearly empty box of bullets, she shook her head and raised her gun. Might as well finish the box. Imagining the expression on the mercantile owner's face when she asked for five boxes of ammo to replace what she'd used made her chuckle.

She forced herself to be serious again. Steady, loosen up, breathe out…

Bang!

With the light fading, Timothy should have returned from wherever he'd disappeared to today. When the others heard her shooting, they'd come by, but Timothy ignored her. Why? He'd been impressed with her slight roping success. Which had made her feel good. As if he'd truly found something to like about her.

Looking to the north, Gwen wondered if it were possible to see the Hendrix ranch from here. Celia would surely be glad to give her opinion on how well she was shooting. That girl never seemed to care how her words affected people. But asking her would have to wait for another day.

Gwen shot the last of the bullets then packed up. If she left the targets out, would Timothy notice?

Rolling her eyes at herself, she marched over and tore the papers down. She'd wanted to learn how to clean the firearm, but hopefully Nolan wouldn't be miffed at her for putting that lesson off. She'd waited too long in hopes that Timothy would show up. Now she risked not getting home before dark.

Pushing backwards through the door, arms full, she stopped at the sound of two male voices laughing. She used her foot to keep the door from slamming shut, letting it close softly.

That was Timothy's voice all right.

Corinne came scuttling in from the parlor, eyes wide. "I'd thought you'd left already. Your shooting must have blended into the background after a while."

"I should have left an hour ago."

"Here, let me take those." Corinne grabbed the empty boxes and put them in the burn pile. "Since it's late, why don't you stay?"

"That's nice of you to offer, but my brother is probably worried already. I'll just drive fast."

"Miss McGill?" Timothy was in the doorway, his hair crimped where his hat band had rested, his clothes covered in dust. "I'm surprised you're still here."

She swallowed and nodded, not sure how to answer him, considering the frustration in his tone.

So he hadn't heard her shooting and purposely ignored her?

Though maybe ignoring her would've been better than that look of annoyance on his face.

Corinne patted Timothy's shoulder. "And I'm surprised you missed dinner again. Are you ready to eat?"

He smiled down at his boss. He ought to smile more often, his face was a touch handsome when he did so. "I was too far out, but I knew you'd leave something warming for me." Then his smile faded as he looked across the room toward Gwen. "But don't bother getting it out. I'll escort Miss McGill home."

If he didn't want to accompany her, why offer? "That's not necessary."

He shook his head. "Your brother would look down on the

lot of us if no one did. You're unlikely to make it before nightfall."

"There's a full moon."

He shrugged and snatched his hat off the rack by the back door.

Corinne bustled over to the stove. "Let me make you a sandwich. It'll be too late to eat when you get back."

"I don't want to be any trouble." She didn't need another black mark against her in Timothy's eyes.

Corinne waved a hand at her. "You aren't trouble. I'm glad to have your help when I need it."

Tellingly, Timothy didn't chime in to agree.

"Here." Corinne placed a sandwich in Timothy's hand and a plate with a slice of apricot pie in Gwen's. "Give this to your brother. Tell him you've been invited to stay anytime you need to."

Timothy flinched at the invitation.

Why had she thought having him look at her bullet-riddled targets would do anything to earn his favor? The only thing he'd ever volunteered to do was escort her off the property.

When she realized Corinne was still looking at her, she shook herself. "That's nice of you, but I'll just make certain I don't stay out this late again. I hope you wake up tomorrow feeling as well as you have today."

"Thank you, my dear." Corinne's smile was beginning to droop.

Tim opened the door to usher her out, but she crossed over to the counter to get her hat. He released the knob with a shake of his head and let the door swing back shut.

"Honey?" Nolan's voice called from the parlor. "Did you give that last piece of pie away?"

Gwen frowned at the plate she'd just set down. She picked it up and held it out for Corinne.

The older woman pushed it back. "I'm afraid so, dear. You've had three slices already."

"But what if I have a hankering for something sweet?"

"I'm afraid you're out of luck then," Corinne called back.

"Don't know about that. There's *something else* you could give me if—"

"Nolan, there are people still in this house." Corinne's face flushed as she made her way toward the parlor.

"Oh? Timothy?" Nolan called out with an amused lilt. "Don't you have somewhere else to be? I don't pay you to eat my pie and steal my wife's attention, you know."

"I see how it is," Timothy called back. "Don't appreciate the hard work I do disposing of the leftovers. Guess I'll go somewhere I'm more appreciated."

"Yes, you'll be much more appreciated in the bunkhouse."

Corinne's giggle sounded from the parlor just as Timothy opened the back door and gestured for Gwen to precede him.

"I think we best go."

"Seems so." Though Nolan being smitten with his wife made her smile, at the same time, her heart gave a sad flutter. Would anyone ever feel that way about her?

She slipped out beside Timothy onto the porch. When he didn't move, she glanced up at him. The sunset shone behind him, casting his face in darkness. Yet the shadows didn't hide the pinched way he held his mouth.

Timothy was certainly not the man who'd one day tease her about needing more sugar. Bo had been dead wrong.

She brushed past Timothy, making her way to the barn. "You don't have to go with me. I'll be fine."

"If I don't, Nolan will feel obligated. I'd rather he and the missus have time together while she's feeling better."

If he cared enough about them to sacrifice his evening, why was he so opposed to helping her when she asked? "What is it you have against me? What do you find so wrong with me?"

He pushed his hat up, his fingers combing through his hair again. "Noth—Nothing's wrong with you."

She sighed and walked off. Why push him to say something

that would only hurt her? After tonight, she'd stay out of his way and concentrate on helping Corinne. *She* at least seemed to like her.

Timothy insisted on readying her buggy, and once done, she climbed up without his help and set off in silence. No reason to wait for him. Either he'd catch up—or maybe he'd just let her go. Clicking to her horse, she started a quick but manageable pace.

A short while later, Timothy's horse loped up alongside her, then slowed to keep pace with the buggy. Thankfully, he didn't seem inclined to talk.

Deep purple shadows clung to the ridges between the shafts of dying sunlight that stabbed through the rocky crags. The bright shards which found purchase on the ground set the sand and sage aglow. A desolate landscape overlaid in a golden haze.

She turned to see Timothy slumped on his mount, his attention fixed on the ruts in front of them instead of taking in God's transient artistry. Had Timothy lived out here too long to notice what a sunset did to the landscape? The buildings surrounding Armelle had made her forget how much beauty could be found in the barrenness, but then, Timothy was rarely in town that she knew of. Even when he'd come in for school, it hadn't been often.

The horses' heavy breathing grated on her nerves. "So what happened your last year of school? You hardly attended from what I remember. I suppose you had to work?" The out-of-town kids often missed for harvesting and such.

"On occasion."

He missed more than occasionally. "Did you get a tutor like me? I hated mine, though I did enjoy getting out of the schoolroom."

He laughed outright.

At least something had dragged him out of whatever trance he'd put himself in.

"No, no tutor."

"So you cut class?" Wasn't that part of why he'd gotten into trouble last year? He, Daniel, Harriet, and Celia had gotten caught up with the men her father had hired for nefarious reasons. "Would staying in school have kept you out of trouble?"

"I wasn't looking for trouble. I would've attended every day of the week including Sunday if they'd let me."

"You enjoyed school that much?" Somehow that wasn't how she remembered him—of course, she didn't remember much more than where he sat and that he'd kept his head down most of the time. She'd assumed he'd not wanted to be called upon.

"I liked it well enough." His horse tossed its head and Timothy returned to a lope, quickening the pace.

Urging her horse to keep up, she dug through her memories for anything resembling Timothy enjoying school. "I remember you liked the skits we were forced to perform. You always knew everyone's lines. That one Christmas when Celia refused to stand on the piano and be an angel with me, why'd you offer to take her place? You had to know you'd be teased for wanting a girl's role."

His jaw hardened. "Nothing said it had to be a girl. And if you don't remember, the nativity this past Christmas featured Spencer flying from the church rafters complete with a shiny halo. And he made sure we all knew the angel names in the Bible are boy names."

"I still wonder why you would've wanted to be on top of that piano with me. Just to have an excuse to stand on the piano? That was all I enjoyed about it. Never could remember my silly line. Miss Jepson should've just had us recite Bible verses, then maybe I would've remembered. 'Harketh all ye shepherds below…'"

Her brain went blank. "Nope. That's all I remember, just like back then."

"'Harketh all ye shepherds below. Hear the good news we bring of peace, joy, and love. Praise the Lord for the gift He has given you this day in Bethlehem. A babe wrapped in cloths, lying in a manger—a King. Go see.'"

Yes, those were the words. She frowned at him. "How come you didn't whisper that to me?" He'd been one of the shepherds who'd been visited by the angels "on high"—but the boys had been given no lines.

He kept his eyes fixed ahead. "You wouldn't have liked me if I corrected you."

Her skin prickled with cold. Back then, she likely wouldn't have cared one way or the other about him. "So since you've got such a good memory and liked school so much, why didn't you finish?"

"Had to help my family."

But he said he'd not left school for work. She squeezed her reins tighter. Seemed he'd no desire to be anything but cryptic. Was his entire family that way? "I'd like to meet them."

"Who?"

"Your parents and siblings. I don't see them much in town."

He pulled up. "Why would you want to do that?"

Before Bo had pushed her to get to know Timothy, would she have wanted to meet his family? Surely she would have, she'd just not…thought about it. "Why don't you bring them to dinner after church Sunday? I know you come in alone most of the time, but if they'd—"

"Miss McGill." He shook his head, his patronizing chuckle setting her teeth on edge. "I understand you were raised to be polite, but there's no need to pretend you want to—"

"Are you calling me a liar?"

His face scrunched up. "I didn't mean to call you a liar."

"Well, you are. And I'll prove I'm not lying by inviting them over myself."

"No!" His voice boomed loud enough to echo off the rock wall they were passing. "Don't do it, Miss McGill."

His intense gaze made her nod in acquiescence, then he quickened his pace too much for any more questions.

Did he not realize forbidding her to invite them would make her wish to meet his family all the more?

Despite Bo's strange insistence she consider Timothy's court if he were so inclined—which he wasn't—a rancher like Nolan would be the lowest social tier she could comfortably marry into. The families of ranch hands depended upon their boss's success and fairness. If she *were* to become a rancher's wife, she'd need to know how families like Timothy's lived and what they needed in order to thrive.

She'd be unlikely to learn any of that over Sunday dinner, but she could certainly find out on a visit.

CHAPTER TWELVE

Tim's mother pushed away from the messy table, shaking her head at his empty plate. "I underestimated how hungry roofing would make you. I'll fry you some more."

He wanted to argue, but if he did, his rumbling stomach would expose him as a liar soon enough. "Thanks, Ma."

She opened the box where she kept root vegetables and grabbed two potatoes.

He could probably eat three or four, but he wouldn't say anything. Instead, he leaned back in his chair, trying not to think about the lunch he could've had at the Keys'. The abundance he enjoyed there always made him feel guilty. He'd not gone to work for two days now and had forced himself not to wonder what they were eating.

He glanced over at his youngest brother, Patrick, smashing potatoes through his fingers. If the two-year-old had been eating instead of playing, Tim would've refused seconds, but Patrick seemed to have had enough. Though "enough" was a relative term. He and his siblings were skinny for a reason.

When Gwen had invited his family to Sunday dinner, the first worry that popped into his head had been the poor impression his family would've made sitting around a dining room table in a genuine mansion. And then he'd realized, that even if she could make them feel comfortable, his siblings would see what others ate.

There was enough discontent in the O'Conner household, no need to add more.

"How long until our roof's done?—hey you, two. Stop." Ma shot a fierce look at the twins, four-year-old Jack and John, who were flicking wood chips at each other near the fireplace. His mother returned to scraping the pan with her handle-less spatula. "I'm worried it's taking too long. You've been here two days already."

"It's fine, Ma. I asked permission. They said I could stay as long as needed."

"But cowpunchers are a dime a dozen."

Must she keep pointing out how replaceable he was? "The Keys aren't like that. If Nolan changes his mind, he'll send Rascal or Sal to fetch me. He won't just fire me."

Though she depended on him to provide—and he intended to do so—it'd be nice if his ability to make money wasn't all she worried about in regard to him. He scanned the near-empty shelves. He'd gone to the church pantry twice this month. What on earth was his father doing?

A spoon clattered on the floor beside him. His sister pushed a book onto the table, dislodging another utensil. Molly looked up at him with her deep hazel eyes. "Want to hear me read?"

"He can't right now. We're talking." Ma slid the plate of hot potatoes across the table toward him. "You should go back to work tomorrow whether or not you're done roofing. If your father hasn't been able to find a job, then—"

"*I* would find another job, Ma." He gritted his teeth at the insinuation he'd find just as many excuses for being unemployed as Father did. "Even if that means cleaning outhouses. Or getting on with the railroad—"

"No." His mother's face turned ashen. "Promise me. Not that."

He couldn't promise. Not if that's what needed to be done—though he understood why she'd fight to keep him from doing so. His brothers, Michael and Owen, had taken jobs with the railroad two years ago. Though only fifteen and fourteen, they'd hired on so there'd be fewer mouths to feed, more money coming in.

But a month later, Owen had sent them a letter. Michael had died in an accident "too cruel to put into words." Owen had enclosed a five-dollar bill, but there'd been no return address, and they'd not heard from him since.

Tim finally had to sneak into his mother's room and steal the letter. She'd not slept for days, agonizing over that horrendously vague sentence, imagining every conceivable brutal exit Michael could've taken from this world.

"Don't worry about my job, Ma."

Her expression didn't change.

Getting caught up in that rustling ring last year had caused her to doubt he had better judgment than his father. But he wasn't the one to blame for her decades of disappointment.

If only his father weren't around at all, maybe they could get somewhere.

Tim rubbed at the furrows in his brow. "If the Keys fire me, I promise I'll—"

Knock. Knock.

They both startled. Hardly anyone knocked on their door. And when they did, good news rarely followed.

Taking his knife from its sheath, Tim made his way to the door. It might be Rascal or Sal coming to tell him he was needed back at work, or it could be one of Father's "friends." If they weren't stopping by to invite him to go to the saloon, they were often there to collect a debt owed or take their pound of flesh.

"Who is it?" he called, trying to instill muscle and mass into his words.

"It's me," a feminine lilt answered.

His fingers froze tight around the doorknob.

If he remained silent, would Gwen wonder if she'd simply imagined someone had answered and take her leave?

Ma cleared her throat behind him.

He turned to shush her, but Ma's eyebrows were up in question.

He released his iron grip on the door and sheathed his knife. With a deep breath, he undid the latch and cracked open the door.

Gwen stood on the step—or rather, the sun-hardened mud that butted up against their door—with a glass dish in her hands.

"Good afternoon, Timothy. I brought your mother a pie." She leaned to the side as if to look past him.

He closed the door a little more. She didn't need to see inside his house more than necessary. The outside was enough to realize it ought to be torn down rather than lived in.

He poked an arm through the crack. "I'm sure she'll be grateful."

Gwen didn't hand him the dish. "I'd like to give it to her myself. I need to tell her how to reheat it."

He tried not to roll his eyes. Gwen likely had no knowledge of what to do with the pie other than whatever her cook had told her. "I'm sure my mother can figure it out."

Gwen just stood there.

He released a groan. "I know you came out here thinking to get around my asking you not to ask my family to dinn—"

"Are you insinuating it's not good to be neighborly?"

He couldn't help the cynical tilt to his lips. "You rode almost an hour to get here—that's not the definition of a neighbor."

"Isn't it Jesus's definition of a neighbor?"

He frowned. Did that mean she viewed them as a charity case? Though he wouldn't deny they needed help, Gwen viewing his family that way rankled.

She continued to stand there, staring at him.

He drummed his fingers against the door, trying not to like her more for her stubbornness. If she'd just leave him alone long enough, he could figure out a way to stop liking her. And he desperately needed to, for she could never be a part of his life— other than a bearer of charity.

That was it. He'd let her see everything, exactly as it was. The two rooms that looked nothing like the Keys' fine house, crowded with pallets and rickety furniture, surrounded by soot covered walls. Once she saw all the dirt and brokenness, pretending any longer that he had a chance at winning her heart would be impossible.

He stepped back, kicked aside the broken chair, and swung the door open wide. "Come in, then."

As he'd expected, her smile died the moment she crossed the threshold. That's what happened when one took in the dirty walls, makeshift furniture, and ragged clothing his siblings wore to keep their one nice outfit reserved for school.

Frowning at the table littered with dirty dishes and scattered pots of rainwater, she held out the dish. "Where would you like the pie?"

"Pie?" Molly looked up from her book just as the twins came scrambling over.

"Is it like da' one we had at church once?"

"Do we get da' whole fing?" Jack's eyes widened as he looked from the mystery dish to his identical brother.

Tim winced. Did they have to act as if they'd never eaten before? Sugar, however, was reserved for Christmas—not that they could always afford it even then. "Ma, Miss McGill has brought us a pie."

"Nice to meet you, Miss McGill. That's quite nice of you." Ma fluttered her hands down to smooth her apron as if that might help her look better beside Gwen's impeccable appearance. Before he'd let Gwen in, he should've thought about how Ma might've wished to appear more presentable. "Uh, let me make room."

Ma started shoving aside pots and then did a laughable attempt at cleaning the newly bare spot before pointing to it.

The twins' gazes stayed glued to the pie as Gwen slid it onto the table.

Jack hoisted himself up onto the bench to get closer. "Can we eat it now?"

"Of course not." His ma let loose a strangled chuckle. "We don't eat in front of guests."

"But she could eat it, too."

Ma's face paled as she surveyed their mess of a table.

Gwen leaned over, putting her cheek next to Jack's. "Oh, I'm not hungry. Thank you for thinking of me though."

"Ma, can't we—" John stopped mid-sentence when he caught Ma's distressed look.

"Later, boys." Tim ruffled Jack's hair, then plucked him off the bench and planted him down by his brother while Ma snatched up the pie and took it to the stove. She must've changed her mind about leaving it in front of the boys—they might've just dug in with their bare hands and embarrassed them all.

He pushed them both back toward the fireplace. "Why don't you two go back to playing with the wood chips?" Such a sorry excuse for toys, though he'd not thought anything of it until Gwen had come in.

But before he got the boys settled, he caught Molly tugging on Gwen's skirt with her grubby hands.

Tim rushed over to grab his sister's arms. "Let's not get Miss McGill's dress dirty."

Gwen blocked him from taking Molly away then kneeled beside his sister who'd taken a silky ribbon and was pulling it through her thin fingers.

"I see you like pretty things, too."

Molly nodded. "I've only got one pretty thing, want to see it?"

"Of course."

"Uh…" Tim reached for Molly, but she ducked under his arm and ran to her bedroll. How to stop her from—?

"Here it is." She pulled out from under her pillow the stuffed doll he'd made her using a squirrel's skin three years ago and ran back. The shiny beads for eyes were the only thing close to being "pretty," considering the innumerable bald spots it had from Molly rubbing it every night. The toy was nightmarish now, but his sister refused to give it up despite being nine years old already.

She placed the ugly thing in Gwen's awaiting hands. "Tim made Susie for me. Isn't she nice?"

He was impressed Gwen was able to keep a smile on her face despite cradling the stuffed squirrel doll as if it were riddled with disease.

Molly took the doll back and grabbed Gwen's hand. "Would you read us a story?"

Where had Molly gotten the notion to ask Gwen to read? The only visitors they'd ever had were Father's drunken friends, and she mainly hid from them—which was a good thing.

After tossing Susie onto the table, Molly grabbed her worn book of fairy tales. "I like the last story best."

Gwen took the book and opened the pages, allowing the middle section to fall out. "Oh, I'm sorry. Maybe we should read from a different book until this one's fixed."

His sister's expression fell as she stooped to collect the pages. "But it's the only book I've got."

"Oh, well…" Gwen scanned the room, as if not believing they owned no other books.

"Here you are, Miss McGill." Ma walked over with Gwen's pie plate, empty and wiped clean.

Gwen took her dish back with a confused expression. "I didn't need this back right away."

"Nobody leaves us with anything nice if they want it back." Ma's face colored. "It's best you take it now."

Gwen frowned down at the plate as if it were the farthest thing from nice she'd ever seen.

"Thank you for bringing us something, Miss McGill." Tim put a hand on her shoulder. It'd be best she was on her way in case Father showed up unexpectedly. "But I'm sure you have lots more visits to make."

"I, uh…" She gave Molly a half-smile then nodded at their mother. "I suppose I do need to get going." She waved to the twins and little Patrick—who'd not stopped smashing his leftover potatoes to take an interest in her—and turned toward the door. Not that Tim was giving her much of an option.

Once she stepped outside, he dropped his hand from her shoulder, but not before he'd felt her take in a big gulp of air.

Being crammed inside their place did that to a person.

"Thank you again for the pie, Miss McGill." He turned away to keep from seeing the pity in her eyes. "Have a good afternoon."

"Are you coming back to the Keys' anytime soon?"

He wouldn't let himself read into what sounded like hope in her question. She'd only latched onto something to say, being too well bred to simply take her leave.

He steeled himself, refusing to look at her too closely. "Once the roof is done. Unless Nolan's antsy for me to return?"

"I don't know about that. It's just I…" She looked past his shoulder, likely remembering the dismal picture she'd seen behind his door. "I'm sorry I dropped by without giving you notice."

Did she think they could've made themselves more presentable if she had? "When someone decides to be neighborly, it's bad form to turn them away, right? My brothers and sister will probably dream of the sugar they're about to eat for weeks on end."

"I suppose so." She swallowed hard and took a step back. "Have a good rest of your day, Timothy. I hope your roof gets done quickly so you can return to work."

95

"So do I, Miss McGill." Though he'd wanted her to see the squalor he'd come from, he liked to pretend this wasn't his life. Which was much easier to do at the Keys'.

Gwen looked at him for a second longer before striding toward the fanciest vehicle that had ever rolled across their yard.

Hopefully she'd sated her curiosity and would never return. Surely one glance at the O'Conner home would be more than enough for the likes of Gwen. The only thing that could have made the visit more disastrous was if Father had been here.

Tim breathed a sigh of relief and closed the door. With any luck, Gwen would never meet his father. Nothing good would come of that.

CHAPTER THIRTEEN

Gwen drifted down the street toward her house, kicking stones. The Whitsetts would be back to eat dessert soon. A few days ago, Bryant and Leah had returned from their travels to visit their newest grandchild. They'd sold their home to help their youngest daughter cross the country to sell her memoirs, so Gwen had offered them a place to stay since their oldest daughter's house wasn't huge.

Though they'd told her they didn't need to be fed or entertained because they planned to spend every day with family, Gwen had remained in town. If they needed anything, she wanted to be available since her brother had traveled to Montana on business.

Gwen stopped at the edge of McGill property and watched the gardener. Father had tasked him with making sure their acreage was always the greenest spot in Armelle—and making sure no splash-worthy mud puddles ever again appeared in their yard.

Nothing but mud had surrounded the O'Conners' cabin. What a disastrous visit that had been. Before going out there, she'd convinced herself she was doing the right thing, but once—

"Good evening, Miss McGill." Mrs. Tate's piercing voice startled Gwen as she came up behind her on the road.

Considering the old woman's opinion of her—made so clear on that day she'd dragged her to church—why would Mrs. Tate even want to talk to her?

"I've heard you've been spending a lot of time at the Keys' ranch."

Of course. Gossip.

"I thought you told us you weren't with that O'Conner boy?"

Gwen's heart rate accelerated. Mrs. Tate couldn't possibly know anything about why she'd gone out to Nolan and Corinne's ranch. "I've been helping Mrs. Key."

"That woman doesn't need *your* help."

Gwen tried not to lash out, but she wouldn't dare hint to Corinne's pregnancy before the Keys did so themselves, especially to Mrs. Tate. "Perhaps it's more she's been helping me."

"I was told you were making a fool of yourself trying to impress that boy."

"If you mean my attempts at roping and shooting, I'm trying new things to improve myself. And if that concerns you, don't worry about it. I'm *not* impressing anyone."

"Improving yourself? If that's how you're trying to attract the men now…" She tsked. "With the way you go about things, if you get into trouble again, and the pastor doesn't—"

"I have no intention of getting into trouble, Mrs. Tate." Of all the self-righteous—

"Then you shouldn't do anything that could get you tangled up with an O'Conner. It'd be a disgrace. And you can't handle any more of that after what your father did." Mrs. Tate exhaled with exasperation. "If you can't see the wisdom in what I'm saying, surely your brother could enlighten you."

"I think you're right, Mrs. Tate. I'll take my brother's advice on this." Should she tell the old goose that Bo had been the one to suggest she get to know Timothy? Could Mrs. Tate be rendered speechless for once? But she'd not tell Mrs. Tate anything worth spreading about town.

"Good." Mrs. Tate nodded decisively, as if she'd just saved Gwen from ruin. "Without your parents around, I know it must be difficult. But stay sensible, Miss McGill."

And yet, Mrs. Tate found it *sensible* to judge people based on tittle-tattle? Gwen clenched her lips tight to obey her mother's demand to honor her elders.

Thankfully, Mrs. Tate hobbled away.

What would Timothy think if he caught wind of whatever rumor must be circulating about them? Gwen closed her eyes. If he didn't simply dismiss it for nonsense, he'd likely stay even farther away from her.

Could she ever find a man who liked her for herself?

"Are you all right, Gwendolyn?" The gritty sound of Leah Whitsett's voice always surprised her. After a run-in with Father's hoodlums, Leah had not only lost her melodic voice, but sported scars she couldn't hide.

Gwen turned to see the little family of three who'd sneaked up on her. She straightened her shoulders. "I'm fine."

"That's not what your expression says." Leah's mouth, stuck in a permanent half frown from her injuries, curved even farther down. "What's troubling you?"

A good hostess shouldn't unload her problems on her guests. "It's only that I've dawdled so long. I haven't made sure the dessert's ready yet."

Leah's husband, Bryant, cleared his throat. "Speaking of dessert, Miss McGill. I hope you'll forgive me if I don't stay. I'm going out to see Jacob's ponies, and I sense you ladies might want to talk without me around." He kissed the top of his wife's dark head and then his daughter's. His blond hair was an even sharper contrast to his complexion than before. Now that he was no longer working in an office but picking up labor jobs as they traveled, the sun had lightened his hair into a burnished gold. "Good evening, you three."

Leah waved at him as he headed off to the stables. "I have a feeling he's tired of being surrounded by females. And though Bryant loves us girls—"

"We've done *a lot* of gushing and cooing today," Jennie finished. A small smile graced the Whitsetts' youngest daughter's face, her focused gaze almost giving off the impression she wasn't blind.

"I'm glad to hear you've enjoyed your day."

"But you don't seem to have enjoyed yours," Leah stated. Seemed she wouldn't let Gwen sidestep her inquiry a second time.

"Ma's not *trying* to be nosy, Miss McGill. Mothers just can't help mothering, you know." Jennie stood by her mother's side, hand anchored to Leah's elbow per usual.

How had Jennie sensed she didn't want to talk about her predicament? Could her worries not only be seen on her face, but felt?

Gwen swallowed and looked away. How many times had she wished she could talk to her mother about things? Perhaps God was granting that wish in a fashion. Since the Whitsetts wouldn't be here long and could be trusted not to gossip... "Well, you're correct. I haven't had a good day. And Mrs. Tate just made it worse."

"Ah, cranky ol' Mrs. Tate. Did her words smart because there's a grain of truth in them, or did she misjudge you?"

Gwen let out a short, half-hearted laugh. "Can it be both?"

With her free hand, Leah took Gwen's arm. "Why don't we head in. Would you like to talk about it?"

Gwen shrugged. Other than the incident with Eric, Leah knew as much as everyone else in town about her failures at securing a husband. "You already know plenty of men have rejected me, and Mrs. Tate has strong opinions on what I should do about that. Not that her advice will help. But what's wrong with me? I thought I had what most men wanted. I do what I think would please them, but none want me."

She steeled herself for Leah's answer, but the older woman continued to walk quietly beside her as they made their way to the house.

Guess she didn't know what was wrong with her either.

Once inside the parlor, Leah seated Jennie. Then she took Gwen's hand and looked into her eyes. "Every once in a while, I've seen you drop the affectations you hide behind and say what you really think—like you did outside just now. And those are the times I feel most connected to you—as if you're a real person I could get to know."

Gwen blinked against the warmth welling behind her eyes. She did intend to be herself more, but what if no one liked her that way either?

"Why not stop being what you think everyone wants you to be and be who God made you to be?"

But these past few weeks, she'd left her flighty self behind, and Timothy still seemed to express no interest in her. Like all the other men, he rejected her.

Leah put a hand on Gwen's shoulder. "I know this may not be what you want to hear..." She took a quick glance at her daughter before continuing. "But it's possible you won't be asked to marry—at least by anyone worth marrying. And if that happens, do you want to look back on your life and realize you've spent it striving for something that's gained you nothing? There are so many good things you can pursue that don't require you to wait for someone to do them with. What if you stopped aiming for a man who may not exist and let God use you?"

If anyone in this town had let God use her, it was Leah. For who else was as well known for being someone who could be counted on to help at church, to cuddle a sad child, to fill a need that had yet to be made known? And everyone loved her.

When Bryant had been in prison last year, Leah had been bitter over his betrayal, and it was as if Armelle had lost its brightest light. But now the two were once again acting like lovebirds. Their devotion and unabashed affection had always been so strikingly different from what she remembered of how her parents interacted. A love like that was all she'd ever wanted for herself.

But if she sought after what God wanted and discovered His plans for her didn't include being a wife and mother...

Jennie cleared her throat from where she sat. "I can tell you're worried, Miss McGill. But don't forget you're in an excellent position to do what my mother advised. As long as you're careful with what God has provided you, I bet you could live comfortably while exploring all sorts of worthwhile pursuits."

A lump formed in Gwen's throat. Here she was, sad about being unwanted, when the O'Conner children and so many others would never have what she already possessed. She might not end up managing a fancy home, but she'd never have to live in a run-down shack.

And yet, Timothy had to deal with poverty, day in and day out. But he wasn't running after rich women or a better life. He was focused on doing what was best for his family.

When was the last time she'd helped someone for the pure joy of it? Not because it benefitted her or proved convenient, but because it was the right thing to do? She might care about people's predicaments, but when was the last time she'd sacrificed anything to help another? "Would you two pray for me? I think I've let all my worries keep me from being who I ought to be."

CHAPTER FOURTEEN

Tim set down his hoe and squinted up the road. Today felt twenty degrees hotter than yesterday with the humidity hanging heavy in the air.

A liveryman drove an enclosed buggy toward the ranch. A flash of golden hair moved behind a window.

Gwen.

Tim sighed. She must've hired a driver to traverse the washouts left by the previous three days of rain. Since the Whitsetts had come back to visit their newest grandchild, Gwen had remained in town. Considering they wouldn't need her to constantly entertain them, he'd hoped she'd decided to stay home because she'd finally given up on trying to be a rancher's wife.

As the buggy turned into the gate, he peeked over his shoulder to see if Nolan would come out to greet her.

The porch remained empty, and Sal was still in the far pasture with Rascal.

How was it he couldn't seem to keep any space between them? If he rode off now, Rascal would again get onto him for treating the Keys' guests poorly. Gwen couldn't be faulted for being rich and practically helpless.

Tim wiped the sweat off his face and trudged over. Though being near her was not good for his heart, perhaps the constant avoidance was worse. Maybe like chickenpox, if he got a good dose of her, the heartbreak that would come later wouldn't be fatal. Might as well help her get what she wanted quickly, so she could walk down the aisle to whichever rancher got pulled in by her dowry and long lashes.

Jogging the last few yards, he stopped near the front porch. "Pull up over here," he shouted to the liveryman. "There's a huge puddle there."

The driver did so, and Timothy opened the door.

But Gwen didn't step out. A woman with brown hair tucked up inside a cap did—a woman his mother's age. Was she a relative of the Keys'? Unlikely, seeing as she was dressed for work, not travel. He held out his hand. "Allow me, ma'am."

"Why, thank you." Her calloused hand was somehow still soft. Once she was on the ground, she kept her head down and scuttled to the side, as if awaiting an order.

But he didn't know who—

The carriage jostled and a bloom of lavender and golden hair drew his attention like a magnet. With Gwen's long blond tresses trickling down her neck, he had to keep from imagining how it might feel to—

Her hand landed in his, and he tensed. Good thing she was unaware of the electric current she shot through him every time they touched. "Welcome back, Miss McGill, and…?"

"This is Mrs. Barton."

"Mrs. Barton. I'm afraid if you're here to visit Mrs. Key, she was ill at breakfast. We haven't heard that she's feeling any better."

"Is she worse?" Gwen's smile vanished.

"Not that I know of." He glanced toward the other woman, not knowing if Gwen would've told this stranger about what they suspected was behind Corinne's sickness.

Gwen extracted her hand from his—seemed he'd forgotten

to let go—and straightened her shirtwaist. "That's fine, we're not here to take tea."

The carriage squeaked behind him and a girl closer to their age stepped out. He lunged over to offer his hand.

"We're here to clean." Gwen turned to the driver. "Come back for us around six-thirty if you would."

The man tipped his hat and slowly drove away, likely to keep from splattering them with mud.

"To clean?" He scanned the other two women, noting the aprons over their gray dresses. These must be McGill servants.

"I see what you're thinking." Gwen's accusatory tone caught him off guard. "You're so convinced I'm no good at anything I have to hire people to work for me. But I'll be working, too. I just wanted to be done as quickly as possible so as not to disturb Mrs. Key more than necessary."

He held up a hand, pledging innocence. "I wasn't thinking ill of you at all." Though her two servants would surely do five times the work Gwen would.

"Go on up to the house, ladies. I'll be right over." Once the women started off, Gwen turned to him. "You're probably thinking only a spoiled rich girl would use servants for something as simple as dusting. But as you well know, my talents do not lie in that area. But I want to help Corinne, so I decided it best to use whatever assets I have."

"Be that as it may, I thought you were here to learn how to be a rancher's wife." *The quicker she gets what she wants*, he chanted silently in his head, *the sooner she'll leave.* "Ranchers can't afford *servants*."

She narrowed her eyes at him. "They choose to be servants because their wages feed their families. You could leave the Keys if it wasn't advantageous to you, right? You're a servant in a sense, and yet, you don't treat your bosses as if they're spoiled or incapable because they hired you." She shot him a fiery gaze, snatched up her skirts, and rounded the puddle on her way to the women awaiting her on the porch.

It was a good thing she'd marched off—the fire in her eyes made her ten times more enticing.

His decision to expose himself to the "pox" might be just as fatal as heartbreak.

Gwen was likely right about how he and others viewed the McGills versus the Keys. He'd never once thought of the Keys as being spoiled because they hired him on—rather, they were a gift from God, providing the income his family desperately needed. So why had he ever looked down on the McGills for being rich enough to afford the luxury of a servant? That luxury helped those two women survive.

He sighed and followed them into the house. Inside the kitchen, neither of the Keys were present, but Gwen had the broom closet open and was handing the maids buckets and dusters.

He stood behind them and held out his hands. "How can I help?"

Gwen pulled back a little, keeping a firm grasp on her broom. "Don't you have other work to do?"

He shrugged. "Mrs. Key often asks for help when she needs me."

She took a furtive glance toward her maids, then shook her head. "I've enough help in here, but you can help me outside."

Guess he should have figured she'd ask him to help her do the ranching chores he'd tried to avoid teaching her. He pressed his lips together to keep from arguing and returned to the porch.

Why couldn't some people realize that despite good intentions, nature couldn't be thwarted? Gwen was born attractive and rich. He was born to labor. No reason either of them should kid themselves—they'd never be what the other was, even if they tried their hardest.

He touched the underside of his jaw where a blemish had appeared overnight. The newest concoction Corinne had given him stunk to high heaven. She'd said the sulfur it contained would give his skin a chance at looking normal, but chemicals needed time to work. So far, he wasn't sure his face would ever settle down.

After sitting on the porch swing to wait, Timothy gave the dog a good rub.

Minutes later, the door swung open and Gwen came out, a rifle propped against her shoulder like she knew what she was doing with it, confidence radiating, even in the sway of her hips.

He looked up at the sky. *I've never asked you to keep her from getting more attractive, but could you help me out a little and stop her from doing things that make me think her more so?*

She stopped in front of him and set the rifle down beside her, holding it as if she'd carried one since infancy. "I told the ladies I'd be back in a little while to help, but right now, I'd like you to give me all your shooting tips."

"You mean, you want me to teach you to shoot?"

"Shoot better, anyhow."

He raised an eyebrow. "How long have you been shooting?"

"You didn't know? Just an afternoon, though I'm sure I have plenty to learn."

If she couldn't figure out how to pull a splinter in a quarter hour, she had no idea how long this would take. "Don't you think it'd be better to help with the cleaning?"

"You offered your help, and this is what I need from you most. I'll clean later."

He took his hat off for a second, but then slammed it back on. He ought to shut up and let her try. Though it'd be better to start her off with a shotgun so she'd have more of a chance at hitting something, letting her use the rifle might discourage her enough to get him back to his chores within the hour.

"All right." He gestured for her to follow him to the fence line where the men often practiced. Halfway there, he realized she wasn't beside him.

He turned to see her taking an absurd amount of time walking around every puddle.

He plowed through the soggy field and leaned against a post to wait...and wait.

Did she think it possible to be outside and not get dirty? The day she'd tried her hand at roping, she hadn't seemed concerned about the dust. "You planning on getting out here anytime soon?"

She gave him a glare but went right back to walking around an entire section of the pasture to avoid the mud.

Once she made it to him, he held out his hands. "Hand over the gun and I'll load it for you."

"No need." She pulled around the bag hanging off her shoulder, and within seconds, she had it loaded.

Hadn't she said she'd only been shooting for an afternoon?

She lifted the firearm to her shoulder as if she'd done so a thousand times. With her hair blowing in the breeze, she took a shot and the *ting* of bullet hitting metal made him turn to see what she'd hit. A line of cans he'd never seen sat on the far fence.

Once again, he stared up at the cloudless heavens.

I suppose my request that you help me find her less attractive has been answered with a no?

In the space of his prayer, she'd repositioned herself and shot again.

Ting!

He watched her shoot three more times, missing once. Why hadn't the can fallen? "What did you do to the cans?"

She reloaded. "I had Rascal hammer pegs along the rail because I was tired of walking over there to set them back up." She chambered the first round and smiled over at him.

Had he ever seen her so beaming sure of herself?

Oh, Lord, this isn't helping!

Good thing he'd already gotten Nolan's permission to go hunting for his mother tomorrow. Several days of not seeing her would be a very good thing.

He tore his gaze off her smile and looked toward the hole-riddled cans. "I'm not sure why you dragged me out here."

"I wanted you to watch me shoot and tell me if there's something I could do better. Rascal said it was all in how you position yourself." She hiked the gun back up to her shoulder and shot again, hitting a can.

She lowered the rifle and turned to him, awaiting his response.

Watching her so confident and happy kept him from being clear-headed enough to have noticed anything much. He cleared his throat. "If you're hitting them, you're doing fine."

She leaned the gun against the railing and pulled a paper from her bag. "I'll tack up this target. Maybe my groupings will tell you something."

She started off across the pasture, again taking long trips around the ruts that had filled with rainwater.

How could she be a crack shot yet be so averse to mud?

He leaned against the fence and waited. She was taking forever, and he was looking at her too long. Might as well start telling her what he thought, otherwise this would take all morning.

"I'm impressed, Miss McGill. It's obvious if you put your mind to something, you can succeed," he called out. Maybe she'd get that rancher husband she wanted after all.

She smiled back at him as if he'd handed her a hundred dollars. He thrust his hands in his empty pockets and growled under his breath. God evidently wasn't going to help him tamp down his attraction while he was trying to help marry her off to someone other than him.

As she started circling another puddle, he called out, "If you want to be a rancher's wife…" Gosh, that was hard to utter. "Then stop worrying about your dress. You're not being presented to the queen. You're shooting."

"How's that?"

"Means you're supposed to get dirty when you work."

She shrugged, then continued to pick her way around a small lake.

"Let go of your skirts and plow through. Ranchers need things done on time."

Her face lost the confidence it'd been sporting, a strangely wistful expression replacing it. "But that'd not be nice to my maids. Getting caked with mud will cause them extra work."

"Rancher's wives do their own laundry. Maybe you should learn how to do that, see how much work dirty laundry can be. No rancher will skirt mud puddles to keep his wife's sudsy water pristine."

She stood there, head cocked and mouth tight, as if he'd insisted she chew off her own hand. But then she reluctantly let go of her skirts, wincing as if the fabric had turned muddy instantly. She took a step to the left.

"Go straight through."

She shook her head and hollered back. "My boots are too expensive to tromp through water."

Rich people and their need to spend money on useless things. He crossed his arms as she walked around another stupid puddle on her way to the far fence, giving him a glimpse of her fancy leather footwear. How many meals could he buy his siblings if he stole them off her and sold them to—?

No, that's how his father thought. No one should decide who deserved what possessions—he knew that well enough from losing so many things to his father. If only his father spent what he stole from them on food.

After she'd hung her target, Tim waved to grab her attention as she started to avoid a swampy section. "Why not take off your boots? Or are they so fancy tight you can't get them off?"

Her whole face puckered. "I'm *not* walking barefoot out here."

He slipped off his boots, stopping to frown at the holes in his socks. Oh well, by the time he made it over there, mud would keep her from noticing. "Use mine then."

"*You're* going barefoot?"

"Won't be the first time in my life."

He could see her swallow as he came nearer, but she took his arm when he stepped beside her and then leaned down to pull her boots off and slip his on.

Once she was finished, he collected her dainty leather footwear and marched back. "Now this won't take all day."

"You could've volunteered to hang the target for me instead of making me cross this mess."

"I didn't realize you'd take so long. But it's done you good. Now you'll know what it's like to be dirty."

"I already know what it's like to be dirty."

Sure she did. He called over his shoulder, "Prove it."

What a sad childhood the rich must endure. To never make a mud pie, stomp around in the rain, wrestle in the mud, jump in a creek.

Seating himself atop the fence rail, he watched her plod through standing water. Despite today's heat being a great excuse for getting wet, she didn't appear at all as if she enjoyed it. Maybe she didn't realize that even though ranching was hard work, it could be fun if you weren't so prim and proper. Soft mud and lush grass were the perfect conditions for going barefoot.

But once she made it back to him, she appeared more strained than he'd ever seen her.

"You didn't find that at all enjoyable?"

"No," she answered, her fists clenched tightly at her sides.

She just didn't know what fun was then. "Come." He beckoned to her, but she didn't move, so he hopped down and took her arm. "Let's splash through some of these puddles, get you thoroughly dirty. Then you can—"

"No." Her muscles tensed beneath his hand.

"It's fun, trust me." He tugged on her. "Why, I've seen Mrs. Key so dirty—"

Plop!

111

Though he'd not pulled hard, she'd dug in her heels and had yanked herself from his grasp.

And now she sat in six inches of mud, wide-eyed like a flushed-out jackrabbit.

He couldn't keep a chuckle from escaping. "You won't melt, Miss McGill."

He reached down, but instead of giving him her hand, she stared at her muddy palms.

"Don't worry, you're not stained." He squatted beside her, swiped a finger through the mud, and tapped her on the nose. "Mud might even make you prettier."

To his horror, a fat tear slipped down her right cheek as she wiped her hands on a clean section of her dress.

"Oh Gwen, I'm sorry. I was just funnin'."

Her face scrunched up more, like she wanted to say something but couldn't in fear of outright crying.

"I shouldn't have insisted. I should've known this wouldn't be fun for you." What did he know about rich people's fun anyway? Perhaps her clothes were worth a fortune and she'd just ruined them or…well, it didn't matter what her problem was, she wasn't enjoying this a jot. He held out both hands. "Let me help you up."

She didn't resist his tug upward, but she was dead weight. Once he got her to stand, she looked up at him with those glossy blue eyes, closer than they'd ever been before. And with the smudge of mud on her nose and her lashes dewy and her lips trembling…

"I'm sorry," he whispered. "I'll have Mrs. Key get you something else to wear, and I'll do your wash. I didn't realize—"

"It wasn't you." She looked away and loosed a heavy sigh.

"Of course, it was. I'm the reason you're dirty."

"It's not that." She sniffled. "It's the mud."

How was that any different? "I didn't realize you hated mud so much."

"I don't. It's just been a long time since Momma and I—" She looked away, swallowing hard.

What did her momma have to do with anything?

Gwen cleared her throat but continued staring off toward town. "The last time I played with my mother was in the mud, and Father wouldn't ever let me do it again…" Her voice disappeared on those last words.

He stilled. Her mournful expression seized his heart like a vise.

"My momma died of pneumonia." Her words were barely audible. "She came down with it after we'd played in the rain. Father said my tomboyish ways had killed her. He—" A hiccup cut her off. She blinked hard and fast.

He couldn't help but cup her cheek, hoping she'd face him again. "I know what it's like when your father blames you for things you didn't do. And I know it's easy to *tell* yourself he's wrong, but another thing all together to *feel* the truth of it. But Gwen…"

Moments of silence passed before her gaze came back to meet his.

"Your mother was not so weak that you, as a little girl, forced her into doing something she thought was dangerous. She undoubtedly enjoyed that time with you. She died loving you—that's what you should remember."

"But you still have your ma." Gwen's voice was so breathy he almost hadn't understood her.

"I know." He smoothed back the hair that had fallen across her cheek, brushing away a tear as well. He could tell her his ma was so stressed he wasn't certain she could have fun anymore or give his siblings the type of beloved memories Gwen's ma had given her. But that would sound as if he thought her circumstances easier than his. "And I'm sorry yours is gone. It's not fair."

Unable to watch her tremble any longer, he gently pulled

her close, unsure of how she'd react to the offer of a hug. Maybe she wouldn't want—

She curled into him and cried.

Commanding his body to ignore how she felt in his arms, he rubbed a hand up and down her back, murmuring that it'd be all right.

The fact that she felt secure enough to allow him to comfort her was more than he'd ever hoped for in life. To love her in this way was a privilege he never believed he'd have.

After a few minutes, her sniffles waned, and then she pulled away.

He swallowed his disappointment and touched her lightly on the shoulder. "You want to go inside and wash up?"

She stepped back, causing his arm to fall, and looked past him. "I won't keep you from your work any longer. Thank you for what you showed me."

He'd shown her nothing. All he'd done was make her cry.

She trudged back to the house in his boots, shoulders slumped.

Letting her go off alone after forcing her to relive such heartbreak made him feel horrible. But he'd watched his father stomp all over his mother's wishes enough over the years, he couldn't stomach doing so to Gwen. He'd respect her wish to be alone, though it may be the hardest thing she'd asked of him so far.

CHAPTER FIFTEEN

On the Keys' parlor sofa, Gwen shrank into the cushions while Nolan tried to console his wife. Corinne had felt better this morning, had even dressed to go visiting, but was now overly emotional because her husband had suggested she stay home after getting sick again.

Nolan wrapped an arm around his wife's shoulders. "Come on, let's get you upstairs. A nap would probably do you good."

After sniffing a few more times, Corinne shrugged and then allowed him to lead her out of the parlor.

Once they were gone, Gwen picked up the diaper she'd been working on. Thankfully, the Keys had let her in on their "secret", so she no longer felt wrong expressing sympathy without suggesting Corinne visit the doctor.

After re-threading her needle, Gwen examined the diaper Corinne had shown her. A strange, but ingenious way to sew several flannels together to make it faster to fold yet stay attached so it could dry quickly on the line as a single unit. Corinne hoped to sell these in catalogs if they worked as expected.

She'd told Gwen she didn't need help with the diapers since there'd be plenty of time to sew before the baby came—which was probably true. But if she didn't help with this, what else could she do to stay near Tim?

Which of course, she'd didn't have to do anymore now that she wasn't so desperate to get to Denver. Leah's advice had quelled her desire to leave as soon as possible, despite the likelihood of finding a husband in Armelle being as dismal as ever. There were things she could do here for now, like helping Corinne.

And though Tim was not the man for her, he'd make a good friend. But would he find her worth befriending?

The way he'd listened to her the other day, holding her while she'd sobbed over being muddy…

He hadn't pushed her to stop crying or rolled his eyes at how she'd been going on—as if her mother had died just yesterday instead of years ago. He'd acted as if her feelings were important. Which Eric had never done. Neither had Father. And though Bo cared, he'd been so busy since he'd returned from school, she'd decided not to interrupt him for anything that wasn't urgent.

Cupboard doors slammed in the kitchen, and Nolan's voice grew insistent.

Had Corinne not gone upstairs? Maybe Nolan was taking her to the doctor. She'd be more comfortable if they took Gwen's buggy instead of the farm wagon. Gwen put down her sewing and headed into the kitchen.

"Here." Corinne pulled two jars from the cabinet where she stored her medicines and set them on the counter. For a second, she stopped to press a hand to her chest, but then shoved the jars toward Nolan. "These are the ones."

"But why must they be delivered today? Corinne, honey—"

She waved to shush him. "I didn't realize until this morning that he's likely run out by now."

"All right, I'll send one of the hands off with them."

She shook her head. "Timothy's hunting, and Sal's in town for the day. You need—"

"I can go," Gwen interrupted.

"That's nice of you to offer." Nolan gave her a smile. "But that's not necessary."

She pointed at herself. "I'm the least useful person here. Corinne needs you, and Rascal's taking care of the animals." She looked to Corrine, who sported a slight sheen across her forehead. "I'm only sewing diapers."

Nolan glanced at his queasy wife then to Gwen. "But Mr. York lives all the way up on the ridge. You'd have to ride."

"Riding is one of the few things I *am* good at. Just give me directions." Good thing she'd worn her split skirt today.

"It'll take all day." He scanned her, his gaze landing on her curled hair piled atop her head. "I'll go if you stay with Corinne."

"I'm sure she'd prefer you stay with her over me."

"I—" Corinne opened her mouth, then slapped a hand over it and turned around.

Nolan spun on his heel and rubbed his wife's back.

His sweet ministrations made Gwen long for the exact thing she'd decided days ago she'd no longer pine for—and possibly give up chasing all together. She needed to get out of this house.

So much for doing something solely for someone else's benefit.

Gwen headed for the pantry and fished out a basket. She'd pack herself a lunch, maybe something for dinner if it indeed would take all day. While Nolan escorted Corinne upstairs, Gwen wrapped the jars so they wouldn't break then filled a canteen.

As she tugged on her riding jacket, Nolan came back down and dragged a hand over his face as he took in her preparations. "Are you sure about going?"

"Of course. Handing something to someone takes so little skill, even I can't bungle it up." She tried to give him a cheeky smile, but the truth of how useless she was made it feel stiff. "The York place isn't hard to find, is it?"

"No. It's pretty simple. You know the road that goes by the pastor's folks?"

She nodded. They'd hosted several church gatherings in their enormous barn.

"Stay on that road until you get to the two buttes. Take the left fork. The trail gets close to the cliff's edge on occasion, but nothing worrisome. It's a peaceful, scenic ride actually."

"And the house?"

"When you get to a pair of willow trees bent together, you'll see a small cabin tucked up on the ridge with a massive quaking aspen hanging over it. There's no path up, but if you keep the place in sight, you shouldn't have a problem picking your way over."

"Sounds easy enough." Gwen grabbed the basket she'd prepared and threw back her shoulders in feigned confidence, despite never having been past the Lawrences' place and being unsure she could identify a quivering aspen if her life depended on it.

Once he finished writing down the directions, Nolan followed her out and saddled a horse. After helping her mount, he looked up, shifting his weight back and forth—out of worry or the discomfort of his false leg?

"Don't fret." She tried to ignore the flurry in her middle over heading some place she'd never been. "I'll come straight back if anything unexpected comes up. My brother would kill me if I didn't."

"All right then but take this." He disappeared into a small room and returned with a rifle. "I heard you've become a regular sharpshooter."

Assuming that was a compliment, she smiled as best she could. But surely no huge animals would be on the road if he let his wife travel to the Yorks' on her own. "I shouldn't need it...should I?"

He shook his head, but worry still glazed his expression as he slid the firearm into the scabbard that slipped in under her left leg.

After giving Nolan a final assurance and farewell, she set off. Once they were out of the gate, she prodded the gleaming black horse into a gallop. "Let's have fun, shall we?"

As the wind whipped through her hair, she thrilled in the exhilaration of speed. After several minutes, the Keys' place was hidden by the roll of the land, and she reined in her mount, letting him walk at a comfortable pace.

Scanning the smattering of trees, she tried to figure out which ones were aspens. The fact that a tree hung over a cabin should be enough to indicate she'd found the Yorks' place though. Up ahead, she turned onto the Lawrences' road and sat back and relaxed.

An hour later, a snuffling and thumping in the gully beside her made her stiffen. Reaching forward, she put her hand on the gun and prepared to dismount. She might know how to shoot, but could she really kill?

And then a man's hat appeared above the ledge. Then a horse's head.

When the man looked up—

Timothy.

Her heart restarted, and she straightened back up.

Eyes wide with concern, he trotted over. "What're you doing out this far, Miss McGill?"

"I'm on an errand for Mrs. Key." She pointed to the basket tied to her saddle. "I'm taking liniment to Mr. York. How's hunting been?"

"Haven't taken down anything but the rabbit I had for breakfast." He reined in closer. "You been out this way before?"

She raised her chin. "No, but I have good directions."

The expression on Tim's face labeled her a fool. And maybe she was, heading off to a place she'd never been in the mountains, but she hadn't lied to Nolan. The moment she felt unsure, she'd turn back. She'd been paying attention to her surroundings, making note of every visual marker that would help her return. "I've a gun as well. I'll be fine."

His expression didn't change.

Seemed no matter what she did, he'd never think highly of her. If she took initiative, he'd tell her she shouldn't exert herself. If she sat back, he'd look down on her for being spoiled.

But since her talk with Leah, it didn't matter what he thought anymore. "I told Mr. Key I'd be careful and not deviate from his directions. So there's no need to worry."

"Nolan let you go?"

She bristled. "Nolan didn't let me do anything. He wasn't too keen on the idea, but I wanted to help, and my own permission is all I need."

The side of his mouth tilted up and his eyes lost their dullness. "Good for you."

"What?" He was happy she'd gotten riled?

"I'm glad you found the gumption to do as you wish—whether or not some man thought you should. We answer to God, not men—though of course, we don't want to be stupid either…"

The way he trailed off made her squeeze the reins in her hands. "You think I'm stupid, then?"

She waited for him to hem and haw, since clearly—

"No."

She blinked and waited for the "but" to follow.

His jaw worked as if he were debating something, but he remained silent.

"So then…" She backed her horse away and turned to face the empty plains. "I better continue on. Nolan says it'll take me all day."

Timothy trotted up alongside her.

"What are you doing?"

"Coming with you."

"There's no need."

He shrugged. "Probably not, but I have a feeling Nolan was too preoccupied with Corinne to think things through."

Gwen reached into the basket and pulled out the scrap of paper he'd written on. "He gave me directions. You can check and see if they're good."

He took the paper, but barely glanced at it. "I'll still escort you. I don't like the thought of you being alone out here, even if you are an excellent shot."

The compliment warmed her from the toes up. Maybe he didn't think poorly of everything she did. "But you're supposed to be hunting. Were you doing so out here in the open? Don't big things hide?" If they didn't, now she really felt uneasy. Would a bear come running out at her?

"I was checking tracks I'd seen weeks ago. We're missing a cow and calf."

She stiffened. Had Nolan given her the gun because he'd been concerned she'd come across rustlers? Big animals had been scary enough to think about.

"I heard something strange last night near where I made camp. An eerie squawk, but not exactly bird-like."

Her insides twisted. She would no longer attempt to convince Tim she didn't need his escort.

"Might have been nothing other than it was late. Everything's spookier at twilight. But all I've found are some kittens."

"Kittens?"

His mouth tilted up. "Fuzzy balls of big-eyed fear and huge ears. Spit at me as if they could take me on." His mouth tipped back down. "Too bad they likely won't make it."

"Why not?"

His face blanked. "Nature. The dead cat near them was probably their mother. She appeared malnourished. Then of course, there's always predators."

Kittens being hunted for food made her stomach roil. "Why don't we get them and take them to the ranch?"

His brows raised. "Have you tried to catch feral cats? Besides, I have nothing to carry them in."

"I have a basket." She flipped open the lid, imagining several kittens tucked inside. "Are they far off?"

He sighed and shook his head. "Even if I could find them again, there's no guarantee I could catch them. They're probably flea-ridden, too."

"You know what I think would be *the right thing to do*…?" She gave him a look, daring him to refute her.

He took a breath deep enough to make his trim chest puff. "It's nice to rescue them, sure, but it's natural for creatures to die. You don't move ants when they decide to make an anthill in wagon ruts."

"Ants aren't as cute as kittens."

"Kittens aren't cute either when their claws tear into your flesh."

"That's only because they don't know any better."

He stared at her, and she stared right back. Of course, all he had to do was refuse to tell her where they were and she couldn't do a blessed thing. She caught herself fluttering her lashes and stopped herself. What was she doing? Of course, if it worked… She poked out her lower lip a little farther.

His face hardened.

Was he made of steel or something? "Please. If they shred us up, I promise to leave them to God. But couldn't we try? The Keys need cats for the barn."

"The dog takes care of rodents."

"And he has more silver hair than my father. He won't be around forever to dig up gophers."

"It's not as simple as plopping cats in a barn. They're young. They'll require a lot of babying."

"I'll do it."

Tim stared at her for a second, then squinted up at the sun, then west. "We'd be adding an hour to the ride."

"An hour is worth keeping the death of cute, little animals

off our conscience, don't you think? Admit it. You'd feel better if we didn't leave them to fend for themselves."

His body went rigid. "Sometimes having to fend for yourself is what makes you strong."

"Or pitifully incompetent."

He looked at her carefully. "I don't think you're pitifully incompetent."

She chuffed. He could have fooled her. "Then let me prove it by taming those cats and providing the Keys with good mousers. Heaven knows I'm not doing much else for them."

Without waiting for her, he reined his horse around and trotted back toward the ravine. He called over his shoulder, "We can't be long, don't want anyone worrying because you're not back when expected."

She kicked her horse to follow. So much for conversation— as usual. She readjusted herself in her saddle and settled in for a fast ride.

A quarter hour later, they picked their way down a crevasse. The echo of rocks sliding and the wind howling through the outcroppings made her shiver. The horse's hooves sounded louder, and the air was cool and damp. No wonder Tim had been spooked if he'd heard something down here.

Lots of scattered rock and tumbleweed were piled up against bleached wood, suggesting this ravine took in a lot of runoff when the snow melted. "Are the kittens down here?"

He pointed to a hollow log. "I think they're hiding in that tree."

Heading toward the decaying trunk, Tim's horse nickered. A little gray, striped ball of fuzz ran out from beneath a tumble-weed, stopping to hiss at him once before scrambling inside the log.

"Aw, he's scared."

"You might not be so inclined to say *aw* when he pokes you full of holes."

"I bet with some good food and cuddling he'll be purring in no time."

"Suppose we'll find out." He slid off his saddle and scanned the area. "Let's put the horses on that patch of grass. They won't frighten the kittens there. You block the opening at the smaller end of the log. I'll capture them from the other side."

She glanced at the log as they passed. It was easily six feet long. "You're going to wriggle your way in?"

"No, I figured I'd lure them out with your lunch."

She kept the frown off her face as she led her horse to the far patch of grass. If that's what it took, so be it. An empty stomach was easier to face than letting kittens die over the want of a sandwich.

He held a hand up to her as they walked back to the log. "Slow down. Don't want to scare them. They need to stay in there if we have any chance of grabbing them."

While he unpacked her basket, she crept toward the log's far end. The ground in front of the opening was nothing but mud. She groaned.

"What's the matter?"

"There's a big mud hole here."

He stopped messing with the basket. "You don't have to do this if you don't want to."

He sounded afraid she'd fall apart if she got dirty—of course, after her sob-fest the other day, why wouldn't he think so? "I promise not to break down in tears this time. I just hadn't any warning then."

"I'm sorry."

"Don't worry about it. You didn't know." Then she shushed him and padded toward the back of the log. Once there, she knelt beside the opening and grimaced. The ground was spongier than she'd thought. She'd been right about how difficult it was to wash mud out of fabric. Mrs. Barton hadn't been happy when Gwen had insisted on taking over the washroom that evening. And after an hour, she'd had to resist the urge to give up and call her maid back.

Once settled with her body and skirt covering the opening, Gwen signaled to Tim.

He nodded, pulled the ham from her sandwich, then stuffed the bread into his mouth.

"That was my lunch," she whisper-shouted.

He swallowed and smiled. "I set the other half aside for you." Then he squatted down and duck-walked toward the log.

"Here, kitty, kitty," he began in a squeaky staccato.

A spitting hiss answered immediately.

"I think it's insulted by your girly voice."

He rolled his eyes but called again with his lower tenor. Rumbling, soothing, masculine.

Had his voice always been that smooth? Maybe she'd not noticed since he usually used his words to point out she was worthless—

No, he didn't actually do that. He just made sure she knew she was…inadequate. She chewed her lip. Why did she care what he thought, anyway?

Since he was occupied with coaxing out cats, she let herself watch him. His face wasn't as broken out as she remembered. Maybe he was growing out of his acne. Though "growing out of" seemed too childish to describe a man with shoulders as wide as his were, even if they had no meat on them.

Minutes ticked by, and her knees protested the position she'd taken up. If the kittens took forever to trust him, her legs would fall asleep.

At the sound of a sorry little mew, she stayed still despite her screaming joints.

"Yeow!" Tim flinched backward, flicking one hand, but his other was pressed against his chest, a gray bristly tail swinging madly between his fingers. "Got one!"

He waddled over to the basket, shoved the cat inside, and inspected his hand with a scowl warping his lips.

"How many are there?"

"No idea. I'll just keep going until there's no more hissing." Picking up the ham he dropped, he scrunched back down. "Here, kitty, kit—"

The cocking of a rifle lever echoed off the rocks. "What are you doing here?"

Gwen stiffened at the strange man's voice and looked past Tim.

Near their horses, three dirty men held guns trained on Tim. Her heart rammed into her throat. How had they sneaked up on them? She scanned the ravine but saw no other entrance.

"Stand up, woman. Let me see your hands."

"You, too." A different scoundrel gestured at Tim. "Stand."

Slowly, Tim unfolded his long legs and stood.

She ran to him, and he shoved her behind him.

Shaking her head, she scrunched her eyes tight. Why had she run? They might've shot her. Of course, if they wanted to kill them, wouldn't they have done so without warning?

The blood rushing in her ears muffled the words the men were now shouting at them. Her vision went gray as pinpricks of tiny stars crowded in.

Breathe, Gwen. You can't faint. How worthless would you be to Tim if you did?

One breath in through her nose. Another out. Her heartbeat, however, refused to slow.

Tim spoke quietly out of the corner of his mouth. "If they ask questions, you're my wife. If they need the story, everything at the church happened with Mr. Wright, but you married Mr. Wrong."

"You're Mr. Wrong?" Her heart did a sad little flop.

"Sure, we can go with that. And we both work for the Keys."

"Hey!" One man shouted.

"Pray all they want is our valuables. If not, pray I can get us away."

"Hands up. Stand apart!"

Tim moved, but her legs were too jelly-like to even pick her feet off the ground.

"I said move apart!"

Somehow, she got one foot to go, then the other, but she couldn't take another step. She raised her hands, trying hard to keep them steady so they wouldn't see how badly she trembled.

The familiar feel of her knife against her ankle shouted its availability, but she'd not throw the one weapon they had—not that a well-aimed knife would be worthwhile against guns. She'd been a fool to ride out here on her own, and then insist they go off the trail for kittens—but even more of a fool for leaving her rifle strapped to the saddle.

Tim was probably cursing her under his breath right now.

She was definitely more trouble than she was worth.

CHAPTER SIXTEEN

Swallowing, Tim forced himself to obey the man pointing the gun and take another step away from Gwen. Every fiber of his being screamed at him to stay in front of her, and yet, his flesh and bones were unlikely to stop a bullet from reaching her.

"Farther!"

He lifted his hands higher and moved a few more inches, while covertly scanning the ravine. Where had they come from? Where could he and Gwen run if given the chance? The pistol at his side would only buy them—

"Throw your weapon out in front of you."

He lowered his right hand.

"You so much as look like you're drawing, and we'll kill you both."

Slowly, he lifted his sidearm from its holster and tossed it. "We don't want trouble. I can give you my pocket watch and whatever jewelry my wife is wearing, but that's all we have. You've got our horses and guns already."

Though he was certain they'd be surprised by a woman as beautiful as Gwen condescending to marry him, hopefully they believed he'd been so lucky. If they had even a smidgen of morals, maybe they'd leave her alone.

But none of the men responded. Two ducked their heads together, while the third kept a shotgun aimed square at his chest.

"Should I toss them my earrings?" Gwen's whisper was barely intelligible with how her voice shook.

As much as he wanted to assure her things would be all right, he kept his eyes on their captors. "Don't move unless they ask you to."

And why weren't they demanding all their valuables? Gwen had worn something sparkly on each ear today—as far as he knew, they were diamonds.

When the third man turned his head to enter his partners' conversation, Tim took a small step back toward Gwen. He might not be thick enough to stop a bullet, but he wanted to be close enough to try.

The third man's head whipped back, and his eyes narrowed. He waved his shotgun. "Turn around."

Tim's heartbeat ramped up. Was the man too cowardly to face them as he sent them to their Maker?

Tim took a deep breath and did as directed. *Please, Lord, let them rob us blind and skedaddle. Don't let them hurt Gwen.*

As footsteps approached, he glanced quickly at her. She was paler than moonlight.

The man came closer. Tim braced himself.

Please God—

He was quickly patted down. Tim's every muscle slumped. No rifle butt had struck his head. No bullet had ripped through his brain.

"Turn around, hold out your hands, and don't try anything."

He turned to see the other men's gun barrels pointed in their direction.

The cowboy moved to Gwen and tied her hands, too. "Now head to the horses."

Once they traversed to the other side of the ravine, another man began tying Tim to the saddle of Nolan's beautiful black gelding.

Were they going to have the horse drag him? "What's the meaning of this?"

"Shut up."

Pressing his lips together, Tim fought to comply. Gwen might have accused him earlier of thinking her worthless, but right now, *he* was the epitome of worthless. Why had he not looked around before he'd left their horses? He subtly tested the ropes at his wrists. Too tight. He lifted his bound fists like a club and turned, but the man had already backed away.

The scoundrel put his hand on the pistol on his hip and gave him a stare down. "Now take it easy, fella. We're just going for a walk."

"Where to?" He itched to clobber the scoundrel and pulled against the ropes. "Why don't you—"

"I said, settle down." The man took a step back and pulled his pistol—then pointed it at Gwen.

Tim settled like sand through a shattered hourglass.

"If you don't keep your trap shut, I'll shoot her, then you. Or you can do as I say, and she'll live."

Tim let out a slow breath and nodded. The man hadn't said *he* would live, but her life would be enough.

The beefy man left to rejoin the others.

A strangled sob came from Gwen.

"Hey, darling. You heard him. You'll live." *Please God, make them honor that.* "I'll do whatever they ask from now on. I'm sorry. I could've gotten us killed just then."

A stirring caused him to turn to look away from her. The one who'd threatened to shoot Gwen was headed back, shaking his head while leaving the other two who were now headed for their horses.

When the man reached for his hip, Tim stiffened, but the bloke only pulled a bandanna from his pocket. He spun it into a roll and headed straight for Timothy. "Turn around."

Tim did so, bracing for what might be a choking or a—

Blindfold.

"It's time to take a walk." The man's voice was gruff as he cinched the knot tight against the back of Tim's head. "Now your turn, ma'am."

Her utter silence tore at him. *Please, obey.*

A second later, she whimpered.

"Let me hold her hand. She's scared. Don't—"

"She's fine." The gruff voice answered.

An unexpected pull on his arm registered as her hand, then something cinched her thin arm against his.

His chest heaved. Hopefully the men were like his father and his buddies, not malicious, just dumb. He had no experience with truly evil men, but he knew what to do with stupid ones. Best to let them go through with their idiotic plans unprovoked and—

A jerk sent him reeling forward as one of the men called for them all to move. Tim's arms nearly popped from their sockets as the horse lurched forward, the rope around his and Gwen's arm digging into his flesh. He scrambled for footing, but his feet made purchase and somehow Gwen stayed upright. They weren't being dragged after all, thank God.

Minutes passed, but the horse didn't slow. This was far too fast a pace to maintain for long, especially for Gwen. He squeezed her hand against his side. "How are you doing?"

"About as well as one can trotting alongside a horse, I suppose."

Seemed she had a decent amount of fight in her. But that could only sustain her for so long.

After countless steps and stumbles, the men started to argue. Tim tried to make out what they were saying, but between the clopping hooves, creaking saddles, and heavy breathing, he couldn't understand a thing.

Gwen's arm yanked on his, and she pressed up against him.

"Tim," she whispered raggedly.

Had she ever called him Tim before?

She yanked again, so he leaned down.

Her mouth pressed against his ear, her words breathy. "If you could get me closer to the saddle, I might be able to untie something. You think I ought to try?"

He straightened, straining to sense if the men had heard her, but the timbre of the men's grumbling hadn't changed. "Are you not blindfolded?"

"I am," she whispered. "But my fingers can move."

Though he liked her gumption, they were in no position to do anything rash. "No, don't try. I don't want to risk them seeing you attempt something and shooting us dead."

Then again, why hadn't they already?

A warm blanket of sunshine passed over his shoulders. If they were out in the open, hopefully someone would see them— but they were far from civilization. The pace picked up and all he could do was concentrate on moving his feet. They were likely pushing them hard to get across the plain without being spotted.

"Please," Gwen hollered. "I can't go this fast."

She weighed heavily upon him as she stumbled. He pulled her up, but his own strength was giving out, his lungs burning.

Someone's horse trotted up alongside them. Reins creaked and their horse slowed somewhat, but they didn't stop.

After what felt like hours, the rustling of branches and the scent of pine pierced through the focus necessary for him to remain upright. A rock slipped under his foot, and he crashed into the side of the horse, catching himself just in time to keep from sending them both to the ground. The moisture in the air called to his dry throat like a siren's song. Considering the intermittent shade cooling him every few seconds, they were likely following a tree line that met up with one of the creeks that meandered through Wyoming's empty plains.

The terrain now sloped downward and the heat of the sun dissipated. Gwen's breathing became erratic.

"Please, stop," he called out, but his vocal cords were so dry he hadn't even heard himself. He cleared his throat and tried again. "My wife can't take anymore."

She stumbled beside him, and he saved her from falling, but they were seconds away from a catastrophe. "We need to slow down. Please—"

The horse stopped. Gwen's weight lifted off him, and he sank to his knees, his feet throbbing.

The rope around his arm released, and a giant wave of pinpricks traveled from his hands up into his neck. Before he could flex his fingers, he was being dragged backwards across rocky ground. If he was about to be tossed down a ravine or into a body of water, he wouldn't make it.

No escape plan worth an attempt came to mind. He could barely move, every limb felt like jelly. Gwen was likely worse off. "Gwen!" How had he forgotten her for even a second?

A shove launched him forward, and his face smacked square into a tree trunk. His body relaxed despite how the flesh of his cheek shredded against the bark as he slid to the base of a pungent pine. Glory! He didn't have to walk anymore.

His feet were pulled out from under him, and a rope cinched his ankles. Gwen's soft body landed against him. For a glorious moment, his hands were free, but they were wrenched back behind his back and retied.

"Water," Gwen's rough voice called out.

He hung his head. Here he'd thought escorting her to the Yorks' had been some chivalrous act of protection—but now she faced dehydration, pain, and maybe even death because of him. Oh, why had he taken her off the beaten path?

He could hear her gulping, and seconds later, a canteen was thrust against his lips. All thoughts of dignity fled as he tried to keep the water in his mouth, but most of the liquid ran straight down his front. Had his muscles lost all ability to function, or was this kidnapper not even watching what he was doing?

The canteen lifted and with a pop of knees, the unidentified man stood.

"I need more." His throat was sore, but he'd scraped out the plea anyway.

The shadow disappeared and his footsteps dissolved into silence.

Tim half-heartedly tugged against his new bonds. Once his heartbeat slowed, his body pled with him in a different manner —a most uncomfortable one. "Help," he called, but no sound came from anywhere other than Gwen's hard breathing beside him.

He tried to adjust the way he sat, but the rocks beneath him were as painful as the intermittent jolts searing through his body.

"I got my bandanna down enough to see," Gwen whispered.

He turned toward her, only able to see a hint of her maroon skirt through the gap next to his nose. "How'd you do that?"

"Wriggled my eyebrows."

He attempted the same, but the fabric didn't budge. "What do you see?"

"They're near a rock overhang. One's gathering sticks. You think they're setting up camp?"

"I'd assume so." Considering the weariness in her voice, he'd pray they were. If his legs were throbbing, he couldn't imagine how hers felt. Her fancy boots were more for show than anything else. "What time is it?"

"How should I know?" Her tone indicated she was calling his intelligence into question.

"The sun. Can you see it?"

"No." Her voice lost its indignation. "But I'd not be able to tell time that way even if I could."

"Where the light's coming from? What angle?"

He heard her shift, then exhale heavily. "Somewhere to our left maybe. Sixty degrees? Forty? Thirty?"

At least "left" told him where west was. "What else can you see?"

"Rocks, sagebrush, pines."

"Great, now I know we're outdoors." He chuckled but had to quit to cough.

"I'm not much help. Sorry."

"Don't be. Just tell me when they're heading back."

"What should we do?"

"I don't know. Are your ankles tied too? Your hands behind your back?"

"They left my feet free, but my hands are behind my back now, yes."

He tried pulling on his bonds again. "I'm hoping since they didn't kill us right away, we have a chance of surviving."

"What do you think they want?"

"If they wanted something, I'd think they'd have taken it already. So I'm hoping we stumbled too close to something they didn't want us to see, and now they're taking us away to give them time to cover their tracks or relocate something." Were they behind the Keys' missing cow and calf? Maybe they had a bunch of ill-gotten head hidden near the ravine the kittens were in.

"What if they know who I am and want a ransom?"

He straightened. He'd not thought of that, however… "Unlikely. If they knew who you were, they'd not have believed for a second you were my wife."

"Should I tell them who I am? If they knew they could get a ransom—"

He shook his head vehemently. "Don't you dare let them know we're not married. Better to let them think we're worthless poor people and hope they abandon us somewhere."

"My outfit's too nice for them to think that."

With his threadbare clothing next to hers, why *had* these men bought his lie about them being married? Or maybe they didn't, and if so…

That had to be it. They'd noted her dress and realized she had money. "If only you chose clothes because they were practical rather than pretty." He inhaled sharply. "I didn't mean that how it sounded."

"No, you're right. I'm nothing more than uselessness wrapped up in a fancy bow."

He shifted toward her, adjusting his shoulder against the rough bark. "Don't be so hard on yourself. No one of your class cares if you know how to milk a cow."

"It's nice of you to assume I'm competent for my own 'class,' but I'm not. I embroider abominably."

He laughed. "I never figured embroidery was useful. Just thought ladies liked to annoy men by piling up sofas so full of pillows they can't figure out where to park their backsides."

"Shhh!" Amusement colored her shushing him. "If they think we're too relaxed over here, they'll come make us more uncomfortable than we already are."

He swallowed his amusement but couldn't shake the absurdity of how much he was enjoying bantering with her while blindfolded—with death looming.

"So embroidery isn't a skill you're looking for in a wife? Good to know."

He blinked behind his bandanna. She was interested in what he wanted in a wife? For a second his heart faltered, but then his mind fired back up. Women and their matchmaking. She was likely thinking of someone to set him up with if they got back to Armelle alive. Or could it be she was the kind who talked constantly when uneasy?

The sunlight disappeared, probably behind a cloud. Gwen informed him of the men's actions, but they seemed in no hurry to return to traveling, yet they weren't doing anything to indicate they intended to make camp.

With the sun now hidden, the wind snaking through the gully, and the sweat clinging to his clothes, he felt chilled, which only added to his discomfort. How many hours until Nolan and the others realized Gwen wasn't coming back? Since she was supposed to be gone all day, they wouldn't be able to search long before dark fell. There'd be no rescue tonight.

But the longer they were at the mercy of these men, the dimmer their fate would grow.

After a few more reports from Gwen, Tim couldn't figure out what the men were doing. Had they forgotten about their captives? He tensed against the need to relieve himself.

If he were alone and could untie the bandanna and his bindings, he might attempt to run, but with Gwen… He heard a slight rattling sound beside him. Were her teeth chattering? "Are you cold?"

"Yes."

"Come closer. Use my body heat." She had on far more fabric layers, but his mother always seemed to be freezing when he and his brothers were plenty warm. "It's fine. They think we're married, remember?"

Without replying, Gwen scooted closer and snuggled against him.

He swallowed hard. Though he truly was Mr. Wrong for her, having her this close wouldn't help his pining.

Think, Timothy. How do you get her out of here? She deserves to make it out alive and find a man she can make proud.

"Hallo!" His voice scratched out. He had to clear his throat for a second attempt. "Someone?"

"One's coming." Gwen's voice wobbled. "What if they notice I can see?"

"If they do, don't mention you did it yourself. They'll just think it fell down."

Footsteps plodded over and stopped in front of them.

Without preamble, Tim was yanked up by the arm, his shoulder socket screaming. "I didn't mean to be a bother, but I need—"

The man jerked him up farther, and he hissed against the pain.

"Please!" Gwen's voice begged.

Timothy's lungs hitched and he grew lightheaded.

"Please!" she hollered. "I need to, you know…"

Tim was shoved back down, his face making impact with the tree again.

"Oh!" Gwen protested. Then her skirts smacked him in the face. She must have been hauled up as roughly as he'd been. "Please."

The sound of her being dragged off made Tim growl while trying to rub off his blindfold using his shoulder. If that man so much as…

"Gwen!" He cried, but no answer. With frantic movements, he scraped the side of his face against the bark, hoping to get the blasted bandanna off. He might not be able to do much tied up, but if he couldn't see where she was, he couldn't even wriggle his way toward her.

"Gwen!"

CHAPTER SEVENTEEN

"Please, you're hurting me." Gwen kept her face turned away from the man dragging her back to where they'd left Tim. She didn't want the brute who'd threatened to shoot her if she ran while she'd been relieving herself to notice her blindfold was cockeyed. While taking care of business, she'd pulled her hair down to cover her face, hoping to hide that she could see. He hadn't noticed when he'd retied her hands behind her back.

As they neared the tree, she caught glimpses of frantic movements. What was Tim doing? Was someone hurting him?

"Settle, chap." The rough voice beside her sounded oddly kind. "She's back in one piece."

Tim whipped his head toward them, his chest heaving. It appeared he'd gotten his bandanna down over one eye by scraping his face against the tree's bark.

Her insides did a heavy flip.

"Gwen," he breathed.

Why had his whisper of her name pulled at her heartstrings so?

The man behind her pushed her forward, and she stumbled, falling inches from where Tim sat. The concern shining from his one visible eye made her want to reach for him, but she couldn't without giving away that she could see. She hung her head to allow her loosened hair to fall around her face.

The stranger pulled Tim's blindfold back up. The angry, swollen abrasion decorating the side of his face was embroidered with pinpricks of blood.

The man checked Tim's bonds. "No need to go crazy. If you don't try anything funny, she'll be fine."

Could such a declaration be trusted?

The moment the man left, she slumped against Tim like hot butter.

Though his hands were tied behind his back, he somehow curled around her, and she let herself sink into him. Maybe she was just desperate to cling to some assurance that things would be fine, or maybe she wished he felt something toward her other than annoyance, but the way he gathered her in seemed to show he cared. Though of course, he'd be concerned about any kidnapped woman he felt responsible for.

"Is he gone?" Tim whispered. Under the ear she had pressed against his chest, his heart was slowing back to a normal rhythm.

She nodded against him but didn't answer aloud in case the man who'd walked away could hear.

Once the brute was on the other side of the horses, she inched her way up to sit and turned her body toward their captors. No one seemed worried about them escaping.

"Where are they?"

"They're..." Oh, she'd already proven she was no good at describing anything. It'd be better if he could see, so he could decide on a plan—if there was one to be had.

She could pull down his bandanna, but she'd have to use her teeth. She hesitated a second before scooting closer. Why had her heart sped up at the thought? She wasn't moving in for a kiss or anything.

Her heartbeat kicked up another notch. Stupid organ. Inching closer, she whispered, "Hold still."

He took that rather literally, considering he stopped breathing.

She leaned forward but then sat back with a frown. She couldn't see below her eyes. How was she going to do this? She looked back at the men, who were busy eating. If she were going to do anything, she had to be quick.

Trailing her lips against his face, she tasted the salt of his sweat as she searched for the edge of his bandanna. Once she found it, she grabbed the fabric with her teeth and pulled down slightly. She moved back and peered over her blindfold to see how far she'd moved the cloth, then returned to pull it up a smidge. She didn't want the misalignment to be too obvious.

"Can you see?" she whispered.

His breath stuttered out, but he nodded. His eyelashes were hitting the top of the fabric.

Backing away, she caught him scanning her, as if to assess whether she was in one piece. Then he turned to look at the men before returning his gaze to hers. "Go ahead and put it back up now," his voice scratched out.

Her chest froze. "But why?"

"I don't want them to get suspicious, to watch us more closely than they have been. One of us seeing is enough, and your hair has a chance of keeping them from noticing."

She huffed. Why did he have to be right about everything, and she so wrong? She leaned back in, but this time with his eye on her, she found it hard to breathe. She pulled the bandanna back up, taking quick glances toward their captors to be certain they weren't paying attention.

Once the fabric sat taut across his brow again, she felt a strange compulsion to kiss the welted skin covering his cheekbone. He had clearly ignored pain and common sense in his attempt to see how she was faring.

Would he have skinned up his face like that for just anybody? Perhaps her brother knew something she didn't.

When Tim released his breath, it brushed warm against her lips. If she leaned just a fraction of an inch…

Chills broke out along her skin. She'd never felt this way at the prospect of kissing Eric—even when she actually had. Shaking her head, she scooted backward, putting space between them. Why was she thinking about kissing in a situation like this? She cleared her throat. "Do you have an idea of how we can get away?"

She needed to escape this situation in more ways than one.

His shoulders drooped. "No. But whoever brought you over here mentioned they didn't mean to hurt us, so we keep our eyes out for a chance to get away while praying hard that they simply let us go."

"Do criminals truly let hostages go?" Maybe all day in the sun had affected his ability to think. He *had* lost his hat at some point.

"I can't take it anymore." Tim growled and convulsed as he pulled against his bonds. "Hello, someone!" he hollered. "I need to be relieved."

The same man who'd taken her to the bushes headed over.

Her heart raced. "Please don't run without me. I know you might be able to get away and find some help, but I'd be all alone—"

"I won't."

Their captor kicked a stone toward them, and they fell silent. Gwen hung her head, shaking her hair down once again.

"Why does this have to be my job?" the man muttered as he stomped over to wrench Tim up. "Let's get this over quick, shall we?"

With every yard he dragged Tim away, she willed her breathing to slow. He'd said he'd not leave—

"Ah!" she yelped as she was yanked upward.

"Come on, pretty lady. Time to move." One of the other men's rough hands had clamped around her upper arm and forced her to stand. Too bad her bandanna didn't also cover her nose. His breath reeked of tobacco and spirits. His rotten teeth—

She ducked her head, letting her weight hang heavy on his arm. Hopefully he hadn't noticed she'd seen him.

"Relax, miss. I'm just taking you back to the horse." He tightened the knot of her bandanna, and now all she could see was reddish light filtering through the fabric. He then untied her hands to move them back to the front. Were they really going to make them march or be dragged by the horse again?

Her heart sank as he hauled her forward, her feet and legs protesting. Her chest clamped. "I can't walk anymore. I just can't. Please leave us here. You'll be so far away by the time we hobble back to town no one will ever catch you."

She received no answer other than a rough shove forward.

If these men weren't going to kill them, what were their plans?

The story of Joseph flashed into her mind—his being dragged up from a cistern, tied to a camel, sold in Egypt.

Sold. Trapped into a life she couldn't return from.

Her blood pulsed in her ears. Her lungs fought to pull in air.

A man's voice seemed to be shushing her, but the words were all jumbled. Her vision grew blacker than the blindfold could account for.

But then her arm was lashed to Tim's, and she gripped him as tight as her numb fingers could. She wasn't alone. She had Tim, and he'd fight for her.

But what if that wasn't enough?

CHAPTER EIGHTEEN

The flames flickered in the small fire in front of Tim as an owl hooted above him in the tree they slumped against. He attempted to stretch his tingling fingers and toes as his body fought against the sleep it needed after so many grueling hours of walking.

At least his blindfold had been removed—though all that did was increase his anxiety. He couldn't sleep until he'd had a better look at the man who'd recently joined camp. If this newest lowlife was bad news, he'd not take his eyes off him for a second.

Against the side of the tree, Gwen's skirts rustled as she squirmed about with her ankles bound and her hands tied behind her back just like his. At least the men had built a fire for them. Once the sun had gone down, the air had turned crisp.

The new man walked in their direction. He had to be six foot something, with a lot of muscle.

Tim sighed. Why did they all have to be bigger than him?

With spurs clinking, the tall man walked over and shoved aside a low-hanging branch. His eyebrows rose when he caught sight of Gwen.

Tim scooted toward her, trying as best he could to shield her from view.

The man sneered. "Guess it's a good thing I caught plenty of fish, since there's two of you. Hungry?"

Tim eyed him. If he said yes, would they be denied food?

The man shrugged and headed back to the main fire. Seconds later, the man's gravelly voice informed the others he hadn't recognized them. Then he stooped to open a basket and pulled out fish.

Fighting his heavy eyelids, Tim scanned the camp's surroundings. Nothing about this gorge looked familiar—not that he could see much.

"I'm hungry, and I just want to sleep, but my feet hurt so badly." Gwen's voice sounded thin.

"Try to sleep. If they bring anything over, I'll wake you up." He blinked hard a few times to be certain he could stay awake long enough to do so.

Gwen didn't answer.

"You aren't going to sleep over there, are you?"

A snort mixed with a yawn sounded, as if he'd startled her awake. "Where else would I sleep?"

"If you stay so far away, we won't look married." He'd prayed all afternoon their marriage ruse would be enough to keep the men from acting on any base desires.

"How's that?"

He couldn't tell whether she'd not understood or was already drifting off to sleep. "I'm afraid they'll treat you worse if they don't think we're married, so we need to act convincingly."

"All right." She murmured sleepily, but at least she scooted over. "Though I'm not sure they could do anything worse than make me walk in my stupid boots for the million miles they already have."

Thankfully she seemed too tired to imagine things worse than walking. He scooted over to meet her, and she laid her head on his shoulder.

Once her weight pressed against him, his body relaxed. Perhaps he was the one who'd needed her near. For so many years, he'd pined for her because she was his ideal, the possibility of leaving his rotten, dysfunctional world behind, of being accepted by people who seemed to matter in this world, but now...

He didn't care what the world thought of him, he cared how the world treated her. And though he'd learned she wasn't his ideal, he'd been impressed by her stubborn desire to improve herself. Though he wasn't sure he'd ever be happy about the reasons behind her quest for self-improvement, she at least was willing to admit faults and work on them. That was the kind of person he could see himself growing old with, striving to grow alongside her. He knew how infuriating living with someone who never sought to better themselves could be.

Gwen's breath evened out but never softened into the sounds of slumber. As much as he wanted to insist she sleep, he didn't mind that she felt comfortable enough to simply relax into him, as if he were the man she would always seek out for solace. If only he could pretend she'd chosen his arms instead of there being no other alternative.

Minutes later, the clomp of hooves and the shiver of dislodged pebbles pricked Tim's ears. Someone else was entering the ravine.

A stocky man rode into the firelight. After stopping near the men, he slid off his horse, blocking out the silhouette of the man torturing them with the smell of frying fish.

Tim tilted his ear toward the campfire, hoping to hear anything the new man said.

Gwen turned her head against him. "How many men do you—?"

"Shhh."

The voices were soft and distorted as they bounced off the surrounding rocks.

"...taking them to base ca—"

"What? Why would you even…?"

The hairs on Tim's neck stood up. The new man's voice wasn't sinister sounding, so why had his body reacted like that?

"…I told him we shouldn't have, but he…"

"That ain't going to work… I'll decide…choose wrong and we're in for…"

Their bickering didn't make them seem devious. Rather, this group acted unused to making decisions. However, the newest man sounded more self-assured. Was he the boss?

"I'll find out myself." The new fellow slashed his hand, then turned and started for the tree where they were bound.

Tim froze. Did he know that voice? If they were recognized, did they stand a chance?

The man's steps slowed as he approached their pitiful fire. He took off his hat and cocked his head.

Tim's heartbeat ratcheted.

The figure, too far away for Tim to make out, spun his hat in one hand, then shoved it back on and marched forward with purpose.

Had he imagined the newcomer's hesitation? With how he'd—

Daniel.

Tim stopped breathing as his former friend walked into the firelight, his face shadowed and hard-edged. Last time he'd seen Daniel was the day he and Celia were released from community service. Since Tim had managed to escape full involvement in Gwen's father's schemes, he hadn't been sentenced. He'd heard Daniel had been sent off to live with an aunt, but perhaps his parents had made up that story to cover for him.

Tim studied his former schoolmate, noting the hardness of Daniel's face. He'd always acted tough, yet he couldn't count the times Daniel had shared his lunch with him when he'd noticed he'd brought nothing to school. Daniel had never asked questions and always acted as if he'd intended on sharing his lunch.

Daniel turned toward Gwen, and Tim froze. His friend

would not be fooled into thinking Gwen had condescended to marry him.

Daniel took a step back, his eyes hooded.

Tim dug his fingernails deep into the flesh of his palms. He'd thought posing as Gwen's husband would've given her a better chance at safeguarding her innocence. But now, things might be worse because of it. If Daniel informed the others they weren't actually married…

Daniel put a hand on his hip holster and thrust his chin out. "Where you folks from?"

Tim moved to scratch his head, but the sharp bite of rope reminded him he couldn't. How could Daniel not have recognized them? Which meant he was pretending. What was he imagining would happen if the other men knew they were acquainted?

"Armelle," Tim pushed out, his voice wobblier than he would've liked.

Daniel took a quick glance at Gwen and turned back to address Tim. "Your *wife*?"

He gave a sharp nod.

Though he had to know Tim was lying, Daniel said no more. He walked over to crouch beside them. "Now, don't fight me."

Tim tensed as his former friend patted him down. He evidently hadn't trusted the others to have done so.

He then sidled over to Gwen, and she inhaled sharply.

Had she recognized Daniel, or was his "friend" letting his hands wander?

Giving them a harsh glare, Daniel stood. "Behave yourselves." And with that, he marched back to the others.

Gwen let out a heavy rush of air.

"Did he hurt you?"

"No. I was afraid he'd find the knife in my boot."

"The what?" He swung his head toward Gwen.

"My throwing knife—but he didn't."

"You mean…?"

"If we can get to it, we might be able to free ourselves, but I'm too exhausted right now to make a run for it."

"Why didn't you tell me you had that earlier?"

Her shoulders scrunched against his side. "I'm so used to having it there and didn't think it'd be worth much against guns. I didn't think about cutting ropes until now. I'm so sorry. I was too scared to think straight." The tears clogging her voice caused a lump to form in his chest.

"I'm not mad at you. And you're right. Sleep is what we need most at the moment."

Her head bobbed against his shoulder.

What other fascinating things did he not know about her? He wanted to ask why she even carried a knife, let alone a throwing one, but that could wait.

"Do you think Daniel recognized me?"

So she'd recognized him. "Of course he did."

"What do you mean, 'of course'? I never talked to him in school. He was even younger than you."

Tim let loose a chuckle. "Every boy in our school was in love with you at some point, whether you talked to him or not. If we weren't talking about hunting or riding, we were talking about you."

"*You* talked about me?"

Oh, why had he said the first thing that had come to mind? "Some."

"What did you say about—"

"Shhh." He pretended to be listening to what the men were murmuring around the fire—which was what he ought to be doing anyway.

Once Daniel returned to the group, nothing he said seemed to change the men's demeanor. They stayed huddled around the fire, talking in low hums. "You were right earlier. We need sleep. I'll wake you if they bring food."

"But—"

"Close your eyes." Since a coyote was currently running along the top of the ridge, that'd be best. She'd get no sleep if she realized the smell of fire-roasted meat was torturing more than just their empty stomachs.

Besides, nothing would entice him to divulge what he'd said about her in school. If they survived this, he didn't want to make things any more awkward between them than they already were.

And he certainly didn't want her to realize that his past infatuation with her was nothing compared to the growing feelings he had for her now. Whether it was the bond they shared in the face of danger, or that he was learning in bits and pieces who Gwendolyn McGill truly was—she seemed to find new ways to impress him with each passing hour.

CHAPTER NINETEEN

Though Gwen had closed her eyes as Tim had insisted, her body was too uncomfortable to sleep. Tim's bony shoulder was pressed into her cheek, her stomach rumbled at every whiff of frying fish, her backside protested every stone she sat on. And yet, her mind was hazy, and every limb felt like dead weight.

She readjusted herself against Tim and stretched her legs as best she could, but the pinpricks in her feet doubled. If only she could take off her boots. How was she supposed to sleep trussed up like this? She needed rest if she were to survive whatever lay ahead tomorrow—if surviving was even an option.

She swallowed hard and pressed into Tim, wishing she could curl up enough to disappear. Long ago, she'd been able to curl up against her father whenever she'd needed reassurance. But after her mother died and her father's grief had turned to anger, he'd never granted such affection again. Bo had only been a boy of ten then, unable to give a nine-year-old girl the comfort she'd sought. Going so long without a person willing to hold you when you needed it...

The feel of her mother's soft embrace and the smell of her lilac perfume drifted in like a ghost. How she wished Momma were here and not a figment of her desperate imagination.

But strange, after all they'd been through today, not until this moment had she wished for anyone's presence other than Tim's. Not Eric's, not her brother's. Nor her father's or her mother's.

Though they weren't safe, though they had no path to escape, Tim's nearness had been enough to anchor her heart when it had gone wild, whenever a captor came too close, when the what ifs had plagued her as they'd trudged across the plains.

If anyone would fight for her well-being over his own...

No, she was being ungracious. Her brother would've protected her with his life if he were here. But if she'd been kidnapped and tied up in the middle of nowhere with Eric...

She couldn't keep the derisive snicker from escaping. She'd be panicking far more than she was right now. If she and Eric had freed themselves and made a run for it, what good would he have been in getting them home? But then, what did she know about his skills or hobbies? She might've been fine with him, but she just didn't know.

She didn't know him well enough to have any idea how they'd fare.

Swallowing, she clamped her lips against the desire to sigh heavily at herself. Tim had been right. She'd not known enough about Eric to be assured she would've been happily married to him if he'd bothered to ask.

A movement near the camp arrested her attention. Though she wanted food, half of her wished their kidnappers would simply forget about them. Once she identified the movement as Daniel heading off alone, she relaxed. But then, if Tim was right and Daniel had recognized her, why hadn't he exposed them?

She turned to look at Tim. His eyes still open. "Do you think Daniel pretending not to know us is because all three of us would be dead if these men knew we were acquainted?"

"I have no idea." Tim stared at the shadowed gap in the rocks where Daniel had disappeared. "I'm sorry I got you into this."

"It's not your fault," she whispered against his shirt.

"I'm the one who suggested we pretend to be married. If Daniel tells the others we're not and they think you and I—"

"Still not your fault." She glanced over at the men eating around the fire. "Kidnappers forcing you into snap decisions isn't anything to feel guilty about. You did what you thought best."

"If we do escape and Daniel tells people about our charade…" His chest rose with a huge inhale and stayed tight. "I'd do the honorable thing if that's what you wanted, but you don't deserve to be forced into marrying me because of what I said to a bunch of lowlifes."

Why did people's opinions have to hold so much sway? "The townsfolk already don't like me because they think I turned a blind eye to my father's wrongdoings. So, well…" She stopped when her mouth went dry. Why did her heart stutter at the thought of leaving? Had his heart tripped a beat as well? She listened to the thumping against her ear but noted that while the rhythm might be a touch quick, it was steady. "I've always wanted to move to Denver anyway. I'll just leave."

"If what I've done makes that necessary, I'll pay to get you wherever you need to go."

The sincerity infusing his voice made her sad. He knew as well as she did her brother could do that far more easily. "You don't have to."

"Yes, I do."

She shook her head against him, listening to the crickets as if there might be wisdom to glean from their monotonous song. "I'd always planned on marrying someone who'd take me away from here, so you shouldn't pay for what I already intended to do."

"All you've wanted out of a man is the ability to get you away from here?"

"No." Were they going to fight over her choice of beaus again?

"Then what is it you're after, exactly? Hendrix wouldn't have left Armelle. The railroad man would've been all over the place, that redheaded guy…"

"William Forthing."

"He certainly didn't have money to go anywhere."

She frowned. "He no longer lives here."

"He's likely just a cowhand somewhere, in a county no more populated than this."

Picturing William's smile, she sighed. "But he was nice to look at." His smile had been a bit like Tim's—when he bothered to smile.

Tim's chest grew tight and stiff, so she darted a glance toward the men at the fire. All accounted for, except Daniel. Straining to see whatever had caused Tim alarm, she scanned the camp, but saw no one else.

The crickets' lullaby was working its magic, and she yawned.

"So if they don't have money…" Tim readjusted himself, which caused her head to roll off his chest and against his arm. "A man's looks are what's most important to you?"

Why was his tone so biting? "Perhaps what I said sounded shallow, but I wouldn't have married William. Though I have money, security's important, especially since I'm not as talented and capable as Corinne or Celia."

"So money's all you want?"

"No, of course not." She yawned again, her legs numb enough to no longer remind her of how uncomfortable they were. "But who doesn't want money? Don't you want money?"

His shoulder lifted against her back, but he remained quiet.

She closed her eyes and whispered, "It makes life so much easier."

"True," he answered in a hushed, defeated tone. "Or so I've been told."

"No one wants to hear a rich girl whining about money, I know." She groaned as she tried to make one leg move despite her muscles protesting. "But without knowing I'll have someone beside me forever who'll actually love me, well, I can't imagine loneliness is any better if you're wondering where your next meal comes from."

"You're lonely?"

She frowned at having revealed such, but what good was keeping everything tucked inside when tomorrow she'd likely be dead? "Of course, I have my brother, but what I wouldn't give to be held right now by my mother. I miss who my father had once been, I miss…"

Her breath stuttered out. "I miss knowing that when life gets hard, someone's there to wrap their arms around me. Though my brother loves me, we've never had an affectionate relationship and he's so busy, and I'm too old for that, you know?"

"But how would money make that better?"

"It wouldn't. Just wouldn't make it worse." Tim had to understand that. She'd seen how little he had in school, how he'd been forced to scavenge for food. Surely he knew poverty was not just a hardship a woman might fear, but a threat to the happiness of any future children as well.

The crickets sang for a bit before he answered. "I'm sorry you've been lonely."

She turned her head, trying to glimpse his expression in the darkness. "Do you ever feel lonely?"

"Yes." His answer had been forced out, his whisper cracking a touch. "But you learn to deal with it."

"If I die and somehow you survive—"

"Shhh, don't talk like that."

She sat up, trying to meet his eyes so he'd know this was too important to shrug off. "My brother has no one else other than me. But I don't wish for him to go through grief alone. Please tell him I love him and that I hope he won't bury himself in work. That I won't be mad if he doesn't even wait a day to pursue a woman if she'll help comfort him. That I wasn't afraid to die." Her throat got hoarser by the second. "Tell him I'll hug Mother for him."

He swallowed hard enough for her to hear. "I'll tell him, but let's not think that way—"

"But we have to, Tim." If she could have, she'd grab his hands. "Is there something I could tell your family if I survive and you don't? Of course, if that happens that will be entirely because you'll have saved me somehow. Know I'll have my brother set up a fund for your mother and siblings for whatever daring thing you end up doing to save my life."

"You believe I'd do that?"

His voice had broken, not out of incredulousness, but something that had sounded like disbelief. "Tim, you're too good not to. Just earlier, I'd been thinking about how safe I feel with you despite the fact those guys over there could kill us any second. And though I wish we weren't in this mess, I'm glad I'm with you."

He stared at her but said nothing. The night was too dark to see his expression, to guess what he was thinking.

"Tell my mother…" Tim's voice was nothing but a clogged whisper. "I died protecting someone precious and I'm sorry that means I'll no longer be around to protect her, too."

Precious? Gwen's insides fluttered at the tender way he'd said the word. Though he'd surely die for any female under his protection, knowing he at least didn't think he was dying for a spoiled brat made her feel more worth the sacrifice. "Let's not either of us die, all right?"

He nodded and took a deep breath, as if he'd been holding it. "Yes, of course. I'm not ready to die—not because I'm afraid for myself, but my family."

"I can't imagine how hard it is to feel financially responsible for so many. Is that why you've never courted anyone?"

He cleared his throat. "No."

Oh? "Then you've not found the right girl yet? What is it you're looking for?"

He was silent so long, that she figured she'd probed too far. Though she could point out he'd needled her for such information earlier, there was no need to argue with the person she depended on for survival. "I'm sorry if that was too much to ask, I'll be quiet now."

"I'm actually…"

He was quiet again for so long, she'd begun to wonder if she'd imagined he'd said anything at all.

He readjusted himself to sit higher against the tree, making it impossible for her to remain against him. She tried to reposition herself, but she simply couldn't maintain her position without rolling down into his lap. Just as she was about to push away, he slid down an inch which kept her from falling and put his chin against the top of her head. "What I'm looking for…" His voice rumbled against her hair. "Is a woman who faces difficulties with a good attitude, because I'm afraid she'll have a ton of difficulties with me."

"You don't seem like you'd be hard to live with."

This time, she really did believe she heard his heart skip.

"I don't know about that, but it's nice you think so. But I meant the difficulties of life. I can't promise any woman a life of ease—in fact, I likely can guarantee that'll never happen, no matter how hard I might try. So I'd need someone willing to work hard alongside me, brighten my life when it's tough. Trust that she won't turn on me as I do my best to give her what I can. Care about others. Care about…*me*." He let out a slow breath.

Did she not fit such a description? Of course, he'd been far too annoyed with her these past few weeks to see the good in her, but if Bo thought she'd fit Tim's criteria, what if she could show him—wait, why did she wish he'd consider her?

She tensed against him, suddenly highly aware of the feel of Tim's taut chest under her cheek and his breath stirring her hair. Maybe she was wrong. Maybe she wasn't all right with dying. What if Bo was right? What if she could love…

She moved her head in an effort to see Tim again but he moved too, and she slipped farther down. A yawn overtook her, making her wish she could forget the aches and pains, where they were, where they might never be, and simply disappear into unconsciousness.

"Why don't you lie down, Gwen? I'll wake you if they ever decide to feed us."

Despite being against him, she suddenly felt cold. Of course, he likely couldn't maintain this position all night for her comfort, but the thought of moving to the hard ground, not feeling him close by... "Will you be lying down, too? You can't protect me if you're exhausted."

"I can't protect you at all." His voice cracked. "I can't even scratch my own nose at the moment."

"I know you'd do whatever you could. Plus, I'd feel better if you were—" Her face colored, but if they were going to die anyway, why spend the night before their deaths in lonely misery? "I'd feel better if you were lying beside me."

When he didn't answer, she felt her skin flush even hotter over what he must think of her asking such a thing. Closing her eyes tight, she forced herself not to ask again. "Good night, Tim." Then she scooted down as quickly as she could, despite the way she had to push against his body like an awkward inchworm to keep the ropes from biting into her ankles and wrists too harshly. She finally made it down to the musty ground and tensed against the urge to sniffle.

Tim didn't make any move to follow her.

Between heavy breaths and the haze of her thoughts, she fought to find a comfortable position despite her tight bonds. With his body heat gone, she began to shiver. And yet, moving to the ground had made her brain decide sleep was far more important than the rocks jabbing into her, the gooseflesh crawling up her arms, or the ropes digging into her wrists. As the numbness in her hands increased, her mind grew duller.

Tim mumbled something she couldn't make out, and then he lay down beside her. His body blocked the wind, his steady breathing comforting against the background of the coyotes yipping from atop the ridge.

"Sleep well," he whispered.

As if he'd uttered magic words, the last remnants of tension drained from her body. "If only…" She fluttered her eyelids for a second but couldn't get them open enough to see him. "If only one of the men I could marry made me feel like you…do…"

Had that groan come from him or was her body still protesting being awake?

Her thoughts unraveled as she sank into the dark bliss of unawareness.

CHAPTER TWENTY

A shadow jolted Tim awake. His hands attempted to move into a defensive position, but they chafed against the bindings behind his back. Squinting against the morning sun, he sucked in a painful breath. With his heart beating double time, he peered up at the cowboy hovering over him. "Dan—?"

A swift kick to his shin caused him to groan.

"Get up, you two." Daniel's voice was serious and hard.

Tim's limbs sprang back to life in a shower of prickles. He winced as he tried to move his neck. He'd not thought he could sleep with how tight they'd done up his hands, but he'd succumbed at some point.

"Up!" Daniel shouted again.

"I'm tied, you weasel." He gritted his teeth to keep from calling Daniel anything worse.

"Watch your insults, mister. Unless you want me to gag you."

Tim sneered up at Daniel, but the look his "friend" was giving him held a soft warning.

Daniel stooped to untie Tim's ankles then nudged Gwen's shoulder.

Startling, she rolled back, hitting Tim square in the chest, eyes wide, breath short.

"Steady." Daniel moved to untie her feet.

A man carrying a rifle walked up. "Free her hands, too. We'll have them take care of business before we give 'em coffee. Take the girl over there." The golden-haired man caked with weeks of trail dirt jabbed his boney finger toward a clump of trees. "I'll keep my gun on him. He won't run off without her."

Seemed Daniel hadn't informed them of who they were. Was he pretending ignorance to save his hide or theirs?

Daniel pulled up Gwen none too gently.

She whimpered, likely from the blood rushing to her feet.

Tim couldn't keep from scowling at Daniel as he dragged her away. But then, if Daniel treated her too nicely, perhaps their familiarity would be exposed.

Tim eyed the man in front of him. Of the five in the group, he was the leanest. Once his hands were untied, could he take him?

Unfortunately, another man came to lead him away while the first kept his gun aimed at his head. At least Daniel was with Gwen—not that he was certain he could trust him, but he was less worrisome than the others.

After he'd relieved himself, he was returned to the tree where he'd spent a fitful night—half because of the danger they faced, half because he'd been sleeping next to Gwen. Even in such dire circumstances, he'd had to keep his mind busy to ignore the sound of her breathing, how she smelled, her hair brushing across his face.

Gwen returned, rebound at the wrists in front instead of behind, ankles free, same as he now was. How soon did these men expect them to return to walking?

After rolling up a bedroll, Daniel pointed at a man who appeared younger than the rest. "Take them food along with that water. But only untie the woman. She can feed them both."

"But why?"

"Just do it."

If Daniel was the boss, what did that mean for them?

The other man tossed a canteen and pouch toward Tim before stooping to untie Gwen. After releasing her, he stood and crossed his arms over his chest. "Get to it, we haven't all day."

With trembling fingers, she picked up the canteen. After they took several gulps each, she opened the bag beside her and pulled out thin slices of jerky. The skin below her eyes was puffy, and the side of her face had been imprinted by grass and rocks. Had he ever seen her look so rough? Of course not, she'd likely never worked as hard as she had yesterday just to survive.

Over the sound of his chewing and the near steady breeze, he strained to hear the men's conversation.

Daniel slashed a hand through the air, his words indiscernible but definitely condescending. After grabbing items from around the campfire, Daniel strapped his things onto a black horse Tim hadn't seen yesterday. Must've been the horse Daniel had ridden in on.

He gestured to the man who'd brought them food as he walked his horse over to them. "Tie her back up and put their blindfolds on."

She whimpered. "Please, I—"

"Shut up." Daniel glared at Gwen then turned to the other man. "I'll take care of them."

A shiver ran down Tim's spine at Daniel's sinister tone. Seemed they should've been more worried about what Daniel would do *to* them, rather than for them.

The other guy sighed and gathered up the rope. "Good. I told Joe they'd only be trouble however we ended up dealing with them."

Tim swallowed hard and looked at Gwen as the man tied her hands back in front. Her skin had achieved a paler hue than he'd thought humanly possible.

"Joe's an idiot." Daniel leaned over and spit, as if this conversation were as mundane as speculating on hog prices.

"He should've taken care of them to begin with, but he's yellow."

The man beside Daniel tipped his head slightly and pulled out the blindfolds. "Good thing you came along, then. Now we can get back to—"

"Hush." Daniel gave him the eye.

The other man shrugged. "It's not like they'll be able to tell anyone anything."

Tim's world went dark as the bandanna slid atop the bridge of his nose. He swayed at the thought of not being able to see Gwen anymore—or ever again.

"Joe's name is enough to get us in trouble if things go wrong."

"There's hundreds of Joes in the territory."

"Doesn't matter. Now go. I'll catch up with you later."

"Yes, boss."

Boss. Though every part of him insisted Daniel couldn't have become this bad in so short a time, Daniel's words rang through his head.

"…should've taken care of them to begin with…"

"Now, stand up."

Tim obeyed, forcing himself to ignore the desire to ram himself into Daniel. He'd not been told his life would be spared, but perhaps if he cooperated, hers might be.

Something hard jabbed the flesh between his shoulder blades.

"Move." Daniel pushed what was surely a gun barrel into his back with so much force, Tim had no choice but to comply.

After they were both tied to a horse, the animal jerked them forward. Gwen tumbled in front of him, landing atop his feet, causing him to stumble.

Her cry rang out as he stepped on something hard but squishy—possibly her arm. He caught himself before he fell flat on his face. "Stop! Wait! She's fallen."

The horse kept going, the sound of her being dragged

ripping out his heart. "Good heavens, man, she's in enough pain already!"

After a lifetime went by—or mere seconds—the horse halted and Tim rotated in complete helplessness, not knowing where Gwen was to try to help her up.

"Back on your feet!" Daniel barked from somewhere ahead of them.

"Gwen?" Her name scraped through his throat.

"I'm all right. I…" Her voice sounded shaky, yet strong somehow. "I'm up."

The horse started slower this time, and then it was all he could do to keep himself upright as they scrambled. Within minutes, the sun was back in full force. They'd left the gulley.

Considering the heat, it was probably mid-afternoon already. Was anybody searching for them this far out? Would hollering for help only bring death sooner? Could he plead enough to change Daniel's mind? Oh why had he decided to play the chivalrous knight, thinking he could protect her when all he'd done was get them into this mess?

Gwen's fingernails dug into the back of his arm where she'd clamped onto him, working to keep her balance.

He leaned close to whisper. "Do you think you're fast enough to lean down and get a hold of your knife? Do you have enough slack to reach?"

"No," she whispered back, barely audible over the sound of rocks crunching beneath hooves and feet. "That's why I fell just now. I'd hoped to pull it from my boot, but I couldn't."

That's why she'd fallen? Moments after hearing they were going to die, she'd had a clear enough head to attempt to spring them, risking injury to do so? "You remember how you once told me you were worthless? Well, you're wrong. Don't think that way about yourself ever again."

"But I couldn't get—"

"Shhh." He turned his head toward Daniel, though of

course he couldn't tell if his former friend could hear them. And was it only Daniel who was leading them out?

No more than a quarter hour had passed when the rocks beneath Tim's feet started to trip him up. Were they going into another rocky crevasse? Tim listened hard, trying to determine if anyone other than Daniel accompanied them.

Just when he'd given up trying to discern anything above the sound of his labored breathing and pounding heart, Daniel called back, "We're about to head downhill. There're lots of rocks. Watch yourselves."

Immediately, Tim was sore pressed to stay upright. After an exhausting twenty minutes or so, Daniel called the horses to stop. Tim ran into their horse's side and Gwen slumped against him.

Their horse began walking again, dragging them a few feet, the sound of ripping grasses signaling the beast would pull them no farther. Water babbled to their right, and the temperature had dropped enough with the shade to cool his sweaty skin.

Gwen shivered next to him, and he braced himself for Daniel or someone else to untie them. In the silence, his heart-beat sped up so fast he wondered if he'd die from sheer anxiety, but then…nothing happened.

The horse's belly gurgled beside him as the animal continued to rip and chew. Tim pressed closer to Gwen to do what he could to comfort her, but minutes ticked by. Had they been abandoned? Surely not. This horse was worth a decent amount of money.

Attempting to wriggle his brow like Gwen had to force his blindfold down, he worked to achieve a sliver of light. If the men had left, even if only to talk outside of earshot, Gwen could try for the knife again.

He growled at his stubborn bandanna and tried to swipe it off with his shoulder. No luck.

A saddle creaking made him startle back to attention. That was the telltale sound of someone dismounting.

After a thump, footfalls approached.

Tim tried to get between Gwen and whoever was coming. Were they to be shot without a word? He puffed out his chest as much as he could. "Hold up."

The footsteps ceased somewhere beside him. Gwen gave a yelp.

Tim whirled. "Take your hands off her!"

"No need to get your petticoats in a twist. I ain't gonna hurt her."

Tim stopped short. Daniel's tone was more like his past obnoxious self.

Gwen groaned and the plop of rope dropping upon dirt followed.

"You're letting us go?" He should've felt relief, but he couldn't help being wary.

His arms were yanked out in front of him. "I will, if you promise not to strangle me once you're free."

Though his body relaxed somewhat, he spoke through gritted teeth. "Would've been nice for you to have told us you meant us no harm."

"So, are you going to behave?"

Tim's blood pulsed hard against the tightness of his bonds. His behavior would depend upon Daniel's actions, but he nodded anyway. Lying to a criminal wasn't a sin now, was it?

His wrists throbbed as the pressure of the ropes increased as Daniel sawed through their middle. The second his hands were free, Tim pulled down his bandanna, his eyes fighting to focus on his former friend in the light.

Sheathing his knife, Daniel stepped back and sighed as if he'd been the one dragged across half the state of Wyoming.

Tim tried to rub some feeling back into his arms. "What's the meaning of all this?"

Daniel held up a hand. "It's best not to ask. But I had to be sure no one followed us before I released you." He returned to his horse and unhooked a canteen from his mount's saddle. He tossed it at Gwen's feet, tied the other horse's reins to his, then pulled his pistol.

Tim held up his hands. "Now, look—"

Daniel waved his sidearm at him. "Go stand by the water."

Being too far away to rush him, Tim obeyed, keeping Gwen behind him as they shuffled over.

Daniel swung up onto his saddle and raised his gun. Gwen gasped, and Tim flinched as a bullet exploded in the cottonwood behind them, the report echoing loud against the rock walls.

Daniel didn't lower his sidearm as the horses pranced in agitation. "If you don't hear shooting within the hour, then you should be good to follow the river toward Armelle that way." He tipped his head to the right to indicate downstream.

"Wait. Tell us—"

"It's best I don't. If there's any shred of friendship left between us, you never saw me." He cocked his pistol and shot again.

Gwen sank to the ground in a heap, and Tim's body drained of heat. Daniel kicked his heels in, hollering at the horses. They raced up the trail which led out of the gorge.

Falling to his knees, Tim yanked Gwen onto his lap, running a furtive, probing hand across her pale, clammy temple. Had the bullet ricocheted? "Sweetheart, don't leave me, I—"

The narrow-eyed look she cast up at him, followed by the questioning tilt of her brow, made him pull back.

She'd not been shot.

He caught himself in time to keep from shoving her off his lap and gently set her back on the ground. Hopefully she wouldn't read too much into the desperation that had just cracked his voice or how frantically he'd pulled her close hoping to feel her heart still beating.

"What'd you say?" Her voice sounded rough.

Ignoring her question, he looked to where Daniel had disappeared. Nothing there but dust swirling. "What happened? Are you hurt?"

"My legs gave out. I don't want to move again for a million years."

"Unfortunately, you have to. We need to get out of sight in case he was right and someone was following us."

Pulling her to stand, he noted an outcropping of rocks thirty yards up the river and took her arm. "Let's go this way."

She started walking with him, but soon became so unsteady he was practically dragging her as they moved upstream. How had this woman just endured an hour's trek after yesterday's ordeal without missing a step, but was now as weak as pudding?

Once they reached the outcropping, he found the alcove was deep enough for them to crawl into. When he got them inside, he propped her up against the wall. "You must be exhausted. Were you able to sleep last night?"

"Not much." Her head lolled back against the earthen wall, her eyes closed. "Since you couldn't put your arm around me, I kept waking up, scared you weren't there."

She'd missed him in her sleep? "I told you I'd keep watch."

"You should've slept."

"I dozed off toward morning." And if he could've put his arm around her at that point, he might have. Not so much for her comfort, but his own.

"Do you think we're far from home?" Her voice was breathy and soft, just like his little sister's when she got so sleepy she couldn't keep up with the fairy tale he was reading her—despite knowing every story in their worn-out book by heart.

Tim scooted back toward the alcove's opening and scanned the area. They were too deep in the gully and the trees too thick for him to see the ridge. "I won't have any idea until I climb up for a look, but I think it best we hide for a couple of hours."

He turned, noting she hadn't moved. "Might as well take a nap while we wait."

Her head rocked slowly from side to side against the wall

behind her. "I couldn't. Not with how hard these rocks are. Not until we know those men aren't returning."

There was no way to know that for certain, but as long as they didn't hear gunshots within the hour, Daniel assumed they'd be safe. "I bet you could sleep if you tried." She looked halfway to dreamland already.

He backed out of their shallow cave and stood, his legs protesting. "I can gather some pine branches to make the floor softer. Are you capable of filling the canteen while I do so?"

Her eyes opened as she yawned, then she scooted forward.

Handing her the canteen, he watched her limp toward the river. She might not be cut out to be a rancher's wife, but she was far better at donning a brave face and doing what needed to be done than he would've expected of her—or any woman, for that matter.

Before he went scavenging for branches, he swept out all the rocks he could and piled the larger ones across the opening. The crude wall ought to keep the little critters out. After gathering enough thin branches and making a pile on the floor, he arranged the extra boughs against the over-hang to make a screen. Hopefully they'd seen the last of Daniel's men, but no reason to take chances on being spotted.

A soft sigh turned him around. Gwen held the canteen out to him, looking as if she barely had enough energy to lift it.

"Thank you."

She nodded slightly and moved past him, crawling inside the shelter without a word.

He downed half the water then walked backward, checking his setup. Satisfied that no hint of her maroon split skirt was visible from the outside, he returned to the nook. Ducking in, he couldn't help but smile. She was already asleep. Her whisper-soft breath was interrupted by a slight whistle. She probably wouldn't wake for hours unless he prodded her. And he'd not do so for the world.

Scooting in beside her, he lay down, stilling when he accidentally bumped into her. She didn't wake.

Hesitantly, he brushed a strand of hair off her cheek.

It was too bad she couldn't marry him. No use in trying to convince himself any longer that the dream of having her beside him for the rest of his life would ever go away. But worrying about how he'd survive watching her marry another man would have to wait until later. His body had been kind enough to get him through this ordeal, but now his head was pounding, begging for the relief of sleep.

He closed his eyes, but the long blond hair tickling his face kept his thoughts on her rather than sleep. He smoothed the strands back, forcing himself to do no more than brush them away, to not touch her more than necessary. His throat tightened at the memory of her asking him to lay close to her last night. He couldn't pretend she'd wished that because of any feelings she had for him. She would've welcomed the comfort of human contact from any man or woman she knew wouldn't harm her. But for her to be comfortable enough to ask him to do so made him…sort of…hope…no, he couldn't…

His mind grew heavy, blanketed by the thick scent of pine and the softness of her breath.

CHAPTER TWENTY-ONE

A slow, steady throb pulsed in Gwen's head. Every inch of her slowly became aware of the unforgiving ground beneath her. Her eyelids fluttered open. Daylight seeped through the makeshift wall Tim had placed across the opening of their stony recess.

She turned her head and blinked at the spot beside her —empty.

Her heart tripped, and she forced herself to take a deep breath. He'd not abandon her unless something terrible had happened. She rolled over and half crawled, half scooted to the alcove's edge to peer through the brush.

Tim sat by the river, staring across the water at a sheer wall of rock.

She collapsed back onto the dirt, eyes sliding shut, lungs releasing. Fighting against the exhaustion trying to drag her back down, she crawled out from under the low ceiling. She took a few hesitant steps to be sure she wouldn't embarrass herself by landing in a heap like she had when Daniel had shot past them the second time.

She pressed a hand against her throbbing temple and encountered a rat's nest of hair. Finger combing would likely do little good. And yet, she attempted to smooth her hair and dust off her skirts. Once she'd done what she could, she tried her hardest not to hobble the entire way over to Tim.

When she was ten yards away, he looked over, eyes heavy with fatigue. Had he not napped at all?

He pushed something beside him in her direction. "I found some berries."

Gooseberries were not her favorite, but her stomach rumbled anyway. They were a tempting deep purple upon a large green leaf. She lowered herself to the ground, suppressing a groan.

"I wish Daniel had seen fit to leave us a fishhook. Watching the trout surface has been torture." He gave her a wan smile. "I'm sorry there's no coffee—the wilds of Wyoming are plumb out."

She tried to return his smile but was fixated on the small pile of food awaiting her. Would eating so little make her hunger pains worse?

"When you're finished with the berries, we can head home." He handed her the canteen.

"Won't it be dark soon?"

He looked over his right shoulder toward the sky. "From what I can tell, it's three in the afternoon."

She squinted at the sun, unsure whether it was in the east or the west. "I'm sorry you got stuck with me through all this. I can't tell time, don't know where we are, have no idea where to find gooseberries."

"You shouldn't be so hard on yourself. I didn't do much to keep us alive either. If it weren't for Daniel, we'd likely both be dead."

But he was just being nice—too nice. What happened to the man who listed all of her faults and criticized her ridiculous goals? "All I had of any use was a knife I couldn't retrieve."

"Potential is worth something. Just because everything and everyone conspires against you doesn't mean your efforts get written off." He looked past her, his voice far away and distracted. "Intent and integrity mean something."

"You think I have those?"

He nodded, but his eyes were focused on something behind her. She turned to see what he was looking at. Seemed he was looking at the trail that Daniel had taken out of the gulley earlier. "You're thinking about Daniel, aren't you?"

He picked up a stick and stripped it of its bark. "I'm torn over what to do once we get home."

His saying 'once' instead of 'if' made her relax. If he thought they'd make it home, then they would.

"Not only did Daniel save us, but he acted one way with the men and another way with us. When I asked him to explain…" Tim tossed his now stripped stick. "His plea for me to pretend we hadn't seen each other makes me think he's got a reason to be with those men that isn't what it appears. That exposing him would be dangerous. If we told Deputy Dent, and he took out a posse, and Daniel got killed…"

"What if Daniel's afraid if you turn him in, he'll get in trouble for the crimes he *has* committed?"

Tim picked up another stick. After turning it over in his hands several times, he dropped the stick and stared up at the clouds. "You might think I'm stupid for believing he's not just trying to evade the law—that his saving us likely put his own life in danger. But I know him well enough to know the toughness is mostly act—his father's not as neglectful as mine, but that doesn't mean he's an easy man, and acting weak would've only made his growing up years harder. Daniel might have messed up last year, leaving Celia alone with your father's rustlers and Mrs. Whitsett, but he walked because he knew he couldn't hurt a woman. Just like he couldn't hurt us."

She recalled Daniel being rough around the edges, but he'd never been scary. Didn't mean he'd not turned into a terrible man since they'd last seen him though.

Tim snatched up the stick again and stabbed it into the

ground. "After we got hauled in last year, he stopped talking to me because I'd jumped ship so early. Not because I was wrong to leave trouble behind, but because I left despite knowing Celia intended to stay. Daniel would never admit it, but I knew he went along with the rustlers because he didn't want to leave her alone with them. And truthfully, I'm not sure I could've run to save my own hide if I'd thought he wouldn't stick with her. When he'd skipped town, I figured he'd done so because he couldn't forgive himself for leaving Celia when he did."

Tim turned toward her, his forehead furrowed. "Turning him in would be a rather rotten way to thank a friend for saving our lives, don't you think? The others deserve to go to jail, of course, but would they?"

"They seemed fine with Daniel killing us."

"Pretty sure you can't convict someone for intention, just action. We're not dead. And though we have rope burns to prove we were kidnapped, will our accusations get them convicted? Will it make us feel better if the man who saved us gets punished, too?"

As much agony as the group had put them through, would she sleep better knowing they had been caught? She stared at her bruised wrists. She might be more afraid they'd retaliate if they were sent to jail and later released. "It's clear they're up to no good though."

"Likely so, but we don't know what they're doing."

"So you don't want to tell anyone we were kidnapped?"

"I know what it's like to be caught up in something far worse than what you expected it to be." Tim turned tormented eyes toward her.

If only her father possessed a shred of Tim's remorse for past mistakes. "But you refused to go along with the men my father hired. And if I recall correctly, the judge fined you because you *didn't* tell anyone what you knew."

"Yes." He turned to stare at the wall again. "But I kept those secrets to avoid getting in trouble, and I certainly hadn't saved anybody. Daniel's not avoiding trouble—he knows if his men find out he lied about killing us, he'd be in trouble. And if we turn them in, he's in trouble. He did what was right anyway. I see no way to honor Daniel's request to pretend we'd never seen him and turn in the kidnappers. It's either one or the other. If we tell Deputy Dent without mentioning Daniel, and he actually captures the men, how will we explain why we didn't mention Daniel's name? The only hope we'd have of not getting into trouble for keeping Daniel's identity secret is to pray they aren't captured, so what good is it to report them then?"

"But if we don't tell anyone what happened, how do we explain our disappearance?"

He turned toward her, worry creasing his brow. "I'm not sure saying we got lost together would satisfy those who thrive on finding fault with others. If Mrs. Tate and Biddy believed your reputation in shambles after spending a half hour with Mr. Wright…"

She crossed her arms over herself. It'd been hard enough enduring these past two days. Would it ruin the rest of her life as well?

At the church, he'd said he would marry her if she asked. Was that what he was worried about? That she'd ask him to stand by his word, forcing him into a marriage he didn't want? "The only people who know we were together are our kidnappers. You're supposed to be hunting, remember? I can say I got lost and had a terrible time finding my way back. That's not a lie."

He turned a serious face toward her. "I usually go home every night when hunting, but if I get nothing, it's not unusual for me to stay at the shack on Holden's Point until I do. No one's likely worried about me yet."

She nodded and grabbed some berries. Tart juices from the less ripe ones slid down her throat, making her eyes water. She gulped some water, then stared at the stains on her hands. Keeping what had happened to herself was uncomfortable, and she doubted Daniel had a good reason to act like a criminal. But if he was doing something wrong, he'd likely continue doing so and would eventually get caught with more evidence available to convict him. Tim might be grasping at straws to feel justified in trying to save an old friend, but surely if he was wrong and Daniel wasn't as good as he thought, he'd get caught at some point.

Tim pulled a stem from a gooseberry. "Besides, by the time we get home, there's little chance anyone could catch those guys. They didn't seem intent on sticking around."

"And if they were caught at some point for something else, they'd think Daniel killed us, so they'd not admit to being accomplices to murder—or attempted murder. I doubt they'd volunteer anything about us if we didn't."

"True. So we agree? You're lost, and I'm a hunting failure?"

She gave a slight nod. She had time to change her mind on the way home if her misgivings grew.

He scanned the sky, patted his knee, then pushed off the ground. "Better start moving. We won't make it home today, but hopefully tomorrow. Once you're safe, I'll head to the shack and stay a night. That way there'll be more hours between our returns to keep anyone from suspecting our disappearances are connected."

The thought of walking for another couple of days made her want to crawl back under the overhang and curl up like a petulant child. "Should I go to the York cabin instead?" If God were merciful, their cabin wouldn't be as far as Armelle. "Then they could drive me to town."

"If they're closer, sure." Tim held out a hand to help her stand then picked up the canteen and walked to the river.

Sadness washed over her at how quickly he'd marched off. She'd gotten used to hanging on his arm, having him close like a shield. When he turned to head to the path ascending the ravine, she forced her feet to follow.

After an hour at a slower pace than they'd endured the last

two days, the knots in her muscles worked themselves out, and after seeing no one for miles as they followed the tree line tracing the river, she breathed easier. Weaving through high grasses and trekking over soft sands—alive—gave her the weirdest sense of freedom, stronger than any she'd ever known.

Coming across a rise, they changed direction to climb it. Tim hoped he could figure out where they were from the top. As they ascended, Gwen took in the horizon spreading out farther and farther, bumping into buttes and ravines—a patchwork of rocks, rabbit brush, and tumbleweed that turned into beautiful swirls of colors, light, and shadow the higher they went.

A quarter of the way up, Tim walked to the rocky ledge, lifted a hand to his brow, then pointed to his left. "I think those ruts might lead to the road that goes to the Yorks'. But I don't want to drag us over there and be wrong. It would add hours to our walk."

"Don't worry about making me walk more than necessary. God got us out alive. I'm sure He'll get us home at some point."

"I wish I felt as certain as you, but we're not out of the woods yet." He continued up the trail and called over his shoulder, "If God's listening to you though, keep praying."

"Wait, I thought you believed in God, too?" She knew he wasn't often in church, but if any O'Conner showed up on Sunday, it was him.

"I do, but…"

"But what?"

"Well, maybe it's easier to pray when you get what you want."

She jammed a hand on her hip. "You know I don't get what I want."

He shook his head as if that weren't true. "Getting a man you're chasing to notice you is nothing like praying for food when there's none to be had, for your father to stop harassing your mother when—" He clamped his jaw and walked off as if stung.

For a minute, she watched him hike away. No wonder Tim was always so perturbed at her for grumping about her life—even if she did have a no-good father of her own.

"You're right," she called after him as she hurried to catch up, being careful of the rocks underfoot since the path had narrowed as it skirted a rock wall. "Not everything I pray for is dire. But if God's our friend, I figure we're allowed to ask Him for what we want."

Tim looked back for a second. "So you've asked God for every one of those men to marry you?"

She slowed, not liking the bitter bite in his tone. Maybe boys were different. Every girl she knew prayed God gave her favor with the boy she liked—not that she'd liked everyone she'd flirted with, but now was not the time to admit to purposely toying with some of those men. Tim might understand that she'd done it for the greater good of getting her father tossed into jail, considering he was willing to believe Daniel might be doing something wrong in order to do something right, but—

"What is it about Mr. Wright that made you think God would want you to marry him?"

Concentrating on the ground beneath her since she was near a precipice, she worked to come up with an answer that might shame him for his mocking tone. Though by the time the ground leveled out, she hadn't come up with anything. Tim would consider Eric having a good job, a nice smile, and her brother's friendship shallow reasons to pledge her life to him. And though she'd liked him, what exactly had she liked other than he was pleasant to be around?

Tim turned to look at her, eyebrows raised.

She shrugged and stared out over the vast plains, which seemed far duller now. "He was nice."

"That's not why." He shook his head and sped up as if to leave her behind.

"So, he's handsome and has money. But I don't know why you think I'm the only girl who wants those things. And it's not as if I have many options! You claim every boy in the county has been in love with me at some point, but they sure aren't lining up to court me."

He took several steps before answering. "You're intimidating."

She snorted. "How so? I act like I've got cotton for brains most of the time."

He stopped short and looked at her as if he didn't believe she'd admitted that.

She shrugged. "Well, I do. You've pointed that out already, so I don't know why you're acting surprised."

"Why do you do it? You haven't acted like that these past few days."

She kicked aside a small rock. "Men seemed more interested when I didn't come off smart. You just said yourself they don't like intimidating women."

"How you act has nothing to do with it. You're the prettiest and wealthiest woman in the county. And your father was mayor."

She snapped her head up. "If you can disparage me for going after men who have money and good looks, why would you be all right with people dismissing me for the same things?"

He waved his hand as if her argument was no good. "It's different when it's the other way around. Besides, if you pretend to be dumb and a man musters up the courage to court you, how can he make an educated decision on whether or not you're suited for each other?"

Crossing her arms, she looked toward Armelle. Of course he was right—that was exactly why Eric had so easily forgotten her and had evidently started considering other women in Denver.

Before today, she would've shaken off Tim's concern as meddlesome, just like she would have Mrs. Tate's. But with how Tim had let it slip his mother had fared badly in marriage, perhaps she shouldn't be so miffed at his penchant for worrying about the men she pursued.

At the top of the rise, Tim scanned the land. "I know where we are now." He gave a single resolute nod and started back down the way they'd come. "We're farther out than I hoped though."

She turned to follow, groaning at the pace he set. Were his feet not covered in blisters? Halfway down, she took a drink of water as they walked, but her foot hit an uneven patch, and she crashed onto her backside, skidding down the slope with a bunch of loose rock. She brushed dirt from her scraped-up palms, sucking in air through her teeth. Oh, why couldn't she be home already?

"Are you all right?" He rushed back to kneel beside her. "What happened?"

"I'm fine. I slipped."

He helped her up, then scanned the ground. "Where's the canteen?"

She grimaced and stepping to her right, spotted it. He might've insisted this morning that she wasn't worthless, but now he'd surely change his mind. "It went over the edge."

The canteen lay next to a young tree clinging to the steep drop-off, the shoulder strap draped across its skinny trunk.

He walked up beside her. "That's no good."

Though she was no wilderness expert, neither of them ought to attempt retrieving it unless they were willing to risk their lives over a canteen. "Good thing we're following the river, right?"

"Yes, but without water we probably shouldn't take the shortcut to the Yorks'."

She sighed at her dream of a wagon ride going up in smoke. "How much farther is it to town?"

"Probably an extra day of walking."

She stared down the slope, rubbing at her forehead, which was pulsating like the new wounds on the heels of her hands. They could survive without eating, but not without water. "What if we got a branch? Could you fish it back up?"

"I'm just as likely to knock it off the edge, but I guess we can try."

"Wait a minute." She pulled the knife from her boot, then threw the blade deep into the sapling between the canteen's straps. She couldn't help her smile. "There. That should keep it from falling down."

He stared at the knife, mouth agape. "How?"

"I told you it was a throwing knife."

He continued to stare at the knife as if it might not be there if he blinked. "I can't get it back for you."

"That's all right. I have more at home."

"So that wasn't just luck?"

"Nope." Had she finally impressed him? Though this was the first time she'd ever found a use for her hobby other than releasing pent-up frustration.

After shaking his head, he scanned craggy terrain. "Let's see if we can find a branch that'll reach. Hopefully we won't have to go all the way back to the river for one."

Half an hour later, they'd dragged a limb back up from the bottom of the rise. Tim lay on his stomach above the canteen's resting place, hooked the strap, and dragged their water back up.

She clapped. "Good job."

He shrugged and handed her the water.

She grabbed his hand instead and squeezed. "Though I know you're eager to be rid of me, and I don't blame you, I'm glad you're with me. Not only because you just saved me a day of walking, but I would be so much more frightened without you. Just want you to know that before we separate."

He scrunched his mouth and looked away.

Though the thought of that separation created a knot deep down in her stomach, she couldn't keep ignoring his obvious desire to be left alone. "I know I've bothered you a lot lately. You don't have to pretend otherwise. So once we're home, I'll stop pestering you at the Keys'. And in light of your worry over the men I pursue, know that I know you're right. I will wait for someone worth my time, someone who likes me for who I already am. And when I find him, he'll have you to thank."

Tim's expression contorted.

She squeezed his shoulder. "Tim—"

He ran a hand down his face, and for a moment, she thought she saw conflict in his eyes, but then he nodded sharply. "For that to happen, I've got to get you home." He stepped away from her. "We ought to walk as far as we can before the sun sets."

She frowned at his retreat. Every man she'd ever known had seemed happy whenever she'd admitted when she was wrong and he was right—even when she hadn't really meant it. But her confession hadn't satisfied him.

No matter what she did, Tim never acted pleased with her for more than a handful of moments, even when she was being more real with him than she'd ever been with any other man.

They weren't suited for each other, just as she'd told Bo weeks ago.

So why did it hurt so much to admit it this time?

CHAPTER TWENTY-TWO

Clearing a small rise, Tim released a sigh. The cabin they'd seen miles ago was no longer far away. A rough log affair with one door and two windows with a large tree overshadowing it. The building was tucked into the hillside, as if someone had dug a square hole and shoved it in.

The cabin door opened, and he pulled Gwen down to a crouch beside him. If they were seen together, their story would have to change. Hopefully a quarter mile was too far away to be spotted. They should've moved to the trees when they'd crested the rise.

A black cat with white paws ran out, followed by a muffled shout. Whatever was cooking on the outdoor fire wafted toward them, the faint smell of smoky meat causing his stomach to clench.

No one came out after the cat, and then the door shut.

Groaning, Gwen leaned heavily on his arm.

"Do you need to rest before going farther?"

"I'd rather sit in a chair than against another tree. Might as well keep hobbling forward."

He shook his head as he helped her up. She had proven herself persistent before this ordeal, but he'd never thought to call her brave. Despite the grueling amount of walking they'd endured, she'd been amazingly tenacious and uncomplaining. Her ability to persevere without grumbling gave him new feelings for her—deeper feelings.

As if the feelings he had already weren't enough to deal with.

"If we walk inside the tree line, I could go with you a little farther. But I'm sorry I can't go the whole way."

She squeezed his arm. "You've done plenty. I'm alive, right?"

"If I hadn't distracted you with kittens, none of this would've happened."

She frowned.

Had she just now realized this was all his fault? Probably a good thing. He didn't want her kindness or gratitude. He wanted his life to go back to normal as soon as possible, and thankfully, she said she wouldn't be seeking him out at the ranch any longer. Which was necessary since his longings whenever he saw her would surely be stronger now.

Because he loved *her*, not just the fantasy of her anymore.

Gwen shook her head slowly. "No, I insisted on retrieving those kittens." She glanced out across the valley and frowned. "It's too late for them now, isn't it?"

Her face awash in compassion for those wild fuzzballs was not helping his heart one bit. Once he got home, he'd arm himself to the teeth, return to the ravine, and check if they were still alive. "Hopefully God showed them mercy."

His feet dragged as they walked alongside the trees, and she made no protest at their slower pace.

"When will you leave?"

He stopped beside a gigantic oak. "I'll stay right here for a while. After you talk to Mr. York, come back outside. I'll see you, and I'll be able to tell by your expression if you feel safe. If you do, I'll head to the hunting shack."

"If only we could…"

Noting the furrows above her brow, he gently turned her toward him, tipping her chin so she'd look at him. "Things will be all right. If you don't show up soon after you go in or if I hear anything suspicious, I'll shove my way in to check on you. I won't leave you until I know you'll get home safe."

The creases in her forehead didn't go away, but the way she was looking up at him now, with her eyes soft and a stray thatch of blond hair caressing her temple…

Somehow his hand had moved to cup her face, his thumb skimming over her wind-chapped cheek. He stilled, peering into blue eyes that had entranced many a man. If only he could tell her things he ought not to admit. "I'll be right here," his voice scratched out. "If you need me."

And without warning, she launched on tiptoe and pressed her lips against his cheek.

His eyes slammed shut. A heat he'd never known coursed through him at the touch of such soft skin pressed lightly against his.

Was she kissing him far longer than necessary, or had time stopped?

"Thank you," she whispered against the stubble he sported.

When she stepped back, he nearly stumbled forward, as if he'd been tied to her. He tried not to shake his head too much, lest she notice he'd lost touch with reality for a moment. "I can't go any farther, don't want us to be seen together."

She looked up at him with a faraway expression—likely just a heavy need for sleep. Then she nodded as if she'd made a decision, turned, and walked away.

His lungs seized, but he forced himself to breathe. She wasn't walking out of his life. They were simply going back to how things were—how they were supposed to be.

How would he ever manage?

As she stood in front of the log cabin, Gwen's heart knocked wildly—probably loud enough to call attention to her presence without lifting a hand to the door.

Looking over her shoulder, she checked to be sure Tim wasn't visible from the tree he'd swung himself into after she'd taken leave of him.

A part of her wanted to go back and insist they give up this plan to protect his friend so he could come rest, too. He had to be as hungry and worn out as she was, and yet he was going to head off to an ill-equipped cabin, with no gun, no food, and an empty canteen. This might be best for her and Daniel—but not for Tim. Yet he didn't seem bothered having to sacrifice his safety for others.

Trusting she'd see him soon enough, at the Keys' or in town, she knocked.

"Who is it?"

Whether it was the menace in the voice or the fact that they'd run out of water hours ago, her throat constricted and words had to be forced out. "I'm—it's me, Miss McGill, Mrs. Key's friend. I was supposed to come to—"

The door flew open, and a man with graying hair and wizened eyes peered at her as if she were some long lost relative. "Miss McGill, you say?"

He snagged her by the arm. "Are you all right? People were here days ago looking for you. Said you weren't the kind to survive a night in the desert—" He stopped short and scanned her from head to toe, likely taking in the snags in her split skirt, the crazy way she stood on her feet to avoid rubbing off blisters, the pulsing heat in her face caused by sun and blowing sand. She was sure her skin had been scathed to the point it might never return to the creamy color she'd once considered her most attractive quality.

"I'm all right," she graveled out. Even if she had been forever altered.

"What happened?"

The words she'd practiced so she'd not be lying tumbled out as rehearsed. "I was on my way here and got sidetracked by some animals. Cats, actually, then my horse got away, and well, I've never..." She held a hand to her chest, thankful Tim had been with her. For if she'd had to traipse across the desert alone, she wouldn't have survived, as Mr. York had just said. "I've never learned to navigate by sun or stars or anything."

The grooves in his forehead deepened. "And yet, you got here."

"A miracle. I'm just sorry I lost the liniment you needed."

"Lord have mercy, child. God knows I didn't need liniment so badly to put you through whatever you've been through."

Something in the fire pit collapsed behind them, sending the fragrant aroma of meat to taunt her stomach, which growled in supplication.

"What am I doing standing here interrogating you? Where's my manners?" The man limped backward, swinging the door open wider. "I'm Stephen York. Let me get you something to eat. I hope you don't mind squirrel."

She didn't even feel like grimacing at the thought of eating squirrel or any other woodland creature. "Whatever you set before me, I'll eat, Mr. York. But I'm in dire need of water."

"There's a well over there." He pointed behind her.

She turned and grimaced. What if her sleeves fell back as she pumped water and he saw the rope burns at her wrists? If anyone noticed those, her story would be called into question.

"Follow me." He limped past her, his false leg evidently not as well-fitted as Nolan's. He pointed past the fire pit. "I'll pump for you."

"Thank you." While the old man's back was turned, she faced the oak Tim was hiding in and blew him a kiss. Her hand stilled in mid-air, then she snapped it back down to her side. Why had she done that?

She scrambled to catch up to Mr. York, a shiver going

through her because she knew exactly why she'd done that—though she hadn't planned to.

Just like she hadn't planned on kissing him on the cheek, though she'd done so with countless old men and society ladies. And she definitely hadn't anticipated the desire to kiss him again, which had nearly pulled her back. But not a passionate kiss, rather another simple one that would've allowed her to linger just long enough for him to wrap her up in his arms so she wouldn't have to leave.

But then he'd stepped back as if he were relieved to be rid of her.

She'd thought she'd held her own after losing the canteen. No grumbling, no tripping, no pestering. She'd tried her hardest to be as little of a burden on him as possible, but...

"Miss?"

She jolted and turned toward Mr. York. At some point, she'd stopped following him. She crossed the four-foot gap between them and took the dipper he held out for her. "I'm sorry, I just..." She stopped rambling and took a sip of water. Once the wetness hit her tongue, she couldn't get enough.

"You must be ready to get home, but we've got time enough to let you eat and still get you into town before sunset. Good thing it's summer."

She took several more gulps before handing him back the dipper. "I'm sorry I've turned out to be an inconvenience when I'd come to help. Seems that's what I always am."

Mr. York offered her his arm. "Don't even think about that. Let's get you food, and then I'll find my cousin. He's out in the field with the wagon we'll need."

Though thankful for his support, she didn't put any weight on him. The pronounced way he limped meant he likely needed to get off his feet more than she did.

Upon entering the house, she widened her eyes to help them adjust to the dim interior. The cabin was spare. Seemed the Yorks lived with even less than Tim's family, though this place was less chaotic. The single room's walls were perfectly square and smooth, covered in heavy gray paper, with not a frame or trinket hung upon them. The fireplace was the cleanest she'd ever seen, empty and scrubbed free of soot. The floor was stained and oiled just like the solitary square table he led her to. After seating her on the one chair that had a back, Mr. York left.

Where did the men sleep? She frowned at a worn trunk in the corner. Perhaps they tucked away pallets every morning.

"Here we are." Mr. York returned and pulled a cracked bowl off the shallow shelf beside the fireplace. "I have salt if you'd like, but I don't have any of those fancy spices you're probably used to."

She forced a smile. "Whatever you have will taste like heaven compared to what I've eaten these past few days, I assure you."

He ladled a bowlful to the brim and then placed it in front of her. She looked between what he'd offered and the small pot he'd brought in from outside. How much could there be left for him and his cousin with what lay before her? These men had so little, and yet he was certainly offering her a portion of both his and his cousin's meals.

She toyed with the idea of telling Mr. York she wasn't hungry. But if he were to buy her story about being lost—considering she was the type of woman who had no idea which berries were edible let alone where to find any—she needed to act as famished as she actually was. And after one bite, she hadn't any choice.

A thumping at the door couldn't keep her from shoveling in another spoonful before she turned to look.

"Just my luck. Plow broke on a—Eh? Who's this?"

Swallowing a chunk, Gwen nodded at a stocky man in simple clothing, worn but patched with care. The top of his forehead was a block of white indicating he always wore the hat in his hand whenever he was outside.

"Cousin Charles, this is Miss McGill, the one they were

looking for." Mr. York placed a piece of buttered bread in front of her. "Got lost on the way here. Horse ran off, but somehow she got back."

"Yes," she chimed in. And though it would be best to add detail to the story, she grabbed the bread instead and took a bite. She slumped in her chair and hummed despite how dense it was. Who knew poorly made bread could taste so good?

Mr. York handed her a second piece as the cousins talked in low tones, which she couldn't be bothered to pay attention to as she filled her empty insides.

The moment her stew was gone, another bowl, half full, slid toward her.

She felt her face flush at her poor table manners. "Oh no, I won't take your food." Though she already had, of course.

"I won't starve." Mr. York said as he sliced off some butter. "I've got pemmican if I get famished, but you on the other hand —you probably needed more meat on your bones before you got lost. In fact, you should eat some of my pemmican. It's made for satisfying an empty stomach."

He went outside and returned with a small dark brown brick full of what looked like berries and seeds.

"Thank you." She took what he offered her and gnawed off a corner, glad his cousin hadn't pushed her to accept his small bowl of stew.

But he wasn't eating it, just watching her as if seeing a woman eat was fascinating.

Of course, she was likely making a spectacle of herself. She took a daintier bite this time and chewed slowly and contemplatively as she'd been taught as a small girl.

"Law," the cousin finally said while shaking his head. "You weren't gone so many days to have keeled over unless you couldn't find water, but how does a town lady like you find your way to our cabin once you got turned around?"

She shook her head, happy her need to chew gave her time to think through her answer. "Only by the grace of God. At several points, I didn't think I'd get back. Nothing I did got me here, that's for certain."

If it weren't for Tim and Daniel, this man might've stumbled across her dead body somewhere in the desert rather than staring at her incredulously at his table.

She forced herself not to glance toward the door. Here she was, safe in this house with a full stomach because of Tim, while he was out there hungry. Silently, she chewed as the men finished their paltry portions and discussed how to get her to town.

The stocky cousin took a long gulp of ale, wiped his mouth, then pushed back from the table. "I'd better pack. There won't be time for me to return before nightfall."

She kept herself from telling him not to put himself out for her sake, and yet, she couldn't sleep in this tiny cabin with these two. Though she'd survived sleeping outdoors the past several days, without Tim nearby, she wasn't sure she would've slept at all. "I'm sorry to be stealing so much of your evening, but my brother and I have plenty of room for you to stay with us in town. Or he could pay for a room at the hotel if you'd rather."

Charles's brows ascended, scrunching up his two-toned forehead. "Stay in the mansion?"

"It's the least I can do to thank you for driving me home at this hour and feeding me dinner."

"All right then, I'll pack my fancy bedclothes." Charles guffawed before he turned for the trunk in the corner.

"Don't forget your slippers and smoking jacket." Mr. York's face lit up, then he picked up another piece of bread with a smile. "I'm afraid with how you wolfed everything down, you might get sick. So eat this one slowly, would you?"

She nodded, too grateful to talk past the lump in her throat.

As the York men put together a list of things Charles could get while in town, she leaned back in her chair, enjoying her full stomach and the clean, cool water within reach.

Thank you, God, for these men and what they're willing to do for me. And thank you for Tim. And Daniel…

Seemed odd to thank God for a man who was likely a criminal—or was he truly some sort of undercover infiltrator?

Maybe praying for Daniel wasn't an odd thing to do after all —be he criminal or spy. And she could still be grateful for what he'd done, because shooting them to protect himself would've likely been a safer choice for him. Tim was probably right. Daniel couldn't be all bad. Just because he'd been involved in the trouble with her father last year didn't mean he had to continue being trouble.

Unlike Tim, who had the Keys, and Celia with her parents, did Daniel have someone to point out how his behavior was leading him toward a dismal future?

Taking the tea the older York offered her, she stared at the leafy bits at the bottom of the dingy cup. The only one who'd been brave enough to tell her that her man-chasing ways wouldn't get her what she wanted had been Tim. Though she'd not been as invested in those men as she'd pretended, why hadn't anyone else said anything?

Most of the women in town gave her deference. Truth be told, she'd enjoyed the feeling of importance, but had those women known all along that her way of chasing men would leave her lonely? Mrs. Tate was forthright enough to say what she thought, but her advice was rarely worth considering. She could trust Mrs. Whitsett to tell her the truth, but she'd already left to help Jennie sell memoirs again. If only Momma were alive.

Gwen pushed her drink away, shutting her eyelids against the sudden warmth that came with memories of countless tea parties. Though Momma had gone against Father's wishes and let her play in the mud and chase puppies and climb trees, they'd also made lovely memories pouring tea, embroidering samplers, rummaging through grandmother's old stoles and piling them on as if they were royalty.

And though her brother had always been kind, if anyone had helped her change for the better, it was Tim. Ever since they'd knocked into each other at the station, he'd made her want to be better than she was. His insights, his daring to criticize, his begrudging encouragements, his sacrifice for her good...

"Wagon's hitched."

She startled as Charles came back into the cabin and grabbed the satchel his cousin held out to him.

"Oh, I'm...ready."

She wiped her hands on the towel that served as a napkin. Following Charles to the wagon, she glanced toward the trees though Tim was likely already a mile or two away.

That no one would ever know he'd been the reason she'd "miraculously" found her way back didn't sit well. But how could she repay him without inviting censure or gossip?

What if he refused to accept anything she gave him and went back to avoiding her?

Her heart clenched. Hopefully he'd not do that. She needed someone she could trust to continue to tell her the truth.

CHAPTER TWENTY-THREE

The curl of smoke above his mother's house undulated toward Tim like a beckoning finger. A sane man wouldn't want to go inside and sit by a hot stove on a summer afternoon. But he couldn't wait to change his clothes, eat something filling, and collapse in a chair.

He'd slept the night on the floor of the abandoned shack and washed up as well as he could in the spring nearby, but his stomach complained of neglect.

Ignoring the sounds of his siblings playing in the backyard, he knocked on the open door. Before he could announce his arrival, his insides clenched at the smell of cabbage. How unfortunate. He'd hoped she wasn't skimping on dinner this evening. "I'm home, Ma."

She turned to blink at him through the smoky interior since the wood stove leaked like a sieve. "Where've you been?"

He winced at the accusation underlying her tone. He'd expected her to be worried. Of course, the fact she wasn't anxious was good for the story he and Gwen intended to tell. But it still hurt Ma was so distracted by her own stresses that she hadn't fretted over how his overnight trip had turned into four days. Though maybe he couldn't blame her for not noticing how long he'd been away. She was used to Father always being gone longer than he said he would.

Father never had good explanations for those absences either. And now Tim planned to keep her in the dark just the same. This would be the first time he'd done so since he and his friends had been caught with the rustlers. Though he'd promised a judge he'd never do so again, he'd be keeping his mouth shut for his friend's sake. "My horse was stolen."

A flash of actual worry crossed her face.

He held up his hands. "I'm fine, and whoever stole him is long gone. I know I ought to go report it, but that won't get my horse back, and I don't feel well."

Nothing a few days of sleep and food wouldn't fix. Plus, he needed an excuse to stay out of town to keep anyone from tying his disappearance to Gwen's. She should've gotten into town last night, which meant Mrs. Tate and her ilk had likely informed everybody of her miraculous return and were all speculating to the high heavens.

"The horse is gone?"

"And my gun."

Ma wrung her apron in her hands. "How are you going to get to work at the Keys' now?"

"I'll walk. Might not make it out here on the weekends very often now unless they lend me a horse."

"They're likely already itching to fire you for being gone so long, especially after you took time off for the roof, and now that you're sick…"

"They'll be fine, Ma. They'll understand."

Doubt filled her eyes.

He sighed. Couldn't she be worried about him instead of the money he brought in? He shook his head at himself and plopped onto the bench beside the table. If he got food in his belly, he'd not be questioning her love for him—not that it had ever been a demonstrative one.

She ladled out soup and slid a bowl toward him. "Once you eat, you should head over and explain your absence."

He groaned at the thought of moving any farther than the cot in the lean-to he slept on, even if it was too short for his lanky frame.

"Careful, it's hot."

No amount of cabbage soup could fill him up, but it was better than nothing. Pulling the bowl closer he frowned at what appeared to be meat in the bowl. Hopefully it wasn't rat. He was surely giving her enough money to keep her from doing that again—though she'd chastised him for complaining when she had. Food was food—and hungry children needed it.

He took a tentative bite and his stomach cramped with the desire for more. Chewing, he realized the meat was beef—and not the gristly castoffs from the butcher. The urge to gobble it up despite its lack of salt and pepper was difficult to ignore.

"Well, hello. I see you've finally chosen to come home."

Tim set the spoon back in his bowl and tried hard not to scowl at his father's greeting—as if Tim were always the one leaving the family to fend for themselves. How long had Father been gone this time? He'd not been around when Tim had packed for the hunt.

"Hello," Tim acknowledged, because it'd cause more problems if he didn't.

"Brenna, get me hot water and a fresh towel." Father sat at the kitchen table instead of getting the items himself. As if she had waited around, praying he'd come back just so she could serve him.

He took off his sweaty hat and set it on the table. His damp dark hair as limp as Tim's own. "And get out the brandy bottle from under the bed."

Leaning back, he eyed Tim's bowl. "You enjoying that soup?"

Tim bristled at the smug expression on his father's face.

After handing Father the hot water and towel, Ma started ladling more soup.

"None of that for me," Father said with a wave of a sinewy hand. "I'll have a steak. Fry me up one of those."

Steak? When had they ever had steak?

Ma pulled out a marbled piece of meat from the brown paper beside the stove and slapped it onto the skillet. The instant frying beef permeated the air, Tim's stomach flipped. "How do we have steak?" He looked inside his bowl. With all this meat...

They'd consumed ill-gotten food before. No hungry kid refused what they were given on principle, but now with him working for the Keys... "Where did this come from?"

"You always have to complain about everything, don't ya? Can't you just thank your ol' man for once in your life?" Father narrowed his bloodshot eyes at him.

"It's nice to have meat." That was as close to a thanks as he could muster.

"Then you'll be happy to know we have a side of beef hanging in the barn."

"I hope it ain't one of the Keys' cattle, Father. If I get fired because you—"

"You're always yapping at me about not bringing you food, and when I do, you yap at me more. Can't win with you."

"*I* put food on the table through my own hard work, not that of others."

Father lifted himself from his chair and leaned over the table, eyeing him. "If you can't be grateful, get out from under my roof." He turned to Ma. "You can eat the steak. I'm going to cut myself a bigger one." He pushed back his chair and stomped out the door.

"Father, don't you—"

"Hush now." Ma came over and set bread beside his bowl. "You finish your soup, and I'll give you the steak."

"But Ma—"

"It's dead and cooked already, Timothy," she whispered. "It can't be returned."

Timothy blinked up at his mother, only inches taller than him when he was sitting. "You're all right with us eating this? What if he stole it from the Keys? I told you about that missing pair."

She sighed. "I haven't the energy to pick a fight over what's right when my kids have eaten nothing but cabbage and moldy potatoes the last few days. And since you didn't bring anything home, and without your horse…"

"And what if he gets thrown in jail for this?" When he was little, he'd dreamed he was a ranger or deputy and could arrest his father for how he treated Ma—but he'd learned soon enough the law could do very little in that regard.

She shrugged. "We'd get a few days of peace? There'll certainly be a lot less fighting. And you'll take care of us."

"And if I can't? I told the Keys I was looking for that cow and calf. If that's where the meat's from, and they find it butchered in our barn—"

"Mr. Key refused to hire your pa when he asked for work years ago, and yet he hired you. He knows it ain't you who's bad."

"But what if it's their cattle?"

She wrung her hands in her apron as if to dry them off. The amount of time she spent doing that, one would think her hands were always wet. "They aren't paying attention to what we eat."

The pit in his stomach grew. "Ma, you gotta kick Father out before he corrupts us all. If you're willing to fry up the animal of one of the few men who'll employ me, who pays me—"

"Don't you go blathering about this to them. You didn't bring back venison, you didn't even bring back the horse. Besides, your father's just a petty thief. He's merely an annoyance to people like that."

"'People like that?'"

"They've got plenty to share."

"And they do. They gave us a goose at Christmas, a ham for Easter. They feed me every day I work so you don't have to. We need to ask them if we want more, not force them to share."

She busied herself with wiping crumbs off the table.

"What are you going to do, Ma, when he steals the money I give you, and he *doesn't* bring home food—stolen or otherwise?"

"Call your brothers and sister in, would you?" She pulled several chipped bowls off the shelves, then started filling them. "Don't want the soup to grow cold before they get any."

He looked out the back window to where Molly and Jack were chasing the cat. Once he returned to the Keys, he shouldn't come back home anymore unless absolutely necessary. If he became privy to the stuff his father did, he might be tempted to turn him in.

He blew out a hot breath and pushed away from the table to call in his siblings. Sometimes the urge to tell his mother to leave his father was nearly irresistible. Surely doing so would be better than enduring the man's poisoned barbs and ridiculous rages, having to scrimp to buy necessities only to discover he'd wrecked the house to find everyone's stash so he could buy whiskey.

But he couldn't force the one parent who'd done him any good to do something she didn't want to do.

Once Molly and the boys filed in, he told Ma to split the steak between the four little ones and stomped off for the barn. The building leaned ten degrees, considering the amount of rotten wood his father never found the time to replace.

If Ma wouldn't stop Father from putting them in harm's way, maybe it was time for him to do so. He slowed and unclenched his hands. He'd inherited his father's lanky frame and his inability to pack on pounds no matter how much he ate. Though he was taller, Tim knew a brawl wouldn't settle things. Besides, his father swung insults and derision, not fists.

Inside the barn, behind his father, was a butchered cow hanging from the rafters.

Tim swallowed to wet his throat. "Tell me where you really got that cow."

"Oh, that's right. Your father can't possibly be telling the truth." The carcass swayed as Father sawed through meat with a dull knife. He should have sharpened it long ago. Too bad he had far more important things to do, like play cards. "But I'll tell you, so you'll quit nagging. I found it with a broken leg, breathing its last. Leaving meat to rot in the sun is wasteful, and if it's there for the taking, then it ain't stealing."

Of course, a decent human being would consider taking someone's dying animal for themselves to be stealing, but Father followed his own rules. "You could've informed the owner. They might've rewarded you for being honest."

"Who says I ain't honest?" Father glared at him over the animal's back. "And you know as well as I do no rich rancher is going to give me anything. He'd have blamed me for its death and rewarded me with a visit from that dumb deputy. The rich don't give a hoot for men like me trying to dig themselves out of the dirt—oh, no. They always view us with suspicion."

Or rather, anyone with discernment was wary of his father. They likely didn't look down on all poor people, but there'd be no convincing Father of that.

"They have quite the nerve stomping on men who do their hard work for them, considering God gave them more than they need. But give a working man a loan? No. They want us to stay in the dirt. Makes them feel better about themselves. So if what they ought to share is right there in front of me, and I can make use of it, then I'm going to make use of it."

Tim watched his father walk over to the wooden plank he was setting the slabs of meat on. He didn't seem inebriated, but the man didn't have to be drunk to justify anything he did, let alone stealing a cow because someone wouldn't lend him money.

Father scowled at him for a second before using his arm to shove back his greasy hair, so much like Tim's. "You just going to stand there and be a lazy sack of bones, or you going to help for once?"

Tim stifled his retort. He could point out exactly who was helping this family, but he was too tired after the turmoil of the past few days—not that it would've done any good to argue with the man.

It was a shame he looked so much like his father. Surely the fact he was Alan O'Conner's son reflected more poorly on him than his blemishes or tattered clothes. For when trivial things didn't matter—like when one was kidnapped and praying to survive—a woman as beautiful as Gwen had kissed him smack on his grimy, acne-covered cheek without flinching.

Perhaps other women could look past his appearance, too, but to look past where he came from? Why else would Gwen have said she hoped to find someone like him that she *could* marry?

Because no woman in this county would take the O'Conner name if she wanted to maintain respectability. He couldn't blame them.

If he had the choice, he'd refuse to bear the name as well.

CHAPTER TWENTY-FOUR

After nodding to dismiss her maid, Gwen groaned as she lowered herself back into her parlor chair and propped her feet atop the ottoman. Her right ankle still pulsed hot whenever she stood, despite a week having passed since Charles York had driven her home.

Though most of her wounds had disappeared or scabbed over, one of her rope burns had refused to heal. Surely the salt baths would start working at some point.

Giving a sideways glance to the correspondence on the side table, Gwen sighed and picked up the top one. She'd read it twice already.

Months ago, any note from Eric would've caused her heart to flutter, but now…

Did she even want to answer? The letter was nothing but polite—

Tap, tap.

"Miss McGill?" The butler, Mr. Harrison, stepped into the room. "Mr. Hucket's here to see you."

She tossed Eric's letter back onto the table. It'd take a month to reply with the way things were going lately. Maybe she'd figure out what to say by then. If only she didn't have to stand to greet her guest, but she'd asked to see the schoolteacher days ago. Who knew how long it'd take for him to return if she sent him away?

Once the butler's back was turned, she gritted her teeth to keep from groaning as she stood. Then she tugged down her shirt sleeves, checking to be sure what was left of her abrasions were covered.

The short schoolmaster came sweeping in. "Miss McGill, it's a pleasure to be summoned into your presence."

Her eyes hurt from the effort to keep from rolling them. He'd been hired during her last year of school, and she'd been hard-pressed to respect him, especially since he was not but a few years older than Bo. "Yes, I wanted to discuss Molly O'Conner with you."

The light on his face dimmed. He'd likely expected some compliment for who knew what. He often grandstanded about how well the school was doing, despite the havoc that occurred behind his back. Just because she'd been out of school for a few years didn't mean she forgot what went on.

"I wasn't aware you were acquainted with the O'Conners."

"Not exactly acquainted, but the girl attends school, correct?"

"Yes." He sniveled.

"I'm assuming Molly could use help with books, slates, and such? Are there others? I'd hoped to pay for what their parents may be struggling to afford this upcoming year—anonymously of course."

Mr. Hucket's wiry lips thinned as he smiled. "How magnanimous of you. There are three who have yet to pay for the slates I purchased out of my own pocket last year."

"All right, I can pay for those, too. Just give me—"

"I do my best by the children, you know. When you were in school, the students were far better behaved. The children these days—" He stopped short, shaking his head. "It's not the lack of proper supplies, but of discipline."

She nodded, though his weak authority had plenty to do with their behavioral problems.

"I'm most honored by your offer. And may I be so bold as to say the school could also use—"

"I'm not on the council, Mr. Hucket. I suggest you take your requests there."

"Of course, of course." He hunched in on himself like a scolded puppy. "I shouldn't have dared to have assumed upon your graciousness…"

She'd forgotten how much pointless flattery came out of his mouth.

"…back home in the thick woods of Tennessee, I had a family who was a godsend to the school. Not only did they provide for each student's books, but they took care of my lunches as well…"

Was he asking for her to start providing his lunch?

He shook his head and held up a hand. "As I was saying— sorry for getting derailed—on behalf of the students, thank you for what your family has done for the school, and the town too, if I might add."

She sighed, half afraid to remind him why she'd asked him here to begin with lest she end up enduring another boring monologue. "Please make me a list of what those three students need for this year, and I'll take care of it."

"Thank you, Miss McGill. I could do that immediately, if it'd please you. Or I could return later when—"

"No. That won't be necessary." She crossed over to the roll-top desk and took out a sheet of paper. "Here's pen and paper for you to use."

He flipped out his coattails and sat upon the chair. "It'll take me only a moment."

Thank the Lord for small favors.

After scratching down five things, he stood and flourished the paper in front of her as if presenting her with a royal decree. "Here you are."

She frowned as she read the list. Paying for Molly's school needs wouldn't come close to repaying Tim for getting her home safely.

"Is there more I could do for you, miss? I'm honored you've chosen to use your resources to help my students. I knew you'd grow up to be generous, considering the kind of student you were. If more strove to attain the high quality of character you've always possessed..."

It was all she could do to keep from asking him to leave. His constant flattery—

Wait. Was this how she sounded to the men she flirted with? She stared at Mr. Hucket in horror. Was he trying to flirt?

At the widening of her eyes, he took a step back and nervously shrugged. "I'm letting my tongue run away with me. But I truly am thankful for your generosity. May I hope to avail myself of it again if the need arises?"

She forced herself to nod. On behalf of Tim and his sister, she'd allow Mr. Hucket back in the house if she must.

As soon as he disappeared into the hallway, she plopped back onto her chair. Her throbbing ankle had made that whole encounter far worse.

Harrison tapped on the door again. "A Mr. O'Conner to see you."

A tingling took over her limbs and her breath grew short, akin to the jitters she used to get before reciting in school. She gave her permission for Harrison to send him in.

Once her butler left, she contemplated staying seated, not only because of the pain, but if she stood, would Tim notice the butterflies that had overtaken her? Harrison, however, would wonder what had gotten into her if she stayed seated upon a guest's arrival, especially one she was barely supposed to be acquainted with.

Groaning, she pushed herself back up.

Harrison returned, Tim following with hat in hand, his

expression one she'd never seen before. His eyes seemed bright yet anxious and had his lips twitched at the sight of her?

"Pardon the interruption, Miss McGill." Tim cast his eyes down, fiddling with the hat in his hands. "But Mrs. Key heard about your ordeal. Since you've not been to the ranch, and she's unable to endure the ride in, she sent me to check on you."

Would he send her a glance to let her know the real reason he'd come was to assure himself she was all right? "That's kind of Mrs. Key. I'm doing well under the circumstances. Please, have a seat."

He looked back up, and yes, his cheek certainly had twitched a little. He glanced around at the furniture before looking back toward the door where Harrison was exiting with the empty tea service. "I would've come to check on you myself once I'd heard, but I've been home for several days not feeling my best, and then I was put to work."

So he'd wanted to come see her? She smiled at him though he wasn't looking, but then the throbbing in her ankle took over again. Without waiting for him to look back, she lowered herself into her chair again while he stared at the sofa beside her as if afraid he'd stain it, though he was cleaner than the last time she'd seen him.

"Please sit." With a wince, she placed a foot atop the ottoman, followed by the other. She tried to cross her legs to appear more ladylike but hissed as one ankle knocked into the other.

He stopped staring at the creamy white upholstery, sidled over to a wooden chair, and took a seat. The awkwardness had vanished, as if they were once again out under the stars alone, his eyes full of concern. "Is something wrong?"

"Yes. Didn't you wonder why I'd not yet been out to the ranch?"

He looked at her with big, blank eyes. "I'd figured you were busy."

"With what?" She couldn't keep the astonishment from her voice. Did he think she'd not be worried about him?

"I don't know." He glanced around, fidgeting in his seat. "What you weren't able to do while out at the ranch. Visiting, getting measured for dresses, getting your servants to…polish the silverware?"

She laughed. At least he hadn't assumed she sat around eating prime rib and shaved ice all day, like some did.

He didn't return her laughter. But though he seemed a bit bewildered by her reaction, a touch of a smile came upon his lips as he watched her, his face softening.

She stopped and swallowed hard. Though she never would've said he was attractive before, with how he was looking at her, something caught in her chest. If he filled out a little more, had a decent haircut, he wouldn't be half bad. No, more than that, with well-tailored clothes that fit instead of hung, if he put on the confidence he'd sported out in the wilderness, looked her square in the eye…

He cocked his head. "Gwen?"

And when he said her name breathy like that, with just a little of his rumbly voice peeking through. She shivered.

"You said there was a problem that kept you from the ranch?"

"Oh yes." How had she forgotten what they'd been talking about? "I haven't done much considering the pain. I couldn't visit anyone, especially not Corinne. She's too observant. Even she—"

"You're in pain?" He slid forward on his seat.

His panicked look melted away the pit in her chest. Unbidden, a flash of longing for him to come over and put his arms around her nearly made her petition the Heavens he would. Instead, she nodded.

"Why would it be bad for Mrs. Key to know?"

She held up her hands. "The rope burns around my wrists have healed well enough, but there's a spot on my ankle that hasn't. I think the doctor would notice it's an odd place for a wound, and what if he told someone? Everyone's believed my story so far—as far-fetched as it is, but no one's seen the marks. Has anyone questioned you?"

"No. Sleeping for two days straight convinced my mother I wasn't feeling well." He moved his chair around to sit in front of her. "How bad is the wound? It's been a week already. I don't want you losing a limb to keep Daniel's confidence. Surely—"

"I won't lose my foot." She clasped his hand, reassured when he squeezed back. "Though it'd likely heal faster if I didn't have to wear stockings. The fabric keeps embedding into the wound. But how can I explain myself or hide the problem if I go barefoot?"

"You could pretend to be sick, like I did. Stay in bed."

She was already tired of sitting around all day, though she hadn't wanted to leave the house. Going outside caused her to jump at every noise that sounded. Her heart rate suffered enough at night when the house creaked and groaned. She now had to check the locks three times before she went to bed. How long until she felt safe outside again? "Would some salve you put on animals work? Or could you ask Corinne what she'd put on festering sores?"

"Let me see it."

He wanted to see her ankle? A flush stole over her neck. Which was ridiculous, of course, after what they'd been through.

Tim scooted forward and looked her in the eye. "I think a man who's slept beside you and kept his hands to himself can handle seeing your ankle."

Her chest caved with the sudden loss of breath.

"Gwen," he whispered, in his rumbly sort of way again. "If you're worried about your foot, let me see it."

"All right." She leaned forward and unbuttoned her boot then carefully peeled down her stocking, wincing at the painful pull against her wound and clamping her hands around it. The bandage had slipped again and the festering had dried into the fabric. The last several days, she'd insisted on washing her own stockings.

How long until the maids found the amount of missing gauze and her sudden penchant for hand washing odd enough to alert her brother? If infection set in…

Tim's gentle hands took hold of her heel and tugged her foot closer. Setting the bottom of her leg across his lap, he peeled the rest of her stocking off.

The yellowed flesh around the wound looked worse than it had this morning.

Tim was in no danger of swooning over her bare ankle, that was certain.

He probed around the wound, frowning. He pointed to a worrisome area. "I'd heat a needle and lance this section. Something we put on cattle might help, but I'm going to ask Mrs. Key."

"How will you do so without arousing her suspicion?"

He looked up at her, still holding her foot. "I'll tell her you have an infected blister. She wouldn't need to see that to recommend anything, and surely it'd work the same. I'm sorry I didn't come earlier. I figured it'd be best to stay away so no one could connect the dots about us being together—"

"Connect what dots about you being together?"

At the sound of her brother's voice, Gwen snatched her foot from Tim's hand, causing a flash of hot pain where his fingernail scraped across her wound.

Bo stood in the doorway, glaring at Tim's lap where her foot had been, and then his face darkened. "*You* were responsible for her disheveled state when she came home?"

"It's not what you think." Gwen tucked her foot under her skirt. More to keep him from noticing the rope burn than any embarrassment over what he might think about her and Tim.

"You were *together*?" His eyes narrowed on her. "I knew a miracle brought you home, but for you to have lied—"

"Don't jump to conclusions, sir." Tim's voice was quiet but firm.

Bo whipped toward Tim, his face reddening. "I thought you could be trusted."

She pushed herself off the sofa. "Bo, stop before you say anything—"

"How could I've been so wrong to think you were different?" He slashed his hand at Tim, as if he'd not heard her. "Only this morning, despite my intense dislike for your father, I gave in and told him I'd lend him some money. I thought if it'd benefit you and your siblings—"

"Sir." Tim cut her brother off. "I appreciate you looking past your misgivings to help my family, but doing business with my father will benefit him far more than it'll likely benefit me and my siblings, I guarantee you."

Bo stepped back, his head cocked. "I'll tell him no then. But that doesn't..." He turned to pierce Gwen with a stiff glare. "You are not to spend more time with him. I know I told you—"

"Hush!" She thrust out a hand to stop him.

"—to see if there could be something between you two." Tim's face paled, but Bo drove on, "But heavens, Gwendolyn, I never thought you'd—"

"There isn't anything between us, Bo." She squared her shoulders and glared right back at her brother. "I spent time getting to know him as you insisted so I could get to Denver, but since then—"

Tim pushed past them.

She snagged his sleeve, but the fabric slipped from her grasp.

And she'd thought her brother's mouth had run away with him. "Wait! Don't take that wrong. I didn't mean it like that—I mean, I no longer think..."

The way Tim's eyes were filled with dark thunderous pain made further words impossible.

Time seemed to stop, and sound grew fuzzy. She stared at

him as he shoved his way out of the room, as if looking at him hard enough would make him come back.

When sounds began to register again, she turned to Bo, her every muscle now limp. "Do you realize you just did what you accused me of doing weeks ago? Assuming things based on appearance? Tim saved my life. He was looking at the infected rope burn I have on my ankle to help me figure out if I should see a doctor or not."

Bo blinked, his eyes glassy. "Rope burn?"

She sighed and sank onto the sofa. "We were kidnapped."

The cushions buckled beside her as her brother sat. He was silent, looking at her as if he'd never seen her before. "I don't understand. Kidnapped? Why wouldn't you tell me you were kidnapped?"

She placed her foot on his knee, showing him the infected wound. "Because we were concerned people would jump to the conclusion you just jumped to. When Tim saw me on the way to the Yorks' while he was out hunting, he offered to escort me. If you thought enough of him to send me out to flirt with him—"

"I didn't send you out to flirt."

She huffed. "What else have I done in my attempts to capture a man's attention? Though maybe it only works on men who aren't worth the effort—Tim's not interested."

"But he just came into town to see you."

"I don't know about that." The pitiful way she'd said that made her eyes squinch tight. "Mrs. Key sent him in. And considering I didn't want the doctor to know what happened unless absolutely necessary, I wanted his opinion." She turned her ankle to give him a better look. "So what do you think?"

Bo moved his thumb along the wounded area, pressing against discolored skin. "What did Timothy say?"

"He thought I ought to lance the yellowish stuff."

Bo nodded but kept hold of her ankle. "I can help you do that, but Gwen..." He turned, his face a mask of hurt. "Why did you lie to me?"

"I felt I had good reason. Not just because of what you might think, but I can't share why exactly without Tim agreeing since it's more his concern than mine. Besides, you've been so busy lately. I feel like I'm just another complication for you to deal with."

"You've been as busy as I've been, and you're not a complication."

She shook her head. "I've not been doing anything of importance. Nothing more than chasing after men and pretending to be something I'm not. No wonder Eric didn't want me. There's nothing to me."

"That's not true. You might not let others see what lies beneath, but that doesn't mean what you've shown them is all there is to you."

"But if I showed people what's inside me…"

"You're afraid they'll see the hurt? The insecurity? That you're scared?"

She pulled her foot off her brother's lap to hug her knees to her chest. Unable to look at him, she turned to stare out the window toward town. "I'm blessed more than anyone in this entire county. Our money, the clothes, this house, your protection—everything. I even get kidnapped and return basically unharmed. What right do I have to be insecure and longing for marriage when there are women out there in desperate need of a hardworking man to help them survive?"

She gulped down the lump in her throat. "If I set my hopes on a good one, and he realizes I'm nothing but a pretty ornament…"

"You're more than an ornament." Wrapping an arm around her, Bo pulled her close. "We all crave to be known, Gwen. So tell the truth about yourself. And for goodness' sake, tell me the truth about things before I start hollering at people who've been looking out for you. Today's been long, and all the people trying to hoodwink me the last several hours…"

He sighed. "I better go hunt Timothy down and apologize."

Tim likely hadn't been enraged by Bo, but rather by learning he'd just been one more in a long line of men she'd used to get what she wanted.

"No, I'll find him and explain."

But would he hear her out?

CHAPTER TWENTY-FIVE

Riding the sorriest excuse for a horse, Tim endured the slow walk along the ruts leading away from Deputy Dent's. After stretching his arms from a long day of setting fence posts at the Keys', and then again at Dent's, Tim patted the horse's flabby neck to encourage her to keep going rather than fall over dead. "Sorry, ol' girl, for dragging you back into work, but I'll give you an extra scoop of oats when we get home."

She nickered and lifted her head as if to note how long the road was before them.

"I know. It's a long way, but there'll be hay. Keep your eye on supper." Though eating the beef his father had brought home made him uneasy, maybe, just maybe his father hadn't done anything wrong. At least it was nice to pretend that was true. And it would just go bad now if it wasn't eaten.

He leaned back in the saddle, not keen on pushing an animal that should've already passed over to heavenly pastures. Dent's fence had taken longer than expected, and Tim still had to work on his mother's roof. Not what he wanted to do in the moonlight, but the corner above the kitchen was still leaking and he was expected back at the Keys' early tomorrow. If only he could've left the job to Father—

who might've done it if he'd felt like it—but he'd disappeared again.

After cresting a small rise, Tim noted a lone figure in the distance walking the middle of the road. Squinting, Tim tried to make out the clothes, the hat…

His father? What had happened to *his* horse?

Prodding his nag only caused the decrepit ol' girl to protest. "All right, all right. We'll get there when we get there."

As they sauntered on, his father staggered, and snippets of a one-way conversation made it apparent his father was drunk. Had he fallen off his horse, forgotten it, or gambled it away?

Tim reined in his mount to match his father's slow pace. "What happened to your horse?"

Snapping his head up, Father raised a hand to shield his eyes from the setting sun. "*You* got him."

Tim pulled on the reins to move the ol' girl out of Father's reach. "No, this is Clover. She's my ride."

"Crawford's gray?" Father scanned the horse with a sneer. "She's long past making glue, but she'll do."

Tim moved farther away. "I obtained her for my use, and I'm not giving her up. She's my ride to work—a job I need to keep the kids fed."

"Good thing I taught you how to work, then. At least you're somewhat useful."

Clenching the reins, he kept from arguing. "Where's your horse?" Was he going to have to forget the roof and go searching for it?

"It's George Tatum's now," Father muttered.

Who was George Tatum? Though maybe it didn't matter if the horse had brought in money and his father would be stuck at home. There was plenty to do around the house. "How much did you get for her?"

"Nothing."

Tim sighed. Something else he'd lost to games of chance. He should've known he'd not sacrifice something for the well-being of his children. "I suppose you can take over roofing and splitting the firewood, then."

"I'll get the horse back. Just need to borrow money first."

"From who?"

His father scowled and waved a hand at his question. "Now that McGill's backed out on me, treating me like I ain't worth doing business with. If one of us deserves something, it's me."

Tim worked to keep his face blank since he was the reason Bo was holding out on Father. Thankfully Bo and Gwen lived too far away to hear the rants and insults the family would be subjected to for the next few weeks.

"But the old lady likely has money somewhere. She can—"

"Ma doesn't have any money." And if she did, he'd prod this bag of bones to get to the house first so she could hide it as best she could. "Even if she has some saved up, it's for food, not another horse for you."

"Why, you, ungrateful, sorry…"

Tim tuned out the slurs hurled his way. Though they never failed to sting, he'd learned to harden himself. But maybe he hadn't yet built up walls thick enough to deflect everything.

It shouldn't have stung yesterday to hear Gwen hadn't been interested in him. He'd always known that was true—and yet, Bo must have thought him worthy of her once. But that no longer seemed to be the case, because if he'd thought he'd had a chance—

"Did you hear me, boy?"

"What?" Realizing his father had gotten close enough to grab the reins, Tim steered away, then noted they'd turned down the wrong road. "This isn't the way home."

"I'm going to Earl's. He'll give me money."

Without bothering to respond, Tim reined Clover around to head back to the fork. If Father was intent on borrowing from his lowlife friends, that meant he'd forgotten about Ma's possible stash and had yet to think of something valuable enough from the house to sell. He pushed Clover as fast as she would go so they had more time to hide things from Father's grubby hands.

If only he could convince himself to step away from this mess. To leave town, to never see Gwen again…

Had the woman he'd been drawn to since childhood played with his emotions merely to earn a trip to Denver?

If so, he'd been a humongous fool. During his night at the Holden Point shack, he'd decided his plan to avoid her was childish in light of the woman he'd seen. But then, glimpses of what a person could be didn't mean they'd ever become the decent human God intended. There had to be evidence their heart had changed.

He shook his head, not wanting to recall the part where Bo had insinuated that he was just like his father—and Gwen not saying a thing.

As much as he'd rather never cross their paths again, he couldn't leave his family until his father stepped up. Maybe he could take in his siblings if he married. But the only woman who might have him was Celia. She'd not toy with him. She'd either accept his proposal or tar and feather him for asking. Though since she was only seventeen, maybe he'd think about that in another year or two.

Which would be best anyway. Even prickly Celia didn't deserve being wooed by a man who longed for another.

Once he made it home, Tim slid off the horse. "Clover, though I thank you for moving those rickety legs of yours to get me to work and back, you don't make for a good ride."

The door whined open, and his mother stepped out, wiping her hands against the front of her stained apron. "Have you seen your pa?"

How he wished he hadn't. "Yes, but he likely won't be home tonight. He's gone to Earl's. And before he gets back, hide your money and anything valuable you don't want sold off. Father lost his horse to someone."

Ma's frown lines instantly deepened. Soon her face would resemble that flaky dough at the bakery they could never afford.

He stepped up and placed a hand on her shoulder. Life would go on being difficult as long as Father was around—no use whining about it. "What's for dinner?"

She shook herself as if deciding it best to forget about the looming difficulties, too. "I don't have much stew left. The kids wanted seconds, and I couldn't tell them no."

"No problem. If there's not enough, I'll eat bread to make up for it."

She worried her lip.

"All right, no bread. I'm not that hungry anyway." What did a lie like that matter when he'd not told her the real reason he'd come back so late from hunting last week?

"What's wrong?"

Part of him wanted to tell her all about it, since who else could he tell and she rarely ever inquired after him. And yet, she'd chosen so poorly in marriage, any advice she might give him would be risky to follow. He moved past her and into the house. "Just tired is all."

She followed. "The school things you got Molly arrived today."

"The what?"

"You need to inform me when you take care of stuff like that, so I don't buy them myself."

While his eyes adjusted to the dim interior, he pressed a hand to his forehead, trying to remember what he might've ordered from Mr. Owens, and why he'd have it delivered. Perhaps he *was* working too hard—or his feelings for Gwen were messing with his head more than he thought.

At the table, Molly was hunched over a book. When she looked up, she bounced out of her chair and came straight for him. "Look! The edges are real gold."

She feathered the pages, showing off their metallic shimmer. What kind of schoolbook was that? He took up the collection of fairy tales. Likely not real gold, but far fancier than anything he'd ever seen. When did the school start requiring something like this? If Father saw the book… "Molly, you need to leave this with the teacher once school starts. Keep it hidden for now. Not under your pillow, but somewhere Father won't look. If he sees it, he might try to sell it."

Molly snatched the book back and clamped it against her chest. She usually took Father's raiding of the few coins she amassed with a martyr's patience, but she loved to read. Their one storybook had fallen apart because of her. "I don't want to leave it at school. Mr. Hucket won't let me read anything but schoolbooks there." Her lips twisted with disgust. Then she grabbed Tim's hand and pulled him toward a crate. "But I can leave a slate at school now."

She picked up two shiny slates and handed him one. "She said I had one for home and one for school. You must be making lots more money now."

He took in Molly's beaming face. Who'd have thought someone could be so excited about school supplies? He turned to his mother. "Who is 'she'?"

Ma took a potato from the oven and set it on a plate. "Miss McGill rode up this morning, said she was delivering the schoolbooks this year. I tried to tell her no, thinking we were being treated to charity again, but she told me you paid for them."

"But the fairy tales?"

"Oh, that's Miss McGill's own book. Can you imagine?" Ma stopped setting out food to stare off into space. "Having a book like that and just giving it away."

Molly sighed. "She probably has stacks of them."

"I was gonna tell her we couldn't take it, but she handed it straight to Molly." Ma went back to the stove. "You should've seen her face."

Tim picked up the book his sister had put down. He opened the front cover. At the top was the prettiest handwriting he'd ever seen.

To my dearest Gwendolyn. May your dreams come true.
Love, Mother
1871

Gwen might feel terrible about how he'd learned of her brother forcing her to spend time with him—to get her mind off Eric most likely—but this was too much. He knew how dear the memories of her mother were.

Molly pulled him toward the chair, and before he realized it, she'd plopped onto his lap and opened the book. "Read *The Wild Swans* to me. Miss McGill says it's her favorite."

He contemplated informing Molly they couldn't keep the book, but his mother's weakness must be his as well. His sister was beaming. How could he tell her this gift had to go?

Clearing his throat, he checked the contents, then flipped to the back.

Molly gasped as he found the start page, an intricate wood block print depicting swans flying near a beautiful girl collecting thistles. "She's so pretty."

Gwen would surely want this book for her own children one day. He'd have to see if Mr. Owens could order a copy for Molly. He began reading to keep from worrying about how much it would cost.

After a page and a half, Ma came over and set a glass of water next to his bowl, not even half filled with the remnants of stew. "Now, Molly, Tim needs to eat. After you get the boys in and wash them up, I'll read to you."

His little sister slipped off his lap, slid the book back onto the table, and trudged out the side door.

His mother pushed the butter dish toward him with a soft smile playing on her lips. "Miss McGill asked after you."

Everything within him sank at that look on her face—as if she truly thought he had a chance with Gwen. "It's just because I haven't seen her around the Keys' lately." Maybe she'd come out to ask what salve Corinne had suggested. He closed his eyes and swallowed a groan. How had he let a blow to his pride make him forget to honor his word? But now that Bo knew about her wound, he'd make sure she was all right.

"Felt like there was more to her question than simply wondering where you've been."

"There wasn't," he forced out, his voice more growly than he would've liked.

"I know you've always held a candle for her. Of course, I've said little about it, expecting that candle to get snuffed out the moment you saw the world for what it was, but the way she said your name…"

He shook his head. "It's because she's worried she hurt my feelings, Ma. She's just feeling guilty."

He prepared the heel of Ma's bread in silence, trying not to imagine how Gwen must've sounded to his mother. Trying not to hope she felt something other than guilt.

"You're not over her, are you?"

He looked up, keeping his eyes blank. "Salt?"

Ma gave him the eye, but then reached over to the stove and grabbed the shakers. "I don't blame you. She's quite pretty."

"Ma—"

"Now, hear me out." She put up her hands to ward off the long-suffering he'd suffused into his voice. "When I was not much younger than you, I held my own candle for a boy with slick black hair and piercing eyes named Paul Grossett. His daddy owned Central Bank, so I knew I hadn't a chance with him—not that he ever gave me a thought, being I was three years younger, you see. But do you know who he ended up with?"

He didn't say anything since he'd never been to Ohio where she'd grown up.

"Eugenia Schwemmer. A year younger than me and nothing but a bank teller's daughter—though her curly hair *was* the envy of every girl in town. A real love match, they say." Ma sat back in her chair as if that revelation should change the world or something. "I always regretted staying out of his way, believing he'd want nothing to do with me. Maybe if I'd have talked to him…" She sighed. "But you. You're a man, you could ask—"

"Ma, it's different. A poor but pretty woman marrying a wealthy man isn't unheard of. But an attractive, wealthy woman marrying below her? You don't hear about that. And if you do, it's a whispered story filled with all kinds of pity or scandal, I'm sure."

"So it's not that you no longer like her?"

He chewed as nonchalantly as he could and shrugged. "What boy in the county doesn't? My attachment to her is no different than theirs."

"Oh? She seemed disappointed you weren't here. She even stayed a while to wait. And she wasn't sticking around because of what I offered in the way of tea and such."

He stuffed more food in his mouth. The faster he could finish eating, the faster he could get away from the blasted hope wriggling in.

"When we ran out of polite conversation, she wrote this." Ma pulled a folded paper from her apron pocket and pushed it toward him. "Told me to give it to you."

He tried to ignore the note in order to finish his stew, but his mother was staring at him. Wiping his mouth, he unfolded the paper with as indifferent an air as he could muster.

Timothy,
I didn't get to finish what I was telling Bo before you left. He was right from the start, and I was not. You've proven yourself to be the type of man no woman ought to dismiss. I'm sorry I did. That's a reflection on me, not you.

He kept his focus on the words, though he wondered if his mother could hear his crazily thumping heart. A decent man was all that he'd hoped everyone considered him to be. A man different from his father, a man who wouldn't be the bane of his future wife's existence. Even so, writing such didn't mean Gwen thought of him as anything more than that.

He flicked his eyes over her fancy signature, keeping himself from swiping his thumb across her name, then pushed the note away and picked up his fork. "She's a nice lady, Ma, but——"

"Oh, son, twenty years down the line, do you want to regret not trying to win her?" She put her hand atop his, her face more haggard than normal.

He shook his head slowly. Not to answer her question but to stop his mother from trying to fill him with hope.

For dash it all, he was having a hard enough time squashing down the hope he already possessed.

CHAPTER TWENTY-SIX

Pulling up his neckerchief, Tim wiped the sweat off his face as he rode beside Keys' wagon on Nolan's gelding—Minotaur was a much smoother ride than Clover—and yet he couldn't wait for the ride to be over. Yesterday's torrential rains had made today miserably humid, and the summer sun was a killer. If only his mother could cut his hair short and make it look good. He ought to go to a barber, but keeping the family's credit at the mercantile in good standing was more important. That account was hard enough to keep paid down, and it wasn't as if a decent haircut would do him much good in the weeks before it grew out.

Ma's story of the bank teller's daughter marrying the rich man's son was likely true, but he couldn't ignore the crucial detail about the girl having beautiful hair. A shallow surface quality to be sure, but many men, if not all, desired their wives to have a pretty face and figure. But he wasn't even close to good-looking enough for a woman to marry him for that alone, haircut or no. Nor charming enough to trick a woman into thinking he was. And yet…

He rubbed his thumb over the slight ridge Gwen's note created in his pocket. No, her letter was nothing but an apology.

And though he believed himself a decent man, Gwen didn't need to settle for someone who was simply better than his father.

Besides, what could they possibly tell Bo that would clear things up without unveiling the secret he'd asked Gwen to keep? How could he betray Daniel in some crazy hope he and Gwen could be more than friends? *Friends.* Even that might be pushing it now. His mother might think he could aspire to more, but she rarely left home and didn't see the men Gwen normally chased after.

Nolan slowed the wagon when they finally arrived in town. "Wonder where Miss McGill is?"

The whole ride in, they'd said nothing to each other, the weather being too muggy for small talk, yet Gwen was the first thing Nolan decided to talk about? Tim forced his expression to remain impassive, though he had to tug on his collar—it'd gotten hotter somehow.

His boss turned slightly, his upper lip glistening. "When did she last come out to the ranch?"

Four days. "It's been a while." It was best he just forget about ever seeing her again at the ranch. After Bo had—

"Aren't you wondering where she is?"

Tim startled, crashing out of his thoughts. "Who?"

"Miss McGill." Nolan frowned up at him.

"Oh, uh…" Why was Nolan suddenly so worried about her whereabouts? "She came to the house to give Molly a book a couple of days ago. She seemed fine." She'd returned with another of those gold-trimmed affairs. He'd watched her come and go from the barn loft. She'd walked as if her wound had healed, which was a good thing. Corinne had been holed up in her room—

Nolan cleared his throat.

Tim glanced at him. "Did you ask me something?"

Nolan squinted an eye at him. "I was *saying* it's best not to rule out a woman simply because you think she won't want you for something you can't help."

Tim tightened his grip on his reins. How had Nolan become aware of his attraction to Gwen? Hopefully Rascal had said something to him, or else he really needed to get a hold of himself so Gwen never found out.

Nolan tapped his wooden leg, a hollow sound emitting from it. "If it weren't for my cantankerous father and his manipulations, I'd still believe I had nothing to offer a good woman. But I've learned it's how you treat her that's most important. If you treat her well, she's jelly in your hand."

He couldn't help the snort of a laugh that escaped him. Gwen jelly in *his* hand? *Yeah, right.*

But then, Nolan wasn't wrong about women wanting to be treated well. As a child, he'd often listened from his bed in the loft as his father berated his mother. Heard Father call her names no man ought to call a woman, let alone a wife.

Ma had once mentioned Father had turned every girl's head, that when they'd met, he'd had enough money to impress her. But both his looks and assets had disappeared long ago. If his father had ever treated Ma right, they'd long forgotten about it—or they'd repressed the memories in an attempt to make the present less depressing.

He'd have chosen an ugly, old man with nothing to his name to be his father if he would've been kind to his mother, worked hard, let his kids sleep instead of pick fights.

His horse shied, and Tim tightened his reins. Evidently Nolan's gelding hadn't wanted to step into the huge crater obscuring the middle of Main Street. After leading the black around the gaping pit, he frowned at the other potholes the rain had caused. The streets had turned into a regular mess since Jacob Hendrix had stepped down as marshal. With Deputy Dent only working when he had time, a lot of the city maintenance had been ignored.

Wait a minute, where was Nolan?

Tim turned his horse around. How had he ridden straight past the mercantile, not realizing his boss had stopped half a block back? Nolan was likely regretting bringing him into town instead of Rascal, considering his boss stood beside the wagon now, shaking his head.

Thankfully, Nolan's eyes contained a glimmer. He'd not fire him for being so absent-minded, but all the same, he ought to get his head back on straight.

Dismounting, Tim led the horse to the post. "Sorry about that."

Catching sight of Bo walking their way made him want to find an excuse to get back up on the horse and ride off. Was he coming over to chastise Tim in front of his boss? He gripped his reins instead of wrapping them around the post. What if Bo pressured Nolan to fire him? Nolan might be inclined to believe Tim if he refuted Bo's accusations, but without coming clean with the truth of everything—but even if he did...

Seemed once again he'd made the wrong decision. Daniel better have a really good reason for asking him to pretend he never saw him.

Bo waited for the Masons' wagon to pass before walking straight for him.

Tim steeled himself.

"Mr. O'Conner."

He gave Bo a short nod, his fingernails digging into his palms as he held tight to the reins.

"I've come to apologize."

Tim couldn't help but lose all his breath. What had he expected Bo to do, punch him in front of the whole town?

Nolan cleared his throat. "Seems you two need to talk. I'll head inside. Take your time, Tim."

He turned toward his boss. "You don't need help?"

"I've loaded wagons by myself a time or two. Plus, I've got catalogs to flip through." He turned his back on Tim and marched into the mercantile.

Despite the hubbub of the street, the air around Tim grew heavy and silent.

Bo moved his lips as if debating what to say next.

Best he hear the man out. He flipped the reins around the post and waited.

Finally, Bo crossed his arms and exhaled loudly. "I don't know everything, but I've seen enough of your character and I know my sister well enough to believe what she told me. I'm sorry I accused you of taking advantage of her when I should've thanked you for her safe return. I don't know why you two feel it best not to report this to the authorities, but if you think those men have moved on and are no longer a threat, I guess reporting them wouldn't do much good anyway, what with us being without a marshal and all."

Gwen had told him quite a bit more than he'd expected her to.

"You like my sister, don't you?"

Tim blinked. He surely meant "like" as in finding her agreeable. "Of course."

"Then what's holding you back?"

Holding him back from what?

"I suppose it's because of what you believe I'd think. Well, I want you to know that I try my best to follow the Lord's example, and despite how miserably I failed the other day, the Bible says God is no respecter of persons. He doesn't show favoritism for such things as pedigree and wealth but looks at the heart. I know that what someone possesses or what they look like doesn't always indicate how they treat people." He took off his hat and fiddled with its brim. "My father treated Gwen abominably since the day Mother died. And you've informed me yours cares little for your family, though he'll act worried about them to get what he wants. Both men on the opposite sides of a coin, yet with the same disregard for those under their protection."

Bo looked him square in the eye. "You and I come from

entirely different worlds too, but neither of us plans to follow in their footsteps. Am I right?"

"Yes." Though it was nice Bo McGill was addressing him as an equal, he wasn't sure why he was getting this lecture on the street.

"Then why didn't you call me out on how I treated you the other day? Fight for her harder?"

Fight for her?

His breath hitched. Bo had expected him to declare himself? "I...certainly admire the fact you're willing to look past our completely different stations in life to consider me worthy of your sister." He waited for Bo to look bewildered, but the words didn't even faze him. Seemed he really had heard Bo right the other day, that he'd wanted Gwen to consider him. "But you heard her. She doesn't like me in that way."

"I may have put her up to spending time at the Keys'—and she was reluctant to do so because she didn't want to do anything to hurt you. But since she's gotten to know you, her admiration has certainly grown."

Admiration. Not enough. "I know those of you with money consider mutual respect good enough if the marriage is advantageous—but pairing up with me will in no way be advantageous for her. There will be no money, houses, or material possessions to distract whoever becomes my wife from realizing all she got out of the ceremony was me. And if you're highly attracted to your wife, and she's only—"

"You're highly attracted?"

Tim's eye twitched. "Though you likely don't want to think about it because you're her brother, no man in his right mind wouldn't find your sister attractive."

"Of course, we're all attracted by a pretty face, and you can certainly admire her loveliness from afar, but that won't win you the girl."

"I don't think you understand—"

"That you could be crushed if she doesn't choose you?"

He looked away from Bo, not wanting him to see the truth of it. How cowardly, right? And yet, what good was it to face certain soul-crushing defeat without believing something worthwhile might occur following the sacrifice? "I think it's awfully good of you to encourage me, knowing I can't give her anything. But I'd be selfish to pursue her when others could offer more, when someone out there could surely inspire more than just admiration. I don't want to do anything that will keep your sister from having the best life she can possibly have."

"And how do you know that life is not with you?"

He gave Bo a side eye. Though God may be no respecter of persons, He'd obviously blessed some more than others, and it was human nature to be affected by those charms—or lack thereof.

Bo tilted his head at him. "The next man she meets could be another Mr. Wright."

"Or he could be a man willing to love her until his last breath."

"Maybe she ought to know there's a man in Armelle who's already willing."

He looked away again. Surely that wasn't all it would take to win her.

"I wouldn't be saying this if I thought you had no chance—I don't have fun torturing people. But like you, I want to see her happy. And from what I've learned, you can't do that from afar. I've hung back, let her have her space, but all she wanted was my time. She wants to be known, to be cared for, to be seen. If you hold yourself back, how can you know she can't feel more than admiration for you?"

If Ma, his boss, *and* her brother thought he had a chance…

Tim ran his sweaty hands against his rough canvas pants, and looked back at Bo, unable to come up with words.

Could he really declare himself?

Bo gripped his shoulder. "I'm rooting for you."

Tim shook his head, but Bo didn't notice and gave a quick

excuse to take his leave—which Tim heard little of with the rushing sound in his ears and the oncoming train whistle.

What should he do? Simply telling her he loved her wouldn't be enough. But he couldn't afford to take her flowers, pay for dinner, buy her a single lemon drop, nothing. He might have a job, but he had no savings. What was Bo thinking?

The train's rumble pulled his attention to the big black engine chugging into town.

Gwen wanted to live in Denver. He couldn't even afford a ticket to the next station.

"Have you never seen a train before?"

Tim startled, looking down to his right.

The mercantile owner's daughter stood beside him, an amused, but expectant look on her face. The dark purple dress she was wearing somehow both hugged her well-endowed curves and hung on her like a sack.

"Of—of course, I have."

"Then what's eating you up so much you're planning on getting yourself run over?" Raven's expression lost its lightness. "You'll end up flat if you don't get out of the road, Timothy."

He pulled in a breath. If any woman other than Celia would tell him the absolute truth, it'd be Raven. Their teacher had often made her write sentences on the chalkboard about keeping her thoughts to herself the few months she'd attended school here before being sent back East to some fancier school.

Of course, asking Raven anything also came with the possibility of having to listen to a lot of rambling nonsense. Celia was more straight to the point—but she wasn't here. "What do you women want?"

"That's what you're pondering, standing in traffic, tempting fate?"

He staggered back. Had he really asked that question aloud?

She crossed her arms. "I'm guessing you aren't asking what we carry in the mercantile that will set your lady love's heart to pattering?"

He shook his head, since denying he had a lady love would likely have caused his voice to crack.

"Well, *women*. Let's see." Raven turned toward the locomotive and clapped as if she were about to address everyone as they detrained. "They want what they want. Trying to make them want the same things you do won't change a thing. And I tell you…" She leaned closer. "If it does, well then, you've only succeeded in turning her into another empty head like all the rest. And do men *really* want that?"

That had been more nonsense than he'd expected. "Uh, thanks. I'll just—"

"Hey." She grabbed his sleeve before he could turn away. "More simply, it's not what you buy her—as much as my father would argue otherwise. It's that you care about her—not because she makes you happy, not because she reflects well on you—but because you like her for who she is. That's all we want."

Though she'd spouted gobbledygook earlier, she was right—not just about women, but everyone.

He'd always thought Gwen wasn't as brainless as she acted, that she was a decent woman under the façade. And after tramping across the wilds with him, she'd shown she was far more levelheaded than she pretended to be half the time. But did he really know her well enough to know what she wanted? Bo thought he knew Tim would be enough for her, but was he really? "If a man—?"

Frowning, he stared at the empty spot beside him. Raven must've left at some point. With the amount of people disembarking, heading toward shops and the hotel, she'd be needed inside to—

Gwen's blond head and blue feathered hat bobbed against the small current of passengers as she made her way toward the train.

His whole body turned clammy, but if he didn't go now…

Jogging across the street, he worked at wetting his mouth

enough to get words out. The answer to any question that would lead to them becoming sweethearts would be no, of course. He'd always known the answer would be no.

His heart pumped a hard staccato, like a regiment's drummer boy approaching certain defeat. How to accept with dignity the refusal he was about to receive? Or could he figure out something she might say yes to?

Maybe she'd agree to a walk. That didn't require money and would give them time to talk.

His chest loosened, but his mouth remained dry. With how quickly she was walking, maybe she'd be too busy for that. But if he didn't ask now, despite everything inside of him calling for retreat, he likely wouldn't find the courage to forge ahead again.

He walked up alongside her in the crowd, but she didn't seem to notice.

"Hello." The word came out far scratchier than he'd wished, but at least he'd produced sound.

She glanced over and frowned. She looked back in the direction she'd been going then back at him again, frown deeper, jaw working.

He knew well enough the signs of someone miffed at being interrupted, but well, he was here—he might not be able to muster up the courage to talk to her ever again about this. "Mr. Key asked me to find out when we'd see you next at the ranch."

She nodded but looked past him again. Was she worried others would see them talking together? At least this time she wasn't in his arms. He forced himself from recalling the all too real remembrance of what she'd felt like that day.

"I intend to come out next week sometime. Probably Tuesday. I'm sorry I haven't come out to talk to you, I tried—"

He held up a hand to stop her. "I got your note, and I've talked to your brother. I understand you didn't mean to hurt my feelings, and I understand that…" Well, he didn't understand how Bo could actually believe he had a chance with her, but he was here now… "And uh—and your ankle? How is it?"

She continued scanning the crowd. "Bo got me something to put on it. It's healed."

"Good."

She seemed ready for the conversation to be over, so he took a step back.

He'd thought after their days surviving the wilds of Wyoming together she'd treat him at least as someone she could talk to, but perhaps what had happened the last time they stood in front of the train had embarrassed her more than he'd thought—though she had rarely acted embarrassed by any of her public displays with other men.

So that meant it was just him.

He swallowed hard. Good thing he'd asked her nothing beyond what had already spilled out of his mouth. Despite the hopes of some well-meaning people, he'd known deep down, they didn't know what they were talking about. Gwen was more than he deserved—and though she'd certainly been nice to him, she, too, knew admiration and friendship weren't enough for her to surrender her heart.

Taking a step back, he put space between them in case anyone was watching. How could he extricate himself without letting her know he realized how uncomfortable she was in his presence? "Well, if you're…"

She turned to him, eyes wide. "Look, Tim, I—"

"Gwen!"

The masculine shout came from the train.

Tim turned to face a man he'd thought he'd seen the last of. "I see you're here to meet Mr. Wright."

The man in question strode across the platform, eyeing Tim as if expecting a fight.

"Yes, but…"

"I'm sorry to make things awkward between you two once again. I'll go now." Time to bow out of this nonsense completely. He gave her a swift nod, unable to look her in the eyes, and pivoted, heading back to the mercantile.

Next time, he needed to tell Nolan, his mother, and anyone else who thought he was worth something that he couldn't stand the sight of Gwen. Maybe then they wouldn't insist he had a chance and bolster the hopes he'd been smart enough to keep tamped down.

Being unable to stomach looking at her wouldn't be a lie. If he turned now and saw her latched onto Eric's arm, his insides would lurch. It had always bothered him to see her strolling the boardwalks, clinging to men, fluttering her eyelashes, freely giving whoever had her attention that gorgeous smile.

But he didn't have to turn around to feel his stomach roil— Mrs. Tate's hawk-eyed stare was fastened onto something behind him. He glanced over his shoulder. Gwen was leading Eric off to the creek again.

Mrs. Tate gave Tim a knowing glance, her mouth pursed like that of an exasperated schoolmarm.

Would she attempt to force the pair to marry again? Considering she'd been peeved the last time her peculiar sense of morality hadn't been adhered to by all parties, she'd not go about it the same way twice.

Gwen and Eric disappeared into the prairie grasses without a backward glance.

He'd not be his father or Mrs. Tate and try to force a woman to do something she didn't want to do, but he couldn't do nothing either. Bo should know where Gwen was going and that Mrs. Tate was watching.

CHAPTER TWENTY-SEVEN

Gwen's stomach sank as she watched Tim walk off the station's platform. Could Eric's timing have been any worse? However, what she needed to say to both men shouldn't be said in front of the other. And she ought to talk to Eric first.

His telegram had announced he was coming for a visit, but she'd not received the message until he was already on his way. This time he'd addressed the missive to her, saying he couldn't wait to see her. If he'd decided against the two women who'd caught his eye in Denver and was here to patch things up, she wasn't interested.

"What's troubling you, Gwen?" Eric's inflections were once again as charming as he'd been last year.

She shoved a hand in her hair but then froze to keep from knocking out any pins—that had led to disaster last time. "I'm afraid your arrival caught me off guard, and I'm just—"

"I know I didn't give you much notice. But I'd like to start all over with you." He stepped in front of her and pulled a small box from his pocket. "I was going to give this to you later, but maybe this will show you how much I want this visit to turn out better."

Her body seized.

He took off the lid.

Earrings.

Her lungs restarted. Funny how months ago such a gift would've frustrated her, but now she felt only relief. She wrapped his hand back around the box. "Keep it."

Eric slowly pocketed the gift, his face wary.

"Let's walk." She needed to get out of the crowd so they could talk.

"Sure." Patting her hand as if the previous awkwardness had been erased, he led her away, chin high. His confidence had once been highly attractive, but now she found it pretentious. "The trip here took forever, but now with you on my arm..." He smiled down at her. "The miserable hours were worth it. You look beautiful."

Last year, his way with words had always made her feel like she could walk on air, but why did *she* make the hours of travel worth it? His every word could be used on any girl—and probably was. Did he not think Bo would have told her of his suspicions that he'd been attempting to court several girls in Denver?

Eric gave her a huge grin, though it wavered now—he'd probably expected her to have melted over the fact he'd returned for her. "I'd hoped you and your brother would've come down to visit me in Denver, but when you didn't—I realized how very much I missed you."

She pulled up a stem of prairie grass and bent it around her fingers. Might as well get this started. "I've had a rough time since you left—in more ways than one."

He grimaced. "I understand these country folk likely put you through the wringer, but I'd hoped—"

"The country folk have nothing to do with what I'm talking about."

"Oh?" His grin returned, lending him a roguish air.

Her heart had been broken enough times she never wanted to break someone else's, but something told her he'd not be half as upset as she'd been the last time he'd walked away. "Why did you come now?"

His head moved back. "To see you of course."

"Honestly?"

He sighed. "I know I didn't react well to what happened last time, but that doesn't mean I hadn't wanted things to go better. This time, let's stay away from your Mrs. Tate so nothing can derail us from enjoying each other's company."

"Do you actually plan to get to know me this time around?"

"What do you mean?"

"You've never asked me any real, deep questions. We've only ever sweet-talked and flirted."

"Why would you be mad about that?" He flung a hand out as if she were talking nonsense. "You flirted, too."

She blew out a breath. He was right. All her past actions would've told him she enjoyed such attentions.

"I'm guessing those old ladies at your church have made you think I was wrong for not marrying you on the spot, but I wasn't ready." He started them down the path toward the creek, and her stomach knotted.

If she'd still been enamored with him, she'd have clamped onto the fact he hadn't told her he didn't intend to marry her. But now, she couldn't help but compare his response to Tim's so many weeks back. With no money or house, with a struggling family to support on a measly salary, Tim was in no position to take on a wife. However, he'd considered her reputation worth protecting enough to marry her if she'd asked.

He also seemed to think she was worth getting to know rather than just "enjoying" her company. He had no designs on her, yet he knew her far better than Eric did.

Of course, it wasn't Eric's fault she and Tim had been forced to get to know one another. But even before they'd been kidnapped, when he'd crashed into her at the train station, he'd asked pointed questions and called her out for shallow answers.

He'd not simply flashed her a smile and told her she was beautiful.

If Tim wanted to marry a woman, he'd not waste a year small talking.

But what did Tim—a poor farmhand with a scourge of a last name and nothing in the way of looks—possess to attract a woman?

Everything Eric didn't have.

Loyalty. A desire to protect. Honor.

Eric had none of those in regard to her.

But were Tim's good qualities enough? Exchanging her tarnished last name for his wouldn't improve her standing. Her money might be all they'd ever have. Did she even have feelings for Tim, or was she just so struck by what he possessed that Eric lacked?

"What's wrong, Gwen?" Eric had stopped walking and let out an exasperated sigh.

She yanked up another shoot of long-stemmed grass and picked it apart. How did one tell a man she'd led him on for over a year? No, she hadn't led him on, she'd led herself on. They'd both wasted each other's time. She let out a bark of a laugh. "How stupid are we?"

"How's that?"

She threw down the stem and faced him. "I feel as if I've aged overnight, or rather the past fortnight. Like I've finally grown up."

He didn't ask what she meant.

Of course he didn't. He just wanted her to quit her crazy talk and get back to enjoying his "company," where they talked of nothing deep, shared none of their fears, trusting that their social graces and deep bank accounts would keep them from needing to know if they could weather hardships together.

But she knew for certain now that the kind of relationship they possessed was not the type upon which to stake her future happiness.

"It's time for us to move on, Eric. You and I are not meant to be."

She was no longer interested in being anyone's option.

Glancing into the mercantile as he mounted his horse, Tim noted Nolan was still talking to Raven. The Keys' wagon stood empty. And Bo was not inside.

Though Gwen may desire Eric's attentions, that didn't mean it was a good idea with Mrs. Tate watching. Bo ought to be informed of where his sister was, but he seemed to have disappeared.

Tim hesitated for a second but then hoisted himself up into the saddle and sped toward the McGill mansion. He wasn't telling everyone what Gwen was up to—as Mrs. Tate would—just someone who mattered. Gwen was a full-grown woman and should be able to do as she pleased, but it'd be better if she had someone with her—and it couldn't be him.

As he galloped up the mansion's driveway, he caught a glimpse of a man darting out from behind the woodpile and pulled up hard. He turned to catch whoever was sneaking around.

A pit formed in his stomach upon catching sight of the man's dark limp hair.

Father—stuffing something into the saddlebag on an unknown horse. Was he stealing from the McGills now?

At the sound of the horse's nicker, Father spun around, but his face quickly relaxed.

Tim pulled to a stop. "What are you doing here?"

"None of your business." Father turned back around to finish buckling the last strap on his bag. "Go home."

Tim moved to block his exit. "I asked what you were doing."

His father thrust out his jaw. "The young McGill promised

to give me a loan but then decided against it after I'd already promised someone the money."

"So you're stealing from him?"

"I'm helping him keep his word."

Tim clenched his reins. For years, he'd kept his father's shenanigans to himself in hopes of holding onto what little respect he'd earned for the family by not following in his father's footsteps. But he'd assumed his father's victims were merely fellow hoodlums and gamblers—not that it should've made a difference. "Put back whatever it was you took."

"McGill has plenty to spare."

"Wrong is wrong." Whether or not his family suffered, Father had to be held accountable. Tim dismounted. "Give it to me, and I'll return it."

Father grabbed his reins before Tim could. "Mind your own business, son."

"It is my business. What you do affects us all."

Quickly mounting, his father circled away. "Even if I toed the line, the lawmen around here have it out for me. So if you turn me in, they'll lock me up for nothing—and that'll hurt your ma. You don't want to do that."

What unreasonable hoops of logic had he jumped through to blame his thieving on lawmen?

Father acknowledged his silence with a nod. "Now move." Without waiting for Tim to do so, he rode off at breakneck speed.

As much as he wanted to give chase, should he?

He could pretend he'd seen nothing. Or he could do what was right, despite how his family might suffer—not that they were doing well at the moment by any stretch of the imagination. And why keep holding onto what little good was left in the O'Conner name when a man like Eric got everything he wanted with nothing but smooth words to his credit?

Tim rode quickly over to the stables, but Bo's horse wasn't there, so Tim raced toward Armelle, hoping the deputy was in town. Spotting Dent's roan near the marshal's office, he dismounted and rushed inside.

Dent's gaze snapped up from the papers laid across his desk. "What brings you in?"

"My father stole something from the McGills." Tim pulled off his hat and swiped the sweat from his brow with the back of his arm. "Can't tell you what he filched, but he didn't deny it when I caught him outside their place just now. Whatever he took, you'll want to get it back before he sells it. He's probably headed to Red Buttes through the gap pass. The mercantile owner there is as shady as he is."

Dent rose slowly, his expression wary. "Why would you turn in your own father?"

Did he think he was telling a story to set him up somehow? "Before now, I couldn't prove anything. And I hadn't..." *been so disturbed by my father's choice of victim before.*

Tim cleared his throat. "I'm afraid I've kept my suspicions to myself because he's family, but I can do so no longer. I'll help you track him down."

Dent tapped his fingers across his desk then grabbed his hat off a hook. "I suppose we better go."

As he followed Dent out of the office, Tim glanced up and down the street, seeing no sign of Bo, then looked toward the creek where Gwen had disappeared.

God, please help her stay safe and smart.

Though he'd kept his feelings for her secret, he'd thought he'd gotten through to her that Eric wasn't worth her time. But then, neither was he. He'd fancied himself better than Eric, but how many times had he not turned in his father? Why hate the other guy so much when he had plenty of his own faults?

Though his friends and mother might think him worthy of Gwen, he was so far from being so that it was laughable he'd believed them for a second.

Mounting his horse, he reined over to the deputy's roan. "I'm sorry I didn't report my suspicions earlier. I know the judge told me I wasn't supposed to keep knowledge of criminal activity to myself, but I feared I'd destroy my family."

"You aren't to blame for your father's choices." Dent seated himself in his saddle. "But you don't have to let those choices ruin your family. You're old enough to turn things around for them."

How could he shoulder more than he already did? But with Dent rushing off toward the gap pass, there was no time to think of how he'd survive more responsibility. Now was the time to follow through with what he should've done all along.

Miles later, slowing where the rocks littered the entrance to the gap, Dent pulled back to walk alongside him. "What are these other suspicions you mentioned? Is there something I should know before we confront your father?"

Tim readjusted his hat, keeping his eyes averted. "Just that I think he's stolen plenty of things over the years. Though lately he might be rustling. Not all the time, but if you find a cow or two missing—that could be my father. With how little food we have, my mother doesn't ask questions when he finally brings us something."

"Rustling isn't petty thievery. He could—"

"End up in big trouble, I know. But my brothers and sister have had so little to eat recently, so please don't fault my mother for cooking the beef. Father being sent to jail will be enough punishment for her. Not because he'll be gone, but when he gets back. He'll not be happy with me, but she's the easier target. You couldn't keep him locked up forever, could you?"

Dent slowed. "If he's going to retaliate, perhaps you should head home."

"I might as well face him now, let him know I plan to stand up to him from here on out." He had chastised Gwen for caving to the pressure of others, and though his father was a scary man to defy, that didn't give Tim a pass for choosing to look the other way. "If my father knows I'll no longer watch him steal, lie, and abuse, maybe he'll stop."

Dent doffed his hat to wipe his forehead. "I'm sorry I didn't know what was going on at your place."

"Not many do." Tim shook his head. "No law protects my mother from him, and she can't leave Father without heaping shame upon us all, especially in the eyes of some in town. All we can do is endure."

Dent rubbed his chin. "If that's your decision…"

At Tim's nod, Dent turned. "All right then."

Lord, please help me save my family from the firestorm I'm about to set off.

Miles later after passing through the gap, Dent pointed up ahead. On the next rise, a rider, definitely his father, kicked up dust. Giving chase, they were within fifty yards when Father glanced over his shoulder, wide-eyed and stiff. But when he caught sight of Tim, he slowed.

Would he surrender so easily?

Father tipped his hat to the deputy as they came alongside him. "Howdy."

Dent sat rigid in his saddle. "Get off your horse."

Father sent a quick glare toward Tim, his right hand slowly dropping to his side. "What's this all about, Deputy?"

Dent drew his gun. "Hands up and off the horse."

"What have you done, boy?" Father scowled at him as he dismounted. He turned to Dent with his hands up, shrugging as if he were baffled. "I don't know why you're coming after me. I didn't do nothing."

"Hand over your saddlebag."

"You can't go through my stuff."

"He can if someone's accused you of stealing." Tim kept his eye on him, despite Father's murderous glare making his insides quiver. "I told him you took things from the McGills."

Father hesitated a moment, but then shrugged again and tossed Dent the bag. "All you'll find is my wife's necklaces. I'm going to Red Buttes to sell them, but my boy here ain't fond of us selling stuff to pay for his bread and butter. He hasn't a clue how much it takes to keep everyone fed."

Tim dug his fingernails into his palms to keep from responding.

Dent pulled out several chains from the saddlebag. One necklace had something shiny and green dangling from it.

Tim didn't need to inspect them. Ma had never owned any jewels. "Those aren't my mother's."

"How would you know? You keep a record of your mother's things?" Father sneered at him before turning to the deputy. "Ask the missus yourself. Brenna will tell you they're hers."

"He's right. She'd cover for him. He'd slap her around if she didn't." Tim steeled himself for the coming onslaught.

Father's eyes narrowed. "You better think harder, son. Because then you'll remember they're hers, and if she doesn't get the money she wants from those…" He turned back to Dent. "She's always nagging me to bring in more money. She's never content. You try living with a woman like that. And Tim? He don't obey worth a lick. Thinks he's better than all of us."

"Oh, I've done my best to obey Ma, despite her begging me to cover for you more times than I can count. But she appeases you because she's trapped—but I no longer am."

"You don't know what you're doing, boy." His father's voice was a menacing growl.

Tim kept his chin up. For nearly two decades, he'd shrunk back when Father had given him that look, but he'd do so no longer.

But would Ma ever forgive him for the upheaval he'd just set into motion?

CHAPTER TWENTY-EIGHT

Gwen fidgeted in front of the O'Conners' door. She'd once again mustered up the courage to ride out, hardly breathing every time she crested a rise, worrying she might meet a stranger on the other side. After conquering all that anxiety, it'd be ridiculous to turn back without at least knocking, and yet she hesitated. The horse Tim had been riding lately was yanking up what little grass grew in their mud-filled yard, which meant he was here somewhere.

She'd not seen him since the day Eric had come to town. After she'd left Eric purchasing tickets to return to Denver and took some time to pray at the church, she'd caught a glimpse of Tim near the marshal's office. She'd headed his way but noticed Deputy Dent was escorting Tim's father inside in handcuffs.

Tim seemed to have seen her for a second, but she couldn't be certain. He'd ridden off without a backward glance.

She'd barely slept the last two nights worrying about Tim and his family.

Inside his house, a feminine voice was followed by a lower one, unmistakably Tim's.

She knocked and braced herself. Would he tell her how he

truly was—or respond with a 'fine, thanks' which wouldn't quench her worry at all?

Nobody answered. Had she knocked loud enough?

Maybe she should walk away. What could a spoiled rich girl say to ease their insecurities? Her father may be locked up as well, but his being so didn't cause her to worry about where her next meal would come from. She rubbed her sweaty palms against her embroidered shirtwaist.

The door creaked open, and Tim's mother stood there, eyebrows high.

Gwen wiped her hands again. This time, she had no books or pie to explain her appearance. "Uh…hello?"

His mother didn't respond, just looked at her, though her face had softened a little.

"I wanted to check on…Tim. He's not been at the Keys', you see. They told me he was home but didn't tell me why. I wondered if he'd been sick, or if everyone's sick, if I could bring food or…"

Tim's mother obviously wasn't ill, so now what was she going to keep prattling on about? *I saw your husband get thrown in jail and wondered how you all were doing with that?'* She shook herself. They wouldn't want to discuss that with her. Her shoulders drooped and she closed her eyes. She shouldn't have come.

"It's kind of you to inquire after us. No one's sick." Mrs. O'Conner stepped back, dragging the front door open wider. "But do come in."

"Oh." Her heart raced. She'd wanted to go in, right? To be assured Tim was doing well? He may not care that she cared, but she couldn't stop herself from doing so.

The house was tidier today. None of the younger children seemed to be about. And Tim sat in the one useful chair in the room, sporting a guarded expression.

"Please have a seat." Mrs. O'Conner walked farther into the room and cleared her throat at Tim, who stood to give Gwen his chair.

He was looking at her the same way he'd looked at her when Eric had shown up last. His eyes, which had always carried a little sparkle, even when he'd been annoyed by her, were flat and unfocused.

Upon taking her seat and him the bench, she forced herself not to stare at their feet.

"May I get you water?"

"Yes, please." She didn't need water, but she did need something to occupy her hands. Leaning forward, Gwen caught Tim's eye. "I'm so sorry."

"For what?"

"Your father."

His mother hesitated for a second, but then placed a glass of water in front of Gwen.

Tim cocked his head. "I didn't think you'd feel comfortable around us anymore."

"You think I'd blame you for your father's doings?"

Tim didn't nod, but he didn't have to.

"I know you well enough to know you weren't involved in stealing my mother's old necklaces—and we got them all back. I don't even know where he got them from, a trunk in the attic, I suppose. If it wasn't for you, we might not have known they were gone. We're grateful to you, not blaming you at all. You don't hold me accountable for what my father's done, do you?"

Tim seemed to breathe easier for a moment and gave her a slight shake of the head, but then his eyes dulled again and he turned to his mother. "Considering Dent can't keep Father long, we don't have much time to decide what you ought to—" He cringed. "I mean, what you *want* to do, if anything."

Gwen noted the subtle pleading in his voice. Had they been arguing earlier?

Mrs. O'Conner was pouring herself water, her shoulders hunched as if Tim's question had thrown a heavy blanket over her. But she didn't answer.

After a stretch of silence, Tim's gaze swung back to Gwen. "Do you know if Bo will press charges?"

He sounded as if he hoped her brother would. "Do you want him to?"

"I don't want to force anyone to do anything they don't want to."

Though he was looking at her, his tone suggested he was still talking to his mother. Maybe the worry that had driven her here wasn't ridiculous. "I could find out if you'd like."

He turned to his mother. "What do you want, Ma? *Really* want?"

Mrs. O'Conner took a drink but remained silent. Though she did seem to want something, her posture indicated she possessed no hope of receiving it.

What did she want that she couldn't have?

The O'Conners were looking at each other as if they'd forgotten Gwen was in the room. Never had she seen two people look so hopeless. "Are you in need of something? Could I help you get it?"

Tim shook his head. "I'm afraid once Father's out—well, I know my father appears harmless or maybe just annoying, but he's a good actor and sometimes…"

He let out a body-deflating sigh and turned to face her straight on, looking deep into her eyes. "I know this is none of my business, but I worry about you with Mr. Wright. Since he was more worried about himself than you at the church, I wonder how he treats you—or will treat you once no one's looking."

She glanced over at his mother, who seemed to have found her apron intriguing. "You don't have to worry about Mr. Wright. I told him I was no longer interested in his attentions. He's not at all like you."

Her vision went hazy and her hands began to sweat. Had she just said that out loud?

But Tim did nothing more than look away and fidget.

Tim's mother squeezed her shoulder, and Gwen nearly knocked over her water.

"It's nice of you to want to help." Mrs. O'Conner let out a soft sigh. "But I've thought this through many times before, and sometimes, you just have to live with the consequences of your choices."

Tim looked up at his mother with such a defeated look Gwen wished she could hug him.

He stood and, after snatching his hat off the table, headed out the door. "Excuse me."

Mrs. O'Conner watched him leave, her hand pressing harder atop Gwen's shoulder as if to keep her there.

When the door clicked into place, she turned to his mother. "I meant what I said about helping. Though my choices may have doomed me to be an old maid, I have resources you don't. And your son has done so much for me."

Mrs. O'Conner looked at her askance. "He was rather rude to you just now. Maybe you're giving him too much credit."

"No, I know how worried he is about your situation and how he wishes he could make things better. Whether you need a listening ear, money, shelter, a testimony in court, something for the children, I'd like to help."

Mrs. O'Conner's hand tightened on Gwen's shoulder. "Why would you offer all that?"

"Because if it weren't for Tim, I might've ended up in the same situation you're in. He spoke up when no one else did, forced me to think about what no one else had prodded me to notice." Gwen clasped onto both of Mrs. O'Conner's hands and waited for Tim's mother to frown down at her. "I know we're two different women. Yet nothing we've done, nothing we are, means we have to settle for being treated poorly. I want you to realize you are valuable—just as you are, just as am I. And if you need help to see that, I'm willing to provide it."

Mrs. O'Conner sank down onto the bench. "I'm grateful a woman like you thinks of me that way, but I'm not—"

"God thinks highly of you, Mrs. O'Conner, and His opinion ranks higher than anyone else's—mine, Tim's, even your husband's. He doesn't care what I have and what you don't—but He does ask those that have resources to share them. So if you need to, you can show up anytime on my doorstep. We've got room, money, connections. We can help you get wherever you'd like to go."

Tim's mother's eyes grew wide. "You'd be willing to let us stay at your place? The mansion?" She said that as if they lived in a castle.

Breathing easier, Gwen nodded. Though their house was the best in the county, it seemed Tim's mother had never been to a big city and seen the houses in truly nice neighborhoods.

"Could we, Ma?"

From behind the stacked firewood by the stove, Tim's sister poked her head out, her face smudged with dirt, holding the book Gwen had given her days ago.

"I thought I told you to go play outside. You'll ruin your eyes reading all the time."

"Ma, please. If Tim's why Pa's in jail and he gets out and comes home and Tim's not here…" Molly's eyes were large and anxious.

"Everything will be fine." Mrs. O'Conner held out her arms to her daughter, who crawled willingly into her lap. Mrs. O'Conner peered over Molly's head at Gwen but said nothing.

It'd be best to leave and let them ponder things without her around. Gwen stood. "If you think of anything I could do for you, let me know."

Molly looked up with hopeful eyes, but Mrs. O'Conner's face stayed passive. "Thank you."

Had the woman's voice come out rough because she was about to cry, or was she uncomfortable having someone so clueless trying to advise her?

What did she know, anyway? Only weeks ago, she'd thought she knew what was best for herself, but thankfully Eric hadn't given her the chance to make the choice she would've made.

Looking around her, at the broken cabinetry, the spoiled potatoes, Molly's sad face—being an old maid with money would be far better than marrying the wrong man. Mr. Wright had definitely been...

Mr. Wrong.

Gwen pressed a hand to her mouth. When Tim had called himself that the day they'd been kidnapped, she'd just thought he was making a play on Eric's name. Maybe Tim also needed to hear what she'd just told his mother about paying more mind to God's opinion than anyone else's. For Tim was not as wrong for her as she'd once thought.

But was Tim her Mr. Right?

In this house, she saw firsthand how marrying Mr. Wrong could not only destroy a woman's life but adversely affect the lives of their children.

"I'm sorry." Realizing she still stood there with Mrs. O'Conner and Molly staring at her, Gwen waved goodbye. "I'll go now. Feel free to come see me anytime."

Walking out into their mud yard, she noted Tim's horse was gone and her shoulders slumped. She hugged herself as she headed toward her buggy. She'd practically told him she'd turned away a suitor because the man hadn't been him, but Tim hadn't acted pleased by her admission, nor had he waited outside to talk to her about what she might have meant.

And what had she meant? What exactly were her feelings toward him, anyway?

CHAPTER TWENTY-NINE

"Miss."

Gwen burrowed deeper into her pillow.

"Miss!"

Forcing her eyes to open, she peered through the darkness to where their youngest maid stood in her bedroom doorway. Miss Childress's head and lamp were poking into the room from behind the half open door.

Gwen scooted up against her headboard. The book she'd fallen asleep reading crashed to the floor. "What is it?" Her voice came out rough. She couldn't have been asleep but a few hours.

"You're needed in the parlor."

She checked the clock, barely illuminated by Miss Childress's light. "It's two in the morning."

"Yes, miss." The maid continued to whisper, as if doing so would make up for the inconvenient hour. "Mr. Harrison has gone to wake your brother, but the family downstairs said you'd told them they could come whenever they needed."

She ran her hand along the braid draped over her shoulder. Family? A yawn overtook her. What family...? She straightened. "The O'Conners?"

"Yes, miss. You awake now?"

"Yes, yes." She waved agitatedly at her maid and swung her legs over the bed. She let her body adjust to the sudden movement before picking up the fallen book and retrieving her wrapper.

Following Miss Childress downstairs, she rubbed at her eyes. She had indeed told the O'Conners they could come at any time, but two a.m. was an hour that belonged to the devil.

By the time she made it to the landing, the desire to grumble had faded and she started smoothing her hair—though if Tim's family felt compelled to come at this hour, they likely didn't care what she looked like.

The maid preceded her into the parlor, her lamplight revealing the whole O'Conner clan sitting on the sofa. "Miss Childress, why did you leave our guests in the dark? Fire up the—"

"Gwen." The soft voice that uttered her name made her heart race. If it weren't for the time of night and his entire family sitting there, she might've thought the tenderness she'd heard was directed at her rather than simply an attempt to be quiet.

Tim sat in a chair, holding one of his brothers in his lap. "We asked her not to light the lamps. I wanted to avoid alerting anyone to our arrival."

"We're sorry to disturb your sleep," Mrs. O'Conner started.

"I'm the one responsible, Miss McGill." Tim's voice had returned to his usual aloof tone.

Gwen shook her head. "No need for apologies, just let me know what I can do for you."

"I'd hoped my family could hide here for a few days. Can your servants be trusted to keep their presence a secret?"

"We wouldn't keep Miss Childress and the others if we didn't trust them." She turned to her maid. "As requested, say nothing to anyone outside the household. Please ready the guest rooms."

Once the maid lit another lamp for herself and left, Gwen moved farther into the room. Their arrival under cover of darkness didn't bode well. "I'm afraid my brother might be grumpy when he comes down. He's hardly been home, so I haven't yet told him of my offer."

Mrs. O'Conner hunched around the toddler in her lap and looked to Tim.

Gwen held out a hand. "Don't worry, he just isn't a person who wakes up well."

Tim tugged on his long hair. "You're certain he'll be all right with this? If he's the kind to think a woman ought to stay with her husband even if he…" Tim stood abruptly, placed his brother in the empty chair, and gestured for her to follow him into the hallway. "Come with me."

Gwen hesitated, but decided to take the lamp with her, plunging the family into darkness.

He stopped halfway down the hall, then turned and slumped against the wall. "I don't want to talk about this in front of the children more than I have to."

"I understand."

"I'm now thinking this was the wrong decision. Or maybe the right one, but I've gone about it wrong."

"If you're worried about inconveniencing us, don't. My brother will be fine."

In the lamplight, she could almost imagine Tim was looking at her tenderly—but that had to be because they were both tired.

"I went by the jail yesterday to see how my father was doing. He's blaming Ma for landing him in there instead of me. Everything's always my ma's fault, and since this time it clearly isn't, I —" Tim swallowed and stared across the hall as if he could see through the walls toward the jail. "She mentioned they'd had a huge fight the day before he was caught. Neither of us feels certain he won't hurt her when he gets out, whenever that happens."

"How often does he hurt her?"

He shook his head. "He's physically intimidated all of us too many times to count. I've seen him shove her, but...I'm not sure Ma tells me about anything I don't see." He turned tired eyes to her. "If you fear someone you love might hurt you, something's not right. I can't ignore what we're both fearing, but I'm sorry to have brought you into this mess."

She squeezed his arm with her free hand. "Don't be. I knew my offer to your family might get messy."

A creak on the stairs alerted them to Bo's presence. Thankfully, he only appeared groggy, not murderous. He glanced at Tim then back to her. "What's going on?" He yawned while rubbing a hand over his face.

She moved over to him to keep her voice down. "I hadn't the chance to tell you yet, but I told Tim's mother if she ever needed anything, she could come to us. With Mr. O'Conner being released soon, they'd like to stay here a while."

"Of course, whatever they need." He gave her upper arm a squeeze and walked past her into the parlor, beckoning for Tim to follow.

Mrs. O'Conner stood, still clinging to her youngest, as if she might lose him if she didn't clamp onto him hard. "I'm sorry to wake you, Mr. McGill. Your sister told me she hadn't time to let you know of her offer for us to come if we felt the need. If we're inconveniencing you..."

Bo gestured for her to sit and pulled a rocking chair over for himself. "Whatever Gwen promised, I'll do my best to fulfill."

"Thank you." Mrs. O'Conner sank back onto the sofa. John was sprawled out by her feet, curled around a knapsack, and Molly tucked herself up next to her mother.

Bo lit the lamp beside him. "What is it you need?"

Tim stepped farther into the room. "Once Father is free and finds them missing, we're hoping he just blusters and fusses for a while, but we're afraid he'll be livid about being left to fend for himself. We only need a place to stay long enough to decide where to go, and well…"

He glanced at his mother, who was rocking the youngest in her arms since he'd awakened and whined about being hot. Tim moved closer to crouch beside Bo and whispered, "My mother's prayed for things to get better, but they never do. If she decides to return home, she needs to do so before he's out, before the children's hopes go up, before he realizes she even thought to betray him. But this is the first time she's ever considered leaving —because of Gwen's offer, I'm sure—and it proves how scared she really is."

Bo leaned forward, keeping his voice low. "What do we do if she wants to go home?"

Tim sighed. "I think she finally believes she doesn't have to live with what he puts her through. I don't want to tell her what to do, she's dealt with that enough, but I want to be sure she has all the opportunity she can to do as she pleases."

Gwen rubbed her hands together. She might not be able to help these two figure out the details, but she had at least one useful skill—hospitality. "Considering the hour, may I suggest we get some rest and talk in the morning?" She turned to Mrs. O'Conner. "Would that be all right with you?"

Tim's mother gave her a wan smile and stood, this time with Patrick hanging loose and heavy in her arms. Molly crouched down to wake the twins.

"Would you like us to put all the mattresses in the same room?"

"Oh, Miss McGill, that'd be too much work."

"If it will help you all sleep better, we'll do it."

Mrs. O'Conner's eyes glistened as she gave a slight nod.

Finding their butler in the hallway, Gwen gave him directions for preparing the room and for breakfast in the morning.

Tim's mother scuffled behind her, guiding Molly with a hand to her shoulder. The twins tagged behind, clinging to her skirts.

"Just follow Mr. Harrison." Gwen put a hand on the railing and gestured for them to head up without her. "If you don't care how the room looks, they'll carry in the mattresses so you can go straight to sleep."

Ma gave her a nod as she prodded Molly to start up the stairs. "Thank you for your kindness, Miss McGill."

She gave Tim's mother a reassuring pat then turned to Tim, who'd exited the parlor with Bo. "I don't figure you want us to drag your mattress into their room. It'd be far too crowded, but we can if you'd like."

He shook his head. "Thank you, but I'm not staying. In fact, I'm not even returning. I don't want to accidentally lead my father here."

Her chest clamped hard. "Not come back? Then you'd—" She bit her lip to keep from continuing. Her voice had sounded panicky.

Her brother arched his eyebrows at her.

She shook her head. "If you're worried about your mother's decision making, wouldn't you need to see her? Talk to her?"

"That's part of the reason I brought her to you."

"To me?"

"If I can't be with her, you're the next best thing."

"But you've questioned my judgment so many times."

"But I've seen you make good decisions lately—and you're brave, I know that firsthand. My mother hasn't made any big decisions in a long time, and she's got a scary one to make. I'm sure you'll be able to encourage her more than I can."

He thought her capable of helping his mother after the mess she'd made of her own life? "I'll try my best."

He squeezed her hand. "I know." He took a step back as if to leave, but his fingers scrunched around hers tighter. The look in his eyes held so much concern, she could almost feel it.

Bo cleared his throat.

Tim let go of her and his eyes shuttered, then he turned to Bo. "Thank you for keeping them," he said, his voice cracking.

Bo held out his hand toward the kitchen. "I assume you'd prefer to leave through the back?"

Before Tim could answer, Gwen stepped between them. "Why don't we come up with a project to hire you for, so you can check on your family without raising suspicion?" She looked to her brother. "We could pay him to redo something in the garden, or—"

Tim held up a hand. "That won't be necessary. I don't need to be here, I trust—"

"But what if I need you here?"

Tim froze. He searched her eyes.

Yes, I *want you here.*

She moved toward him, but he stepped back, shook his head, and then took a deep breath. "Of course, I shouldn't place all the burden of my family on you. I'll find an excuse to come check on them occasionally. Good night."

He only thought she wanted him here because his family was a burden? "Tim, that's not what I—"

Bo's hand gripped her arm and gave her a short, fast squeeze. "There are servants and children in need of sleep. I'll meet with Tim sometime this week. After the news of his family's disappearance gets around, no one will question my desire to help him. We can discuss ways for him to visit then."

"Sounds good." Tim tipped his hat to her and then disappeared down the hallway with Bo.

Not once did he look back.

The clock chimed the half-hour. The house was quiet. How would she ever get to sleep with her stomach churning over why Tim still seemed so intent on being in her presence as little as possible?

Of course, her difficulty sleeping was a minor discomfort in light of what ailed the O'Conners. Though Tim might not think much of her, he at least trusted her to care for his family when he couldn't. So she'd make sure they were all settled and double-check that Cook would be ready for extra people in the morning. The least she owed Tim was to follow through on her promise to his mother.

If only he wasn't content with so little from her.

CHAPTER THIRTY

With the fairytale book she'd found in the attic in hand, Gwen descended the basement stairs to where Mrs. O'Conner had been canning and doing laundry the past week. The children were with her since she'd insisted they were too much of a burden for Gwen to watch, despite the foursome being a rather sedate group after being told they couldn't play outside or even look out the windows.

Hopefully new stories for Molly to read aloud would cheer them up.

They also seemed to be missing Tim as much as she was. Though Bo had offered him legitimate ways to visit, Tim had decided against coming. Her mind kept insisting he was doing so to avoid her, though of course he did so to protect his family.

A small giggle sounded far off, like it was deep underground.

Turning left instead of going to the washroom, she made her way to the unfinished section, where odds and ends were discarded and forgotten.

Another little laugh made her smile. Maybe they didn't need a new book after all.

In the corner of the cavernous space, the children had scratched a game of hopscotch into the lumpy dirt floor. Mrs.

O'Conner watched them from her seat on a broken cask. Though the room only had one slender horizontal window up near the ceiling, they seemed to be enjoying themselves.

The day after their father had been released, she'd wondered if Mrs. O'Conner would return home considering how she'd paced the floors. But after he'd been out of jail several days and not shown up at the mansion, she'd settled down enough to sit on occasion.

When Bo had learned Mr. O'Conner hadn't bothered to report them missing or organize a search party but had instead chosen to spend an evening badmouthing his wife at the saloon, Tim's mother had quit pacing altogether.

Gwen had become concerned Mrs. O'Conner would do something drastic since she'd ceased doing much at all. But after a few days, Mrs. O'Conner had marched to Bo's office and given him a list of places the family might go that she wanted Bo to discuss with Tim the next time they talked.

"I found another book Molly might enjoy." Pulling a broken chair toward Mrs. O'Conner, Gwen handed her the collection of fairytales before gingerly testing her seat.

The older woman ran her fingers over the gold stamped cover. "I'm sure she will. We'll read a story morning, noon, and night so we can get through it before we leave."

"She can keep it."

Mrs. O'Conner held up a hand. "You've given her enough books. You ought to keep some for your own children."

"But if I never marry, what good is a book that lies about unenjoyed?"

Mrs. O'Conner pressed the book back into Gwen's lap. "You're too young to be worrying about becoming an old maid."

Gwen let out a short sigh. "If you knew what I've tried in hopes of getting married so I could move away, it might be more worrisome than you think. Of course, I'm glad I didn't succeed." She shrugged and turned to watch the children. No reason to bring up how she feared her choice might have ended up with her hiding in someone's basement just like them. Though Eric hadn't seemed to be a monster, how would she have known? "Tell me if this is too personal, but how can you tell if the person your heart is pulling you toward is the right one for you? Did you ignore any worrisome signs when you met your husband, or is it all just chance?"

After a minute of silence, Mrs. O'Conner put a hand on Gwen's knee. "The first thing you ought to do is stop fretting so much about getting married. When you're desperate, you're likely to fall for the first man who pays you any attention. Now, that doesn't mean those who marry their first loves are doomed, but you're more apt to excuse unacceptable behavior if you're worried he's the only man who'll ever want to walk you down the aisle."

That was exactly what had gotten her into trouble. Gwen folded her hands in her lap and tried not to beat herself up over it. *Lord, thank you for saving me from myself.*

Mrs. O'Conner's lips curled into a weak smile as she stared off into space. "In the beginning, Alan was attentive and charming. I'd been amazed he'd noticed me, and I worked hard to make him happy. Now, I'm not saying it's wrong to make the man you're in love with happy, but you should pay attention if you start making excuses for how he treats you because no one understands him like you do. Thinking over my life these last few days, I see that I gave up everything, friends and family even, because I had to be ready to do as he bid, and the good times…"

She turned to face Gwen. "When the good times start getting farther apart, and whenever they do come along, you find yourself not enjoying them because you know, at some point or another, it'll all come crashing down because he'll get upset with you again…that started subtly and only grew after we married."

She chewed on her lip before turning to Gwen. "I love my

children. I try to choose what's best for them, but that means someone doesn't always get what they want—sometimes that's me, sometimes that's them. But my husband's happiness is vital. Otherwise, we're all miserable."

She pinched her lips together and shook her head. "So much of my life has been spent scrambling to do his bidding to avoid his anger, fixing the flaws he constantly pointed out about me—as if things would improve if I only learned to be a better wife. So I suppose if you feel you have to do what he wants or you'll lose him, that's a warning. Especially if you know, deep down, that you'll fail to do something to his satisfaction sooner or later. And when he's unhappy with you, you take his every insult to heart. Because why else would a man who loves you treat you so poorly unless you earned such treatment?"

Mrs. O'Conner finished on a whisper, a single tear running down her cheek.

Gwen clasped the older woman's hand and held on tight.

After a moment, Mrs. O'Conner swiped at her eyes with her free hand. "Anyway, back to your question." She let out an apologetic huff. "Find a man who doesn't need you to make him happy—even if that's not my son. Don't feel as if you have to consider him because he's loved you since grade school or because he saved your life—though I'm happy you told me he did so and that he treated you well. But definitely don't marry out of obligation. You have to be happy, too."

Gwen's lungs stopped. Had Mrs. O'Conner just said Tim loved her? No, she must've misunderstood. Prior to her brother forcing her out to the Keys' ranch, Tim had practically been nonexistent in her life. He'd mentioned all the other boys had liked her in school, but he'd clearly said he hadn't...hadn't he? "You don't mean Timothy?"

One side of Mrs. O'Conner's face scrunched up. "Well, yes. My other boys are far too young for marrying."

"But Tim?" She let her mouth hang agape. "Are you sure?"

Mrs. O'Conner pulled her hand from Gwen's. "Of course,

he realizes you'd not stoop to consider him. But I thought you were feeling you ought to after what you two went through and your question."

Gwen placed a hand on the older woman's arm. "You say he thinks I wouldn't 'stoop'?"

Mrs. O'Conner pressed her steepled hands against her lips. "That ain't his word for it. I'm sorry, I didn't mean to say something so unbecoming of you. You've treated us as equals without acting high and mighty. Which I hadn't expected, and—"

"No apology necessary. It's not as if I'm known for thinking much beyond myself."

Mrs. O'Conner gave her a crooked smile. "But that's not true, is it?"

"Probably not." She shrugged. "I've always tried to please whoever I'm with. Though I've never been able to please your son."

"I'm surprised to hear that. He's never said a bad thing about you."

Thankfully Tim was kind enough to keep his critical opinions of her to himself.

"Momma!" One twin limped over, a hand clamped on his knee. "I hurt myself."

"Let me see." After a quick inspection, she gave him a kiss, and pulled him onto her lap.

Unable to continue their conversation with John there, Gwen made an excuse about checking on dinner, left the fairytales for Molly to find, then retreated into the stairwell.

Once the basement door closed behind her, she slumped against the wall.

Tim *loved* her?

But then why did he act indifferent?

Of course, she might've ruined any feelings he'd had for her in grade school with her flirtatious ways. Or maybe he'd seen how bad of a rancher's wife she'd make and decided against her.

Perhaps he did think himself below her consideration, as his mother mentioned.

Though why *wouldn't* he think himself below her after she'd practically said so right in front of him while arguing with her brother?

She pressed her palms against the heat filling her face.

Rushing up the rest of the stairs and grabbing her parasol, she found the butler and ordered her buggy to be brought round. She then forced her clammy hands into her riding gloves. No one would think it strange for her to visit Mrs. Key and inquire after her health. Hopefully Tim would be there. If the feelings his mother said he had were still alive, maybe there'd be a chance...

A chance of what?

Even if he did like her for who she was, could she marry him? Buttoning her gloves, she blew out a breath. She didn't have to decide anything right now. She only hoped to discern if she'd misinterpreted his feelings.

When the buggy pulled up beneath the mansion's small portico, her heart half pulled her back, half pushed her forward.

How different her feelings were the first time this buggy had been pulled around to head out to the Keys'. This time, instead of railing at her brother in her head, she was about to jump out of her skin at the thought that Tim might ... *love* her.

Concentrating on keeping her mind blank so she didn't make herself go crazy, she somehow made it to the Keys' main gate, though she couldn't remember taking the turn to get there. She didn't see anyone in the fields. Then she heard the slam of the coop door and her heart banged just as hard at the sight of Tim backing out, scattering corn at his feet.

He glanced her way and his face paled. He dropped his bucket and leaped over the gate.

Her skin flushed both hot and cold as she watched him run

to her. But his expression, the speed of her wagon…he probably thought something was terribly wrong.

How could you do that to him, Gwen? She slowed the horse. Nothing was wrong other than how nauseated she felt at the thought of talking to him again—which had never happened before.

"Is everything all right?" he called out as he ran toward her.

Since Rascal had poked his head out of the barn, she couldn't reassure him as much as she needed to. "Yes. How's Mrs. Key?"

Tim stopped beside her wagon, his jaw tight, but then it looked as if he was forcing himself to relax. His eyes narrowed at her.

I know, I wasn't supposed to come out here. But I had to.

He sighed. "I'm afraid this isn't the best time to see her. She's usually napping now."

She put a hand to her head. "I should've known. Is she doing better?"

He gestured toward the house. "You're welcome to wait in the parlor to see her, or I could go ask Nolan—"

"Oh no, that's all right. I'll wait. However, since it'll be a while, would you mind taking a walk with me?"

Tim glanced toward Rascal. The old man loosed an exaggerated sigh, then turned his back on them and stomped away.

Tugging at his collar, Tim turned back to her. "I guess we can take a short walk, but we can't be long."

"Of course." And now the feeling of her skin wanting to wriggle off made it nearly impossible for her to let go of the reins and put her hand in his. "How about we walk to the flowerbeds behind the cabin?"

He helped her down and took her arm. Could he feel how she was trembling?

Once they were away from the house, Gwen let out a big exhale. "I'm sorry about racing out here like that. I didn't realize until I saw your face the panic it would cause. Everything's fine with your mother. She's still determined to leave town, talking with Bo every day about the places she could go. And to keep people from getting suspicious, he's slowly gathering information on the towns they're considering."

"Is she leaning toward one place over another?"

"Not that I know of." She turned to face him. "Why can't you and Bo come up with a way for you to talk to her yourself?"

He pulled his hat off, ran his fingers through his damp hair, then smashed it back on. "Bo can help her decide where to go better than me."

"But don't you want to have a say in where she goes since you'll—" Her body went numb. "Since you'll be going with them?"

How had she not realized that before?

He stared out at the horizon. "I'm not sure I will."

She ignored the hopeful tremors inside of her. She shouldn't be happy about a family being torn apart. "Why not?"

"I have to be certain Father doesn't notice her leaving."

"And if he doesn't? Then you'd move?"

He licked his lips and kept his gaze pinned on the ridge enshrouded by a summer haze of pollen. "At some point, I suppose." He gave her a sad smile. "Can't live the rest of my life here. You and I both feel the same in that regard."

Leave Armelle? And she'd just thought she'd found a reason to stay. "Nothing would keep you here?"

He shrugged and kicked at a rock. "Not once the inevitable happens."

"What's the inevitable?"

He glanced at her, like he was going to tell her, but then looked toward the house and frowned. "I need to get back to work. Rascal needs me."

She turned to see what had caught his attention. The older ranch hand was tossing hay bales, but she had a feeling Tim was scrambling for an excuse to get away from her again. "Do you really find me so unbearable you can't talk with me more than a few minutes?"

"I didn't mean to make you feel that way." A frown marred his face. "All this time, I've prided myself on not being like my father—"

"You're not."

"But if I've made you feel worthless..."

She blinked, her eyes suddenly hot. "Not all the time," she whispered. Sometimes he even made her feel as if he believed in her more than anyone else ever had.

"Let me be clear." He put a hand on both of her shoulders. "I've seen how you care for others. I've seen how hard you work. Even your tendency to latch onto things and pursue them until the bitter end can be a considered a good thing. So many people don't follow through, and that's not you. You believe me?"

"Yes, but—"

"Excuse me."

Gwen startled at Rascal's voice. When had he arrived?

The older man wiped the sweat from his brow and gave her a nearly toothless smile. "Sorry to steal him back, but Nolan hasn't returned, and we gotta get this hay to the Crawfords' before dinner."

Tipping his hat at her, Tim bid her goodbye and strode up the slight incline with his fellow ranch hand.

She hugged herself, replaying all he'd said, just now and over the last month. Walking back slowly, she watched him toss the hay bales that Rascal had thrown out of the loft onto the wagon. With each toss, he grew dirtier and more disheveled, working hard to support a family his father had dumped onto his shoulders.

Why had she ever thought a man's wealth and position were the most important things to take into consideration when looking for a husband? A man of integrity might lose everything he had, but he could still be counted on.

When Tim kneeled to grab another bale, she imagined him

going down on one knee and looking up at her with those serious hazel eyes of his.

Her heart stilled.

If he proposed, she'd say yes. Not because he could give her the kind of life she'd been chasing after, but because she knew he'd not propose just because he'd finally decided she was the woman who'd fit his life best—but because he wanted her in it desperately.

Of course, people in town like Mrs. Tate…

She swallowed against a dry throat. There was no question what Mrs. Tate and her ilk would say if she and Tim walked down the boardwalk together arm in arm.

Well, the only person's opinion she cared about was her brother's, and she had a good idea what he'd think.

Seemed Tim's mother wasn't the only one who needed Bo's help in figuring out what to do next.

CHAPTER THIRTY-ONE

In the marshal's office, Bo plopped the keys into Tim's hand and held them there as if afraid Tim would give them back—and he just might. Last week, when Deputy Dent had come out to the Keys' ranch and asked him about filling the marshal position, he'd figured at some point he'd wake from his childhood dream of wearing a badge that would enable him to stop his father from abusing his mother.

Why had Bo prodded the council to offer him the job when he'd not asked for it? He wasn't qualified; he knew nothing about the law, and yet, he hadn't been able to turn down an opportunity to provide more for his family. Though Ma and the kids had disappeared to Laramie last week, he'd not sent them with much money. Hopefully he could send more once he figured out how to do so without arousing suspicion. With their only contact being someone Bo had come to know last year as he'd worked to give back stolen land to their rightful owners, Tim had to trust both Bo and God that they were in good hands. Considering the Alperns were no one he or his father had any connection to, they ought to be safe from being dragged back home.

Of course, Gwen likely had something to do with his getting

hired, too. He glanced over to where she stood at the end of the line of councilmen who waited to congratulate him, though they probably would've hired anyone who could've hit the broadside of a barn at twenty paces and was willing. He'd met with the deputy several times the past two weeks to go over the laws and learn the expectations of the position. Most of the job wasn't difficult, or even exciting. Checking streetlamps, road maintenance, corralling loose farm animals. All things he could do, but thinking about apprehending criminals made him feel like a fool for agreeing to this.

Deputy Dent nodded as he walked up to him, looking happy to see Tim with the keys. Though the man wanted a break, did he really want someone twenty years his junior in charge?

Dent's heavy hand landed on his shoulder. "If you realize I've forgotten to tell you something, feel free to come out and ask. Or you can wait until my next rotation. Congratulations, Marshal O'Conner."

The title sounded foreign and clunky. At least the deputy wasn't quitting. He'd been patient with him as he'd gone over his duties and had made him feel as if he might last longer than a few months.

Looking at the council, Tim tried to come up with something to say in gratitude, but the bile rising in his throat made him clamp his lips together and just nod at them all. Hopefully they thought he was merely overwhelmed rather than feeling sick.

Mr. Robertson broke the awkward silence and moved forward. "We have faith in you."

At least someone did. Tim pumped his hand with the strongest grip he could muster.

The next man came up and said something, but focusing on what he was saying was difficult since Gwen was waiting for him down the line.

Tim moved to the next man. If only they hadn't made such

a big deal out of hiring him. For what if he failed within the week?

Finally, he shook Gwen's hand and released her quickly. She was dressed in white, making the pink in her cheeks all the more alluring. The longer he looked, the harder it'd be to turn away.

Stepping back, he scanned the men, having a hard time meeting their eyes but forcing himself to do so. "I'm grateful for the opportunity to work for you." He glanced at the corner bookshelf full of law books. "I've got lots of reading to do and plenty of papers awaiting, so I best get started."

A round of encouragement circled the room as they all headed for the door, several giving him reassuring thumps as they passed.

"Don't work too late," Deputy Dent said as he put his hat back on. "The town's made do with me. They'll continue making do with you until you're up to speed."

"Thanks." Tim moved to his chair, a swirl of panic assaulting him as he took in the stacks haphazardly piled on the desk. Files on recent arrests. Routine town inspections that were long overdue. Supplies that needed ordering. He forced out a slow exhale. If Dent was this far behind and the councilmen hadn't fired him, perhaps he shouldn't be too concerned.

Gwen's dainty footsteps made him look up. She hadn't left?

She set a wrapped box on top of a pile of papers.

"You didn't have to get me anything."

"I know." She pushed the present closer.

Guess he had to open it. He tore the paper, and a picture frame emerged. Behind the glass was an embroidered verse, lopsided, but colorful: "...and what doth the Lord require of thee, but to do justly, and to love mercy, and to walk humbly with thy God?"

He set it down and offered her a weak smile. "Thank you. A good reminder."

She smiled back. "You seem overwhelmed."

He gave her a slight nod. He didn't trust himself to answer

with words, for he might be tempted to tell her this job was a mistake.

"Could you share with me what's worrying you? You bolstered me when I was afraid, maybe I could encourage you."

"I just can't believe you and your brother convinced the councilmen to give me this position."

She moved to perch on the edge of his desk. "The position's been vacant for a year, so why shouldn't you have a chance? Besides, it's a great excuse to travel to Laramie on occasion. Makes more sense for a marshal to visit the city than a ranch hand."

"True, but you should've considered if I was capable of doing the job, rather than how the position would benefit me."

She chuckled. "Jacob always griped he was more of a janitor than a lawman."

Hearing her call the former marshal by his first name with that twinkle in her eye made his heart clench. Jacob had been one of the few men he'd felt all right with her marrying—though that hadn't stopped him from being relieved when Jacob had married Annie last year.

He shook his head, mostly to shake away the jealousy trying to eat him up over something that had never happened. "Maybe so, but it's not the whole of the job."

She pointed to the embroidered words. "You've proven you can mete out justice and mercy. With how you turned in your father, with what you're doing to protect women and children. That's the type of man who'll watch out for the best interests of our citizens."

"That's kind of you to say, and I'm fortunate to be able to curb my father now, but given I'm in this position and know about Daniel…"

"You'll figure it out."

He sighed. If only whatever he figured out was certain to be the right thing. "Guess I can't know unless I try."

"That's right." She smiled brightly. "Time will tell."

"I'll agree to that." He pulled a stack of papers toward him. Though he sort of enjoyed the torturous way she looked like an angel perched on his desk just like that year she'd sparkled atop the school piano, she ought to head out before she distracted him from working at all.

"Now that you've got this position, you won't be thinking about moving away anymore, right?"

He blinked up at her. Why was she wondering about that?

"You know, if the *inevitable* happens?"

His stomach sank at the thought, though she couldn't possibly know he'd been referring to her getting married. That she even remembered that part of their conversation made him squirm. He'd let his tongue wag far too much that day. "I want to do right by the council, so I'll stay if they let me, but the future is never certain. Anything could happen. And it's not like I'm married to the job."

"Good, because I'd rather you be married to me."

The pumping rush of his heart drowned out the sound of birds fighting outside the window. He blinked at her, but she was looking at him as if she'd said nothing out of the ordinary.

Surely she hadn't—his brain had just malfunctioned. Probably wasn't worth having her repeat though, so he nodded since she seemed to be waiting for a response. He then stared blankly at the top page of the pile in front of him, trying to breathe again. "I guess you're right. I better get started."

"Did you not hear what I said?" Her smile had dulled.

He chuffed. "Apparently, I didn't, because what I heard didn't make sense."

"I said I'm glad you don't feel married to this job. Because although I hope you enjoy it, if something gets to have your utmost loyalty, I want it to be me. The moment you propose, I'll say yes."

The bile that had pressed up earlier pushed higher into his throat. She *had* said what he thought. But the thought was pure fantasy, like a story in one of Molly's books. He'd not even gotten up the courage to ask her on a walk again since Mr. Wright had left. Had determined never to ask her. He had too much work to do on himself to keep her from being free to court the man God would bring around for her at some point or another.

Gwen leaned forward and looked at him with narrowed eyes. "Are you all right? You look ill."

He might truly double over at any moment. "I don't feel well, actually. I need some air."

She glanced over his shoulder. "The windows are open."

"Cold air."

She cocked her head. "It's summer."

He stood, knocking down his chair, but he didn't bother to pick it up in case that might release the surging bile. "Excuse me."

And with that, he was out the door, heading toward the butcher's. Surely with all the meat, the man had an ice room or something.

Gwen's footsteps sounded behind him, but he plowed into the store and caught Mr. Hancock's eye. "I'm here to do an inspection." It needed to be done. No time like the present, he supposed.

Martin frowned, his hands stilling atop the butcher paper he'd been rolling.

"Marshal duties."

The man continued to stare at him without protest as Tim headed to the back.

"Mr. Hancock," Gwen said from behind Tim. "There's been no complaint. Don't worry. He's just eager to start. You've heard the councilmen gave him the job, right? He's only…"

Not interested in the rest of Gwen's attempt to explain his sudden need for ice, he entered the back room and found a door leading into cold air. Hanging meat lined one side. A bunch of straw-covered ice blocks on the other. He sat upon the frozen wall and breathed, staring at the sawdust at his feet.

Why had Gwen said that? What could he have possibly done to interest her all of a sudden after she'd so clearly said she'd had no interest in him beyond her brother's crazy deal to help her leave Armelle?

He had said he planned to leave at some point, but he'd not said he was going anytime soon. She had just complimented him for looking out for women and children, though of course he would. They were his own family. Had his mother said something to her about how he felt about her? That was possible, but surely she hadn't betrayed him like that. Maybe she'd helped Gwen see how he'd been right in telling her she needed to find someone who treated her well…and so she'd looked around for the first man who did and latched onto him.

He let out a pent-up breath.

She was back to going after her goal again—marriage had always been her goal. *He* wasn't her goal. She wasn't attracted to *him*. He'd simply treated her right.

The door creaked open and Gwen's gaze landed on him.

His heart had returned to its normal rhythm. Thank God she'd stopped to talk with the butcher long enough for him to figure things out. He'd resigned himself to the fact that though he wished it different, he could not be her husband if he truly wanted her to have the best life she could have. He wanted that for his mother, he wanted that for Gwen, and he'd do what he must to provide that for them, no matter how much it might tear him up inside.

Without saying a word, she crossed the room, hands hugging her arms, and sat beside him. "I'm sorry I sprung that on you. But I couldn't keep the thought to myself any longer. Now that you have this job, I hoped you'd feel better about—"

He held up a hand. "Ma once told me the reason she got together with my father was because he was the first man to pay her any attention." He turned to face Gwen, trying to suppress a scowl. Why did *he* have to be the one to advise her to find someone other than him to marry? "Don't let your tendency to

277

go after whatever man is available ruin your future—unless he's the right one."

"What makes you think you aren't?"

"O'Conners don't marry McGills."

"People marry into new families all the time." Her smile was so genuine, he barely held it together.

He dug his nails into his palms. "What sort of life would you have as an O'Conner?" Hopefully some woman, someday, wouldn't think it too bad. He'd treat a woman better than his father, but that didn't mean he'd be able to provide for a lady of Gwen's station. Even if he saved for years and bought a decent house, he still wouldn't be anything like the men she had fancied herself with before today.

"Tim—"

"I'm flattered." He fastened a hand around her arm, though it nearly undid him to touch her. "But please. Don't talk about this anymore."

"Why?"

He shook his head. Truth would only make her try all the harder.

She leaned closer. "Can you tell me you don't like me?"

He turned his face away. Hopefully she hadn't seen him grimace. "Of course, I like you. But I want to see you happy. That's all."

"Pardon me." The butcher thrust his head into the small room, frowning at the two of them sitting on his ice blocks. "Is there something I need to do for this inspection?"

Tim stood, shivering over the way Gwen's hand slid off his shoulder. "I'm sorry to have barged in without any warning, Mr. Hancock. But I needed to know how things look when run well —and Dent says you do—so that I can tell when someone's not running their shop to the same standard."

The man nodded but didn't seem convinced. He glanced over at Gwen, who was still seated.

She stood. "I shouldn't have come, I—" Looking at Tim for a second, she said nothing more then walked past Mr. Hancock.

Though he'd come in here to breathe easier, his lungs squeezed tight in his chest. He'd hurt her pride—and he was sorry for it—but that was surely all he'd hurt. One day, when a worthy man came along who loved her just as much as he did, she'd thank him for not allowing her to waste any time on him.

For though he intended to be the best man he could be, changing everything about himself through sheer will and determination was not possible.

CHAPTER THIRTY-TWO

Gwen shifted on the hard bench inside the mercantile and glanced out the window again with an impatient exhale. The marshal's office was still shut up tight. It had been two days since she'd left Tim in the butcher's ice room, and ever since then, she'd been unable to catch him alone.

Down the street, her brother walked into the bank. She shook her head and frowned. She should've known better than to take Bo's advice about wooing Tim.

He'd told her Tim didn't seem to be the kind of man who enjoyed the chase, and he'd likely not take hints considering how mismatched they were. So Bo had advised her to let him know up-front what her hopes were for the two of them.

Of course, when she'd told Bo what she'd said to Tim, he'd laughed. He'd said he hadn't thought to tell her she needed to warm him up some—the poor man hadn't even had the chance to invite her on a Sunday afternoon drive, and she'd gone straight to asking him to propose.

But how could she warm him up when he was avoiding her?

Of course, he was bound to be busy with his new job, but instead of reading law books, he seemed intent on doing all the neglected maintenance duties. She couldn't stand in the middle of the road while he filled potholes and visit without appearing desperate.

But today, she'd decided to wait and watch. He had to go into the office at some point.

Not spending time with him wasn't helping her warm him up to anything. Surely she could prove to him he wasn't just the next breathing bachelor who'd crossed her path, but a man who'd truly captured her heart and deserved it to boot.

Ah! There he was. Did he actually look both ways before he left the alley and charge up the stairs?

If he thought he could evade her…

As ladylike as she could and avoiding anyone's eye, she gathered her things, slipped out of the mercantile, and marched across Main Street.

She'd engage in no more empty-headed flirting—with him or anyone else—but serious pursuit. Surely God would honor that. Taking a deep breath, she stepped onto the boardwalk and knocked on his open door.

"Come in."

She did with a big smile, which only got bigger with how he looked up at her warily. "I've brought lunch."

He glanced at the clock, which read a quarter past one, and ran a hand through his too long hair. "I hope you haven't been waiting on me."

"I have."

He let out a small groan he likely didn't mean for her to hear. "I'm sorry. I've been busy."

"I've noticed." She sat in a chair, though he hadn't told her to take a seat, and slid the picnic basket onto the desk. "I've overheard several of the councilmen talking with Bo, and they're impressed with what you've already accomplished. But I'm worried you're working too hard. You need to eat."

"No need to worry about me. Mrs. Emrick feeds me well at the boardinghouse, even if I come in after dinner hours."

"Does she provide lunch?"

Tim tugged at his tie. "She does if I pay for it, but I'm all right with jerky."

How much was he intending to send to his mother? "Is your salary not adequate?"

He shook his head vigorously. "I didn't mean I wasn't getting paid enough—I'm not worth what I already get."

"That's not true. The men are thrilled with your hard work."

"Hard work I can do, but I've yet to do anything with the law part." He eyed the bookshelf warily.

"Anything specifically worrying you about that? I'd like to pray for you if I may."

"That's kind of you. I guess I'd just like to be sure I can understand and remember what I read, along with whatever Jacob Hendrix intends to go over with me this afternoon." He stared at the pile of wanted cards in front of him. "To know where to begin."

"Then I'll pray for that." She reached into her basket. "And you'll have a better chance of retaining information on a full stomach."

He watched her plate up the turkey breast, beans, and corn-bread she'd had the cook set aside from last night's supper.

She pushed it toward him.

"Thank you," he nodded, but he didn't start eating.

She raised her brows.

"You're not going to sit there and watch me eat, are you?"

"I was hoping we could talk."

His jaw worked for a moment, but then he picked up his spoon and filled it with beans dark with molasses. "Is something bothering you?"

"No. I just wanted to get to know you better. To have you learn more about me and my intentions toward you."

He choked, dropping his spoon.

She stood, but he waved her to sit—or maybe stay away. But fearing he needed someone to pound him on the back, she remained standing, poised to go to his aid or run for the doctor.

"I—" He coughed and sputtered again, but the fact he got a word out was a good sign.

The door creaked open behind her. Jacob Hendrix walked in, his worried expression likely mirroring her own, considering how Tim was hacking up a lung.

But Tim's coughing settled, and he pulled in an audible inhale. "I'm all right."

Jacob turned to smile at her. "Smells good in here."

She pushed the chair beside her toward the former marshal. "Have a seat. Though I didn't bring enough to share, I do have an extra cherry tart. I was going to eat it myself, but in hopes it'll make you more patient when you teach Tim whatever you're here to teach him, I'll eat dessert when I get home."

He shrugged and took the chair. "Though I hope I'm always patient, I won't turn down a tart if you're offering. Let's see how much more patient I can get."

Tim sporadically coughed as she plated up the dessert.

After taking a bite, Jacob hummed and leaned back in his chair, then glanced between them. "Did I interrupt something?"

"No." She handed him a napkin and a small cup of water. "Since Tim's been too busy to cook for himself, I figured that was a skill I had worth sharing—or rather a skill my cook has." She cringed and turned back to Tim. "I guess I ought to learn how to cook."

Tim didn't respond, his face too blank to gauge an answer.

She looked to Jacob. "Tim's also not been giving me the time of day—unlike many of the men I've chased before—well, except for you. You often avoided me."

Now it was Jacob's turn to have food go down the wrong pipe. After a short coughing fit, he took a napkin and wiped at his mouth. "Well, you were—are…a bit young."

"Nonsense. Men your age marry women my age all the time. What you mean to say is I acted like I had nothing but

feathers for brains and you wanted a woman of substance—
which you found."

Jacob laughed. "I've seen glimpses of this straight-shooting
side of you before. I'm glad to see more of it."

"Do you think I'm more likely to attract a man this way?"

He shrugged, digging back into his forgotten tart. "It'll likely
work better than your previous attempts."

"Good." She smiled. "Because that's what I'm attempting
this time around. Hopefully, I'm more successful."

"Oh?" Then he jolted in his seat and looked to Tim, whose
face was the color of watered-down wine.

"I've got my eye on a man with as much integrity as you.
Who doesn't take advantage of a woman's admiration if he
believes he ought not to propose—though I intend to change his
mind about that." She pushed the other tart toward Tim with a
grin she allowed to turn flirtatious, for she couldn't hold them all
back. "A woman's supposed to start with the stomach, right?"

"That is the saying." Jacob's words rumbled with amusement. "Anne cooked me a homemade meal complete with
crumb cake before she sideswiped me with a marriage proposal
out of nowhere." He shoved the last of his tart into his mouth,
brushed off his hands, and glanced toward the front door. "I
believe I've forgotten to talk to Mr. Owens about…something.
I'll head to the mercantile now and return after your lunch is
over."

Jacob glanced at Tim with an amused slant to his lips, then
back to her. "Thanks for the tart." He winked. "And good luck."

After he exited, she turned to face Tim, who now was the
color of fried green apples. Maybe he had a weak stomach. "Is
there something that isn't setting well with you? I won't bother
to learn how to cook whatever you don't like."

He said nothing.

She stared at him for a moment and then gave a short huff.
"I don't repulse you, do I?"

"No," he sputtered.

"Then why do you look so ill whenever I'm around?"

He massaged the spot between his brows for a minute. "This can't work, you're—and I'm—it won't be what either of us thinks it'll be. And you have to have noticed..." He finally looked at her, his eyes tortured. "Though looks aren't anything important really, it has to matter to a woman like you."

She leaned over the desk to take off his hat. "Let me see you, then." She dropped the beat-up thing onto the desk, pushed aside the hair that always hung across his forehead—less blemished now, but scarred all the same, and tucked his hair behind his ear. Then she sat back and rested her chin in her hand.

"Gwen—" his voice broke off, strangled and pained.

She scrunched her lips to the side. Though her previous bubble-headed flirtatiousness hadn't reflected who she really was, maybe she didn't have to ignore the urge to flirt if she truly wanted to. She rounded the desk and sat on a cleared off space, then placed a hand atop one of his hands which was strangling the arm of his chair. "The men I used to chase aren't nearly as attractive as you. It's not just the outside that counts."

He shook his head, likely about to negate her, so she leaned down and gave him a peck on the lips to stop him. Pulling back, she noted he'd frozen. But then a rush of air left him and such longing filled his eyes that she leaned in to kiss him again, like she'd wanted to for days—but his lips stayed tight and hard beneath hers.

Her face flushed hot, and a bubble lodged in her throat. Though Eric had walked away from her as if he'd never cared, he'd at least kissed her like she was desirable.

She pushed away, but Tim grabbed her arms, and for the few seconds his lips moved against hers, everything inside of her melted like wax.

Suddenly, he slid his fingers between their lips to break them apart and groaned. Yet he didn't pull away. His breath fanned her face, and she opened her eyes—his were still closed.

"Everyone..." He swallowed and another puff of air tickled her lips. "Everyone will make fun of you—being with me."

Her heart gave a sad little flop—not just because he thought that, but because there was truth to those words. But he needed to know she didn't care. Sliding his hand away, she restarted their kiss.

Within seconds, his fingers were wrapped in her hair, and his kiss was full of such fervor and tenderness and longing, she scooted off the desk and into his arms.

Though his lips stayed connected to hers, he scrambled, pulling her back up to sit on the desk, standing next to her. Breath ragged, he broke away. "You can't be seen in my...*lap*."

She chuckled at how incredulous he sounded at the last word leaving his mouth.

His eyes turned liquid and he moved in again, but suddenly stopped and turned his head as if he couldn't bear to look at her. "I don't come with anything you've ever chased," he whispered. "And as I said, you need to think this through." He looked at her again, his eyes afire. "Your happiness is more valuable than mine."

"Why?" She grabbed the lapels of his jacket to keep him close.

"I've seen what a mismatch did to my parents." His words were soft, and slightly broken. "If things aren't even between two people..."

"You don't think I could make you happy?"

He straightened. "That's not a job you should want to take on."

Her shoulders fell. Did he truly not want her?

A finger slid across her jaw and down to her chin. He tilted her face up to look at him. "A man shouldn't choose a wife to make him happy. He should love her so much he wants what's best for her, even if that means he *gives up* what would make him happy. Remember how I said you and my ma deserve more than you've been offered? I haven't offered because I can't give you what you deserve. You can do better than me."

She put her hands on each side of his face. "Whoever you propose to will be the luckiest woman on Earth."

He nodded and stepped back.

Her body went cold. "Why are you——?"

Heavy footsteps landed on the porch, and she scrambled to smooth back her hair.

From the doorway, Jacob cleared his throat. "Did I come back too soon?"

Hopping off the desk, she took a glance at Tim's stiff posture and cleared her throat. "I'll let you get back to work now. I'll bring lunch tomorrow."

He shook his head, but she held up a hand. "Please, let me. It's the least I can do."

He stared at her for a second, but then gave her a tight nod.

How she made it past Jacob without collapsing into a puddle, she wasn't sure, but she made it through the door. Her fingers and toes buzzed, her head spun, her heart seized. For a second, she'd thought Tim would propose, sweep her into his arms, declare his love——

But then he'd backed away.

Yet she'd seen the longing in his eyes before he'd told her he wasn't good enough. She'd win him over. Not by pushing or flirting, no. She'd just keep coming back until he couldn't stand the thought of saving her from marrying him any longer.

This was going to be fun. Torturous, but fun.

CHAPTER THIRTY-THREE

The poster in Tim's hand fluttered in the summer breeze outside the marshal's office. Some men had recently been involved in the shooting death of a sheepherder. The herder's friend had described one man in the group so perfectly, Tim couldn't pretend he didn't know his identity. At least Daniel hadn't been the one to shoot the shepherd. Tim hadn't wanted to put his friend's name at the bottom of the flyer, but if finding Daniel led to the murderer's arrest, then it was necessary.

Tim tacked the paper up with slow, heart-hurting blows. If Daniel was brought in, hopefully there'd be no hanging offense to try him for. Though convicting and sentencing wasn't his duty, the carrying out of those sentences could potentially fall to him.

God, I hope you know what you were doing putting me in this position.

From somewhere across the street behind him, the soft sound of a woman's laugh twisted up his innards. Gwen's genuine laughter—not the fake kind she used to use to draw attention. When a man's gruff chuckle followed, Tim's insides scrambled in an entirely different way.

She laughed again, but he denied the impulse to turn and see if she was enjoying the other's man's company more than she did his. But the longer he focused on the words in front of him and the more she laughed, the harder it was to breathe. Keeping his eyes on the wall, he tacked up another poster.

She laughed again, and with a low growl, he turned before he combusted.

The man next to her had his back to him, his hat unfamiliar. Tim held his breath.

Then the man pivoted and walked away—a very old man.

Tim smacked the next nail through the poster with one blow. He needed to stop keeping an ear out for her, stop sticking around the office at lunchtime.

If there was any chance to keep his heart whole, he needed to stay far away from her—and yet, that was the absolute last thing he wanted.

It's what she needs that matters, not me.

He tore down an old poster and forced himself not to look over his shoulder to figure out if she was coming over. He'd spent several sleepless nights trying to come up with a way to be worthy of her, but it all came down to one thing—quite simply, he wouldn't be able to support her. The marshal job was better than he'd ever dreamed, but if the councilmen decided he wasn't good enough, he wasn't qualified for anything but ranch work. It'd take years upon years of working for the Keys before he could buy property—if that'd even be possible considering he needed to send everything extra to his mother.

Too many men had strung Gwen along for him to do the same. She deserved more than a hazy possibility of a future proposal. And now that she wasn't acting like a featherbrain and looking for a man of quality, she'd be snatched up in no time.

Thankfully she'd dropped all hints of wanting to marry him the last several days—which was good.

He swallowed to fill up the hollowness. Of course, Gwen giving up on him was good. That's what needed to happen.

And yet, that day when she'd ended up in his lap—if he'd kicked himself once, he'd kicked himself a thousand times for not paying enough attention to the taste and feel of her so he might relive that handful of seconds when he'd died and gone to heaven. Though he couldn't remember much—beyond pure bliss mixed with torture—every day afterward, he'd made her sit on the other side of the desk. And she'd not complained. And his heart needed to stop sagging every time she stayed in that chair.

The tap of her fancy boots sounded on the boardwalk. He forced himself to straighten his spine as if he were a dignified marshal—a marshal who should be getting far more done. He picked up the last poster.

She stopped beside him, the scent of lavender hampering his ability to concentrate. As nonchalantly as possible, he tacked up the flyer then pulled his hat down to hide his new blemishes. Corinne's concoction had seemed to be working, but the last few days had been disappointing. Was the stinky soap no longer effective, or did the fact his body wanted to pop out of itself every time Gwen was around manifest itself in more ways than one?

She sidled closer, giving him a conspiratorial look, and beckoned him to lean down.

He leaned only far enough to hear her whisper.

"Mrs. Tate's about to walk by. You need to compliment her shawl."

"I doubt she wants a compliment from either of us."

"Doesn't matter." Gwen kept her voice low. "I was praising Raven's needlework at the mercantile—just trying to be nice since her stuff won't sell—when Mrs. Tate bought one! That means I laid the flattery on too thick. I wasn't trying to, but—"

"I'm sure Miss Owen's needlework can't be all that bad…" He quit speaking as the shawl in question came into sight. "It's orange and purple, trimmed with black?"

"I know," Gwen whispered back. "I'm beginning to think Raven's colorblind. But I wasn't lying about the stitches being fine, it's just…"

Mrs. Tate nodded when she got close enough to catch them staring.

Tim nodded back, and Gwen elbowed him in the ribs. "Uh, good morning, Mrs. Tate. That's a...new shawl?"

"Yes." She put her chin up.

"Ni-nice," he stuttered.

When she'd passed by, Gwen jabbed him again. "That wasn't much of a compliment."

He shook his head. "Sorry, that's the best I could do. I'm afraid, Miss McGill, you—"

She gave him the glare she'd been giving him ever since he'd gone back to calling her by her proper name.

"— you owe it to her to tell her that thing is hideous. She'd hate to be a laughingstock."

It was bad enough Raven was. And though the mercantile owner's daughter didn't seem to care what people thought of what she wore, Mrs. Tate would—quite hypocritical considering she never stopped to think how her insults made others feel.

"No, Tim, you're not allowed to tell any woman her sense of fashion is off. Though you could tell me. I'd want to know your thoughts."

He swallowed hard as she followed him into the office. How was he supposed to meet the lucky lady Gwen said he'd one day propose to if Gwen kept sticking around, asking him things like that—being exactly what he wanted? Someone who brightened his life. Someone who faced difficulties bravely. Someone who cared about others. Someone who truly seemed to care about him.

"Did you see the new music box at the mercantile with the fairies on it?" She placed her lunch basket on the desk and opened its lid. "Don't you think Molly would like it for her birthday?"

He released his breath. He could talk about family. "If Molly were here, I'd bet she'd talk about it nonstop."

"So how do I get it to her? Could I go with you on your first visit?"

He shook his head despite how badly he wanted to hug her for still caring about Molly though she'd never see her again. Gwen knew she couldn't ever visit them if they were to stay safe. "Unless you and your brother have a legitimate reason to visit Laramie, you needn't get her anything. Besides, we've never done birthday presents."

She unfolded her napkin then handed him his when he took his seat across from her. "I think there might be a way to get it to her without anyone knowing."

"Miss McGill—"

"Now, don't worry. I won't do anything to compromise their whereabouts."

"I know you wouldn't. But the only way I can think to visit them myself is creating an official business reason to go there, and I don't even know if I can come up with one."

"But you can't disappear from their lives altogether."

"I don't plan to, but for a year or two, they'll be better off without seeing me. If Father finds out where they are, he'll drag them back. That's not a chance I'm willing to take."

"Has he done anything to try to find them?"

"No." He took a bite of the egg salad sandwich she'd handed him. Though he ought to be thankful Father seemed content to let them go without a chase, the fact he'd so quickly moved on with his life galled.

"I'm sure you miss them."

Since his mouth was full, he nodded. An awkward silence fell, mainly because she was so fidgety.

She blew out a big breath and leaned forward. "Did you hear there's to be a shooting competition on Founder's Day?"

The mischievous gleam in her eye elicited a soft chuckle from him. He enjoyed how easily she was herself now, nearly splitting at the seams to share her thoughts on all manner of things. "What are you thinking?"

"Oh, nothing beyond making sure I have a good chance at beating everybody. Can you imagine what people would think if I shoot *and* win? How about we practice together every night after dinner so I can?"

He shook his head, thankful that chewing gave him an excuse not to answer. He couldn't spend more time with her every day. Lunch was hard enough.

"So you don't think a marshal's wife ought to be an excellent shot? What about for the times when we're out on a picnic and bad guys show up?"

He choked and grabbed for his water.

She kept talking and smiling as if nothing were amiss. "Of course, I know better than to leave my gun in the scabbard now, though maybe I should get a sidearm?"

His heart *ka-thunked* as he set down his glass. "I don't want you carrying a sidearm."

Her face softened as if he'd said something she'd waited a long time to hear. With an enormous sigh, she slumped over, resting her chin in her hand, giving him a long-suffering look. "Why can't you just admit you love me and kiss me again?"

Though he'd swallowed the bite that had tried to kill him, he could barely breathe. If she didn't hurry and get on with her life, he was going to be a miserable man. "What about Denver?" That's what Bo had promised her if she spent time with him. And she'd put in plenty of time—too much time. "If Bo needs someone to escort you, I could get—"

"Are you volunteering?" She got up and walked around the desk.

He lit out of his seat. There would be no landing in his lap today.

She ran her finger down his arm and looked up at him through her eyelashes. "If I wanted to go, would you be my bodyguard?"

He clamped a hand over her trailing finger. If she got any closer...

She stood on tiptoe and whispered into his ear. "I really wouldn't mind if you were."

All right, he couldn't take anymore. But he'd keep his head about him this time, so he could remember every detail. He swept her against him and poured out every bit of longing he had for her in a kiss that would last as long as his breath allowed.

After a few minutes, he had to pull away, lungs burning.

She sighed and a smile spread slowly across her face.

His heart imploded. She truly had wanted him to kiss her.

He leaned in again, letting himself kiss her achingly slow. If this would be the last...time...

He had to hold her up when her knees gave way.

Oh, who was he kidding?

If he could kiss her like this tomorrow and the next day and the day after that...

He set her back at arms' length, a lump lodged clear up in his throat. "Are you just playing with me? If so, please, please walk away and never come back."

She wound her arms around him and pressed a light kiss against his lips. "I was beginning to wonder if the thought of kissing me made you ill."

He swallowed hard. "It was never the thought of kissing you. It was dreading the moment you'd wake up and realize you should've chosen someone else."

She stepped back and framed his face with her hands. "You wouldn't disappoint any woman."

"I certainly wouldn't want to."

"Which is why Bo pushed me your way." She caressed his cheek with her thumb. "You were never Mr. Wrong. But you'll always be my Mr. Right."

"Then perhaps..." His voice came out more ragged than he intended, but he forced himself to continue. "Perhaps I'm just going to have to let you marry me, then."

"Please do." She laughed. "Though I've tried, I'm terrible at keeping the desire to marry you to myself."

He couldn't keep from chuckling. "Yes, you are."

Her smile faltered. "I suppose I'll have to continue being bad at it until you ask. You *will* ask, won't you?"

His heart crumbled at her vulnerable expression. A flutter started in his gut and he held hard onto her hand. "What must I have before you'd say yes? I've got nothing. No family ring. My money's promised to my mother, and—" He looked to the ceiling. How could he ever afford to marry her? Have a home worthy of her to live in?

He already knew these questions had no good answers. He took a step back.

"Don't you leave me, Timothy." She moved with him, wrapping her arms back around him. "I need nothing but you."

He blinked against his suddenly hot eyes. Could that really be true? She might think that now, but years down the road? "That's all you'd ever get, I'm afraid."

"That's all I want."

He pressed his lips against the top of her forehead, letting out a shuddery breath. Could he be certain what she'd settle for would be enough? Of course, even if he had the looks and money his father had once possessed, none of that was promised to last. Grass withered and flowers faded, but God's Word stood forever—and that Word said the heart was what mattered. The best thing he could give Gwen, what he'd always prayed his father would offer his mother, was choosing to love her every day. To treat her right, no matter what she did or how he felt. To provide for her to the best of his ability.

His breath staggered at the enormity of the question, the commitment, the hope that welled up within him. "If you're willing to take me as I am, then I'll do the same for you, as long as I live. Because I love you. Not just the you I fell in love with so many years ago—but the you that you are right now. And every fiber of my being wants nothing more than to be able to love you for the rest of my life." He swallowed hard. "Will you marry me, Gwen?"

With a childlike squeal, she hugged him tight then popped up to give him a quick peck on the lips. "Yes!" Her glistening eyes made her look happier than he'd ever seen a woman look.

He couldn't help the grin that bubbled up. Joy radiated off her face—the face of the most beautiful woman in the world. And he was the reason for it.

Maybe he wasn't Mr. Wrong after all.

EPILOGUE

Two months later

Pulling back the curtain, Tim stared blankly at the number of people in the McGills' backyard. Had Gwen invited everyone in Armelle? He let the curtain fall, then took a deep breath in, then out.

Bo came up beside him. "You ready?"

Taking inventory of his tight breathing, galloping heartbeat, and dripping sweat, saying yes would be a great, big lie. Tim reached up to pull on his hair, but his haircut made that impossible. "I'm not sure how your sister got me to agree to marrying this soon."

Bo smiled. "When she wants something, there's no stopping her. But as she said, it's a perfect excuse to see your mother sooner rather than later."

They hadn't been courting a week when Gwen had mentioned a honeymoon in Laramie would be an easy way to take his kid sister a birthday present without inviting any suspicion. And then they could visit every year to celebrate their anniversary. That Gwen would want to share their special day with his family made him fall in love with her even more.

He'd told her he'd think about it, and she'd immediately

gone and bought the fairy music box and ordered another gold-embossed book.

What kind of brother would keep presents like that from his sister longer than necessary? What kind of man didn't want to marry a woman like Gwen as soon as he had the chance?

He blew out his breath. Though he might not feel worthy of the gift that Gwen was, that didn't mean he didn't want it with every fiber of his being.

He ran a hand along the sleeve of the nicest suit he'd ever touched, let alone worn, and shook his head at how quickly Gwen and her brother had put this together. It'd been hard to say no to such a grand wedding when she'd looked forward to one for so many years. He could hardly imagine the dress she'd be wearing. Considering the grandeur of the outdoor staging, would he even be able to keep upright when he saw her walking toward him?

Even if she were dressed in rags, he was in danger of fainting at seeing such a dream come true.

The murmur of voices outside increased. Bo returned to the window. "Seems your father's shown up. Do you think he'll make a scene?"

Tim shook his head. "If he does, I've already asked Dent to escort him away. But if he wants to be here, he can be—as long as he doesn't insult my bride."

"If he does, you won't need Dent. I'll take him out myself. And I'll be a lot less nice about it." He pulled the curtain closed. "Do you think he's come because he expects your mother to show up?"

Tim shrugged. "Maybe, but not because he thinks I invited her. When I called him out for being responsible for us never being able to see her again, he seemed convinced I knew nothing. He drank himself to sleep for about a month, and now..." His father had gone on living life as if he were single. How had he done so with so little remorse?

Though he was glad that meant Father would likely never

chase after his family, it hurt to know how little they meant to him.

"Do you think your father will divorce your mother on grounds of abandonment?"

"Not likely, too much work. That is, until he finds another woman, unfortunately."

"Unfortunately?"

"For the other woman."

Bo clasped his shoulder. "Sorry to have dragged you down that rabbit trail on your wedding day. I should be helping you focus on the happiness in store for you, not the pain of the past. Speaking of which, I have a gift."

"The suit was more than enough."

"But this one is for both of you." Bo pulled a slim box from his vest pocket.

He took it tentatively. "Then why not wait until after the ceremony so Gwen can be here?"

"She knows about it already." He gestured for him to open it. "I knew she'd be pickier than you, so I consulted her before getting it."

He took off the lid and looked at a key sitting atop a folded piece of paper. A key to a house. He shook his head.

Bo put his fists on his hips. "Can't give it back. You could sell it, but I'd suggest you talk to Gwen first. She likes the place."

Though he'd been grateful to Bo for agreeing to let them stay in the mansion until he could figure something out, he'd not felt comfortable with it. But for him to buy them something like this? "What place?"

"It's near the church. Two stories. Porch on front and back, tall windows. Could use a paint job."

His body chilled. "You mean the marshal's old place?"

"No, the marshal's new place. Figured if it was good for one marshal, it'd be good for another."

"That place is huge."

"Got to have room for all my nieces and nephews."

Nausea swept over him.

Bo braced him by the shoulders, looking him in the eye. "Get a hold of yourself, man. You expected to have children with her, right? Or did your father not have that talk with you?"

Tim swatted Bo's hands away and grabbed a glass of water. "No need for you to give me the talk."

"Thank the heavens, because that certainly would've been awkward." He laughed then pulled out his timepiece. "You going to be all right? Can you make it down front in a few minutes? It's time I go see Gwen, and she's already worried you'll get cold feet and run. By the look of you, I'm thinking she might have reason for concern."

Tim finished gulping his water, his throat still dry. "I'm not backing out."

"Good. You can't imagine how much I spent finding enough flowers for this." And then with a soft click of the door, Bo left.

Tim pressed a hand to his pulsing forehead. He would make it up front, but whether he could stay on his feet was questionable. After slamming down another glass of water, he drained the pitcher. Then he worked at breathing slowly. A house, a good paying job, his mother and siblings safe, a wife...surely something would mess this up. He looked to the ceiling. "Not that I don't want it all, God, but goodness, it feels like I'm asking too much to keep from waking up and discovering this is indeed a dream."

The door creaked open behind him. His best man, Nolan Key, poked his head through the doorway. "There's going to be a delay."

He jolted. "Is it Gwen?"

"Yes, but don't worry." And then Nolan disappeared.

Don't worry? What did that mean? Tim stared at the empty water pitcher, willing himself not to watch the clock. He prayed for them both as coherently as he could until Nolan showed up again nearly half an hour later.

"It's time."

Tim just blinked at him.

"You ready to get married?"

"I'm getting married?"

Nolan rolled his eyes and opened the door wider. "Sure are."

Thank you, Jesus.

Glad he had Nolan to follow out since his legs were the weakest they'd ever been, Tim concentrated on getting to the archway entwined with vines at the far end of the yard. None of the other groomsmen waited up front for him. Weren't they supposed to be there already?

With the amount of people in the crowd, his heart re-accelerated. Now where had Nolan gone? Not wanting to meet the eyes of anyone, especially his father, lest they see the panic creeping in, he stared at the insane amount of orange tiger lilies lining the center aisle stuck into bundles of cattails.

He couldn't help the sudden smile. He'd thought the fancy flower and weed combination strange when he'd seen the women carrying them out earlier, but now he saw the cat theme. So many times he'd called himself a fool for going off the trail to rescue kittens. But now, he might just try to rescue every stray he could to see what good might come of it.

The violin player changed songs and a pat on his back made him look over to see that the pastor had joined him. Remembering the man's advice not to lock his knees, Tim tried to relax, but his vision started going dark when he noted the first attendant couple walking down the grass aisle.

Wait. Those weren't attendants, but Mrs. Tate on the arm of her son, who was carrying his shotgun.

Mrs. Tate's face was about as placid as he'd ever seen it, though he detected a slight gleam in her eye. When the Tates got to the end of the aisle, Ivan raised his eyebrow with a mock expression of grave seriousness, as if to ask Tim if the gun was necessary.

He dismissively waved at them to sit down but couldn't help his grin.

Then the attendants started walking down in a line, and Tim couldn't help but laugh at seeing each of his groomsmen holding their own shotguns. Celia, walking with her brother, seemed to be frowning over the fact she had to hold the bouquet instead of the firearm. Poor girl appeared ill at ease in the fancy dress Gwen had bought her. Even so, he couldn't deny the dress made her look less like a kid sister and more like a woman who could be a good friend to his wife.

His wife.

His knees buckled, but he caught himself. He should've insisted on scaling back this wedding, he was going to embarrass himself in front of the entire town. He took a deep breath but couldn't release it when Gwen and Bo appeared.

Instead of a bouquet, Gwen held her grandfather's fancy muzzleloader, which she'd become quite adept at using during their after-dinner practices.

Bo held the flowers.

The unexpected switch made Tim chuckle, which helped him breathe at least. He smiled as he took in the sight of the woman he loved in the fanciest, whitest, shiniest dress he'd ever seen. A dress she'd never have the opportunity to wear again in this town—a dress made just for him.

He teared up as he noted the color in her cheeks, which could be seen despite the gauzy veil falling in folds in front of her face. For as long as he lived, he'd be in awe that this woman had chosen him. She might be gorgeous, but her heart, her playfulness, her generosity, her willingness to accept people for who they were was what really made him have to pinch himself.

Once she and Bo arrived at the front, the pastor stepped forward. "Who gives this woman to this man?"

"I do." Bo gave his sister a kiss on her cheek through the veil, but she kept her eyes on Tim.

She gave her muzzleloader a slight lift. "Do I need the gun, or can I pass it to Bo?"

Tim took her free hand. "There's absolutely no need for a gun. I'd be a fool to run away from you."

"Good," she whispered, her voice wobbly. She passed Bo the gun and took Tim's other hand and stepped in close. "Someone told me you'd gotten awfully serious—I figured I needed to make you smile."

"Oh, but I am serious." He lifted her veil, encrusted with thousands of little reflective beads which couldn't hold a candle to the sparkle in her blue eyes. "Seriously in love with you." His voice came out in a barely audible whisper.

She winked up at him. "And I, you."

He stepped back and gave her his arm. "Shall we?"

The second her arm laced through his, his heart settled.

By some miracle, he'd won the right to love this woman, and for the rest of his life, he'd praise God for the privilege of doing so.

I hope you enjoyed *Marrying Mr. Wrong*!

If you did, please take a moment to share with others. You can do so by posting an honest review wherever you purchased this book and also on social media. Every review and mention helps!

More stories in the *Frontier Vows* series are being written. In the meantime, if you missed why Leah and Bryant left Armelle and have only come back for a visit, check out *Depending on You*, which is the third story in this series.

If you've already read *Depending on You*, you might like to start another of my series to hold you over while you wait for book five! If you've enjoyed Gwen and Tim having to figure out how to navigate a relationship when they're on such unequal social footing, you should check out *A Heart Most Certain*, where the hero and heroine have to deal with that as well. It's the first full-length story in my *Teaville Moral Society* series!

To keep up to date with my news on book releases and events, subscribe to my newsletter at melissajagears.com

ACKNOWLEDGMENTS

None of my books are written in a vacuum. I agonize over them so much there's no way I send them out into the world without asking people I trust to tell me if I'm not doing so great at this writing thing. Thanks to Heidi Chiavaroli, Judy DeVries, Sarah Keimig, Myra Johnson, Stephanie McCall, Naomi Rawlings, Andrea Strong, and Anne-Marie Turenne for helping me make this story better than I could have made it myself.

Thank you Najla Qamber for designing this novel's cover, to my daughter who allowed me to "steal" her hands to hold the gun, and my husband who made me the beautiful muzzleloader she's holding.

Thanks also to my loyal readers who waited so patiently for this book. Hopefully I'll be quicker with the next one!

And to God who blessed me with my penchant for words, may they bring you glory.

ABOUT THE AUTHOR

Much to her introverted self's delight, award-winning writer Melissa Jagears hardly needs to leave home to be a home-schooling mother and novelist. She lives in Kansas with her husband and three children and can be found online at BookBub, Goodreads, Instagram, and melissajagears.com. Feel free to drop her a note at author@melissajagears.com, or you can find her current mailing address and an updated list of her books on her website.

To keep up to date with Melissa's news and book releases, subscribe to her newsletter at melissajagears.com

© 2022 by Melissa Jagears
    Published by Utmost Publishing
    www.utmostpublishing.com

Printed in the United States of America

    All Rights Reserved. No part of this publication may be reproduced, stored in a retrieval system, or transmitted in any form or by any means—for example, electronic, photocopy, recording—without the prior written permission in writing from the publisher. The only exception is brief quotations in printed reviews.

Publisher's Cataloging-in-Publication Data

Names: Jagears, Melissa.
    Title: Marrying mr. wrong / Melissa Jagears
    Description: Wichita, KS: Utmost Pub., 2022. | Series: Frontier Vows
    Identifiers: LCCN 2021924996 | ISBN 9781948678100 (pbk.) | ISBN 9781948678117 (ebk.)

Scripture quotations are from the King James Version of the Bible. Extracts from the Authorized Version of the Bible (The King James Bible), the rights in which are vested in the Crown, are reproduced by permission of the Crown's Patentee, Cambridge University Press.

    This is a work of fiction. Names, characters, incidents, and dialogues are products of the author's imagination and are not to be construed as real. Any resemblance to actual events or persons, living or dead, is entirely coincidental.

Cover design © Qamber Designs and Media
    Author represented by Natasha Kern Literary Agency

Made in United States
North Haven, CT
21 January 2022

15055678R00188